T4-AEC-171

The Jewels of Allarion Book Three

Allarinth
The Star King

By

Theodora Fair

Copyright © 2003 by THEODORA Fair

All rights reserved. No part of this book shall be reproduced or transmitted in any form or by any means, electronic, mechanical, magnetic, photographic including photocopying, recording or by any information storage and retrieval system, without prior written permission of the publisher. No patent liability is assumed with respect to the use of the information contained herein. Although every precaution has been taken in the preparation of this book, the publisher and author assume no responsibility for errors or omissions. Neither is any liability assumed for damages resulting from the use of the information contained herein.

This is a work of fiction. Names, characters, places, and incidents either are the product of the author's imagination or are used fictitiously. Any resemblance to actual events or locales or persons, living or dead, is entirely coincidental.

ISBN 0-7414-1688-3

Published by:

INFINITY
PUBLISHING.COM

519 West Lancaster Avenue
Haverford, PA 19041-1413
Info@buybooksontheweb.com
www.buybooksontheweb.com
Toll-free (877) BUY BOOK
Local Phone (610) 520-2500
Fax (610) 519-0261

Printed in the United States of America
Printed on Recycled Paper
Published August 2003

Dedication

To my Cat
Allar

The Lord High King of Woodsmeet and surrounding territories,
Fearless adventurer and fearsome hunter,
But mama's baby boy at home.
taf

Lizelle's Prophecy

You will know death but will not die.
You will see one bird but hear the song of two.
You will soar to winged heights but never fly.
You will plant a seed but never pluck a flower.
You will know the Dark but come home to Love.

Prologue

Armina Weatherwatcher felt the calling. She was tired, but the insistent pull back to the rocky headland could not be ignored. She had spent most of the day there, watching the ominous clouds roll in from the sea. She had not foreseen the storm, neither yesterday when the fleet had left, nor today when dawn broke calm and clear. But it had come, black and raging, and she like every other woman in Westshoren squinted a hopeful eye toward the sea for a glimpse of the men racing ahead of it. When the storm broke over the land she was forced to retreat. The cold wet wind drove her along the path. She stopped for one last look from the shelter of the porch. Lightening forked and cracked, striking the promontory where she had stood just moments before. As quickly as it had come the storm swept inland toward the hills.

The calling urged her out into the moonless dusk. She took the lantern, wrapped her bony shoulders in her still damp shawl, and walked out onto the cold, stone-dotted moor, letting the inner voice guide her. The yellow circle of lantern light swung along the foggy path until she heard a sound riding on the shifting mist. Like a soft whimper of exhaustion, like the rasp of a voice too tired to cry, the calling persisted inside her. She walked faster. Who or what was lost on such a night? Then caution slowed her. "This must be magical," she said to herself. "No lost child calls with the inner voice." She stopped and held her lantern high.

"Where y' be?" she asked the dark beyond the security of her light.

"Mommy! Mommy!" called a small weak voice.

"Come out. I'll not harm y' child."

"We can't. We hurt," said the voice between sobs.

Armina picked her way through the rocks, holding her lantern before her like a shield.

"Mommy! Mommy!" the voice called again.

"Armina's comin' little 'n..." Then she saw the child. This was no lost fisher brat. She stared at the embroidered dress and the tiny, mud-stained velvet slippers. She stared at the torn ribbon and heart-shaped locket clutched in the child's hand.

i

"Help us! We hurt!"

"Don't fret now. Armina don't know what y' is but she loves y'." She picked up the child and smoothed back her wet, matted curls. She kissed her smudged, tear-streaked cheek. Her eye caught a red stain oozing through the child's once-white stockings.

"Owie! We hurt!" the child cried pushing Armina's hand away.

"Armina's gonna fix y' up good again. She's gonna take y' home, salve and bind those hurts, and then she's gonna give y' some warm sweet milk and a soft warm blanket," the old woman crooned as she carefully made her way home. The child whimpered weakly and fell asleep on her shoulder. By the time she reached the porch the evening fog had lifted. One by on the stars sparked into being and the moon rose round and golden out of the cradle of the hills.

Chapter 1

King Jasenth received the Frevarian messenger. The lengthy formal phrasing of the memorized speech was more than tedious. The king's mirror bird flitted from perch to perch in its cage on the windowsill, imitating its master's impatience.

"...therefore his Royal Highness is pleased to accept Arindon's most considerate invitation to celebrate the attainment of majority of our cousin Allarinth, High Prince of the Twin Kingdoms, at noon, the first day of Vernal Equinox, this the eighth year in the reign of Keilen the First of Frevaria," the messenger finally concluded.

With barely disguised amusement King Jasenth reached for the mechanical device beside him on the desk. After a quick reference to the chart underneath, he tapped a lever in a pattern of clicks and pauses. The Frevarian messenger stared with eyes wide and jaw dropped open. When Jasenth finished tapping he waved his dismissal.

"But Your Majesty," said the baffled messenger. "Will there be no response?"

"I just sent my response."

"But...?"

"As we speak, an Arindian messenger is riding from the Star Castle gatehouse toward Frevaria."

"Am I not to be given a return message, Your Majesty?"

"Sure. Do you want the same or a different one?" said Jasenth choking back his laughter.

"The same, Your Majesty, as a check for security reasons, these being tense times and all, Your Majesty."

"Alright, the same message then. I said, Hey Kylie, got your acceptance. This would get to you twice as fast if you would build your half of the communication line. Love, Jay."

The messenger still stared.

"Do you have the message?" Jasenth asked.

"Yes, Your Majesty."

"Do you wish to repeat it so I know you have it correct for security reasons, these being tense times and all?"

"If Your Majesty wishes…"

"I don't. Now go." Jasenth waved at the awed messenger. "Be sure to stop by Armon Beck's kitchen before you return and put whatever you like on my tab. There's no need to hurry. My message will be in Frevaria long before you are."

When the door finally closed Jasenth unstoppered his laughter, spilling it out with a merry jig around the room. His purple-feathered mirror bird joined in the fun with a shrill staccato, "Yes, Your Majesty. Yes, Your Majesty."

"Shut up Ame, you purple nuisance," Jasenth teased back.

"If Your Majesty wishes, ha, ha, ha."

"After tea, my winged Amethyst, I want you to make a social call on Frevaria Castle," said Jasenth.

"Good, good, Ame like Frevaria Cook. Give good treat."

"See my message delivered first. I want to see Kylie's face…"

"Yes, Your Majesty," said Amethyst as she lifted the door of her cage and flew away.

King Jasenth went back to his desk, but soon was interrupted by a familiar tap at the door.

"What is it Ben?"

"A visitor, sire," answered his manservant. "She says to announce her as Aunt Jane."

Jasenth jumped to his feet. "Aunt Jane! Send her up. Don't make her wait. Whatever could bring her here? Send her up and bring us tea, a special tea for a lady."

A bent old woman dressed in a hooded black cloak allowed herself to be ushered into the room. After Ben left she straightened up, removed her cloak and looked critically about King Jasenth's apartment.

"Not bad for bachelor quarters," she said at last.

"I have all I need here," said Jasenth fearing where her remark could lead. The sorceress Janille rarely came to Arindon. She had not visited him here in his apartment in the entire four years since he had been crowned king.

"It was wise to repair the gate house first. This is just room enough for a bachelor king to live and hold an informal court," she said standing with her hands on her hips. She turned to look out the window. "The view is excellent with the village on one side and the castle reconstruction on the other."

"You said 'bachelor' twice, Aunt Jane. Is that why you're here?"

"No, it isn't, but when the business I have come about is finished then you must settle yourself into Arindon like a real king."

"I am a real king. I lead my people well. You have said so yourself."

"You're only a heartbeat away from chaos until you marry and produce and heir."

"Then you have come about Lizzie?" said Jasenth pushing a strand of unruly red hair away from his eyes.

"No, I came about Allar. Lizzie will have to cool her ardor a while. Allar's majority rite will be no peasant holiday like yours was. There are important plans to be made. He is the High Prince after all. I'm glad Kylie agreed to attend. That will make things easier."

"But his acceptance message just came..."

"That's why I waited until now to come."

Jasenth did not question further. He knew she had magical powers. He knew she was mother to the High Queen and grandmother to both Prince Allar and Lizelle, his betrothed. Yet he had grown accustomed to thinking of her as Aunt Jane, the quiet resident of Woodsmeet Cot, the gardener's quarters on his aunt and uncle's farm. "You mean we can't have a peasant potluck just to annoy His Majesty King Keilen the First?" He laughed to dispel his unease.

Janille smiled. "The degree of formality is not the issue, but we must do things exactly right. The event will take place at the Star Castle..."

"The Star Castle! Kylie would never..."

"He has accepted our invitation. He cannot go back on us now."

"But why there?"

"I have said, this will be no peasant frolic. We will need magic, strong but discrete magic, to perform the rite. Allar was conceived by magic at the site. He must first become a man and finally be crowned High King at the same if we are to achieve the balance between Light and Dark in this age."

"If you say so," Jasenth agreed with reluctance. "It won't be a popular idea, not even in Arindon."

Janille ignored his remark. "We must work quickly. The site must be cleared and the pool dredged. There are fifteen years of neglect to overcome in two weeks."

"We are going to dunk him in that pool?"

"The High Prince does not get 'dunked' like a peasant boy," she said with a note of impatience in her voice. "He leaves the arms of his mother to enter the Water of Life. His father and brothers receive him, wash away his childhood and he is born again, a man in the sight of the Light," she quoted from the ritual.

"Who is going to officiate? Who is going to receive and assist him with the ritual?" Jasenth carefully rephrased his question. "He has neither father nor brothers."

"He has two cousin kings."

"Kylie would never…"

"King Keilen's rule is bound by tradition. He cannot refuse the honor and that is where your informality will help, Jay. The place and the ritual itself will work the magic. The family, the food and the fun must disguise it."

Ben returned with their tea and almost dropped the tray in amazement when he saw the transformation of his king's guest. The strong, confident woman who stood by the desk was not the tottering gram he had assisted up the stairs.

"Don't gape, Ben," said Janille. "You do not see anything but the old woman you brought here and you will not hear anything except what I tell you to hear while I am in this room. You know who I am?"

"Yes, My Lady," he said blinking to clear his eyes.

"Now listen to what must be done…"

The list was long but between Janille and Jasenth all the preparations for Allar's majority rite were made, from the clearing and cleaning to the gifts and the picnic feast. When it all was agreed and done, Janille put on her black cloak again and tucked her hair back into the hood. "Shall I give Lizzie your love?" she said with a sly grin.

"You said that subject could wait until this is done."

"Do I sense reluctance or is it fear in the voice of Arindon's king?" she said breaking into a smile.

"I fear what I cannot control," he said with honesty.

"Then you have not yet learned to be a good king or a good husband. As we said, the subject will have to wait."

4

Ben saw their guest down the stairs. When he returned, Jasenth was by the window watching a dark bent figure slowly making her way to High Queen Avrille's house.

Mill Manor was not the quiet retreat Mabry had hoped for. He should have known better. Lady Cellina ruled their household with a driving force. But life was good. Darilla his eldest daughter was finally pregnant. Don, her husband of almost fifteen years, was proud and protective. They had almost given up hope for a child of their own, fearing her ill-fated star twins sired by King Will had left her barren. Mabry was overjoyed, not only for the prospect of being a grandfather again, he was also glad that Darilla still loved him. He had wronged her. He had put her in King Will's way and let her bear him bastards. He had stood by and said nothing when Will put her and their twin sons away for their "safety". The girl had withdrawn, but with the efforts of Princess Maralinne and later with the High Queen herself, Darilla rekindled her feelings of self worth enough to accept Don's love. The simple, hardworking man accepted her twins without question and when only one baby came home from King Will's Equinox folly at the Star Castle, he loved and accepted the confused boy that remained. Varen babbled in strange voices, often falling into fits. Don protected him from the curious and critical townspeople who feared the child and kept their own children safely away from him. When Varen shouted and threw stones, Don carried him to the mill. He trained him to help with the work and when Varen came of age Don made him a place to live in the loft. There the young man often sat chattering to himself, imitating the sounds of the great wheel as if it spoke to him.

Mabry watched Don tie a knot of string around the opening of a flour sack and toss it to Varen who neatly stacked it with the others. With the rhythm of long-practiced cooperation they loaded the wagon. After they drove away to deliver the sacks, a Frevarian messenger galloped down the road to the mill.

"What news?" Mabry called.

"His Majesty King Keilen the First of Frevaria wishes to announce his intended visit to Mill Manor this evening at dinner. His Majesty specifically requests the meal be simple and there be no other guests except immediate family as His Majesty has a matter of importance to discuss with his former regent, the Lady Cellina."

"Go on to the house then," said Mabry.

"His Majesty instructed that the message be delivered only to Mabry the master miller at the mill, not at the manor. His Majesty wishes that you convey the message to the cook so as to spare the Lady Cellina any anxiety preparations would cause."

"He knows her well," Mabry chuckled. "Tell Kylie we will look forward to his visit."

"I will, sir," the messenger replied as he turned to leave.

"Will you stay for a bite of lunch here at the mill? The lunch pail should be arriving shortly," said Mabry.

"Thank you sir, but I was instructed to return immediately."

"A cool drink then?" Mabry handed him the dipper from the water bucket.

"Thank you, sir. That I can do, sir," he said gulping a swallow.

When the messenger had ridden away Mabry fell back into his reverie. His wife, the Lady Cellina, was not a tolerant woman, although she had mellowed somewhat after their marriage ended her long spinsterhood. Her huntress instincts had been replaced by fervent domestic efficiency. He had grown to love this large, powerful woman. First he had admired her strength and skill as she executed her role as regent for young King Keilen, successfully balancing her Frevarian heritage and her Arindian loyalties. But now he loved her most for the rare glimpses beneath her formidable exterior at the sensitive, vulnerable woman who needed him. When Kylie reached his majority and no longer required her presence in Frevaria, she had retired to the luxurious manor house Mabry built for her. There they officially married with the simplest of ceremonies.

"Grandpa, I got the lunch," called Timmy, Mabry's three-year-old grandson, as he lugged the pail up the path to the door. "Cook said some is for me too."

Mabry greeted the boy with a big hug. He set him on the bench and unwrapped the fresh loaf of bread and a pot of new cheese. "What's this?" he said pulling out a small jar.

"That's jelly. Cook said for me too."

"Jelly? Berry jelly? Only good boys get berry jelly on their bread."

"I'm a good boy," said Timmy. "I bring the lunch and it was heavy."

Mabry spread a cloth on the bench between them. "We must save some for Don and Varen," he said. "They're out delivering."

"Jelly too?"

"Varen likes jelly. But I'll give him my share," said Mabry as he spread the dark, sweet treat on Timmy's bread.

When they had eaten and tucked the rest in the pail for Don and Varen, Mabry boosted the boy onto his shoulders and headed for the house. "I have to see to something," he told his grandson. "But don't tell Grandma Cellina I'm here because I have to get right back to the mill. She likes me to stay if I come home and today I don't have the time. You won't tell her now?"

Timmy nodded solemnly. Lady Cellina did not grandparent unobtrusively. The child already knew her well.

Just as dinner was announced, King Keilen arrived at Mill Manor without escort. Mabry wheeled his wife's chair into the dining room. The table was laid with meticulous precision. The service pieces steamed in the dumb waiter beside the buffet. The windows were half open for fresh air with the folding screens arranged in front of them to prevent a draft. The clockwork fan whirred in the ceiling. Everything was just as Lady Cellina liked it.

"Kylie! O my gods! Tell the cook! Set a place! Why didn't someone tell me?" Lady Cellina gasped and sputtered.

"He wanted to surprise you, dear," said Mabry with a wink at their royal guest. "Cook has already added to the menu."

"Kylie, don't do this to me ever, ever again," she exclaimed with a hand dramatically placed on her heaving bosom. "You want my weak heart to faint?"

King Keilen knelt by his retired regent's chair. "Aunt Cellina, I need to talk to you…"

"Get up, get up before someone sees you. Kings don't kneel."

"Then how can I hug the most important woman in my life?" he said sinking into her voluminous embrace.

"And that brings up another matter…," she began.

"Cellina, dear, Kylie is not here to discuss a royal wedding," said Mabry wheeling her chair to the table.

"Not so close, Mabry. You know I can't breathe if my chair is too close."

"Yes, dear," he said minutely adjusting her chair.

"You know, Kylie," Cellina continued. "I'll not rest in my grave until you marry and there is a prince in Frevaria's nursery."

"Now dear," Mabry tried to soothe her. "We already know that is not the reason Kylie has come."

"Where is my Dulcie?" said Cellina anxiously looking around the room. "Such a sweet girl she is, so talented. You should see her delicate embroidery, Kylie. Where is she? Dulcie! Dulcie!"

"Yes, Mother Cellina," answered Mabry's shy younger daughter as she rushed to attend her stepmother.

"Be a good girl and wait on His Majesty. Mabry will look after my needs tonight."

Mabry gave another knowing wink at Keilen. This time it was to tell him to say nothing and to go along with the scheme.

Dinner was simple but tastefully prepared. In spite of Lady Cellina's protests that she was too unnerved to eat, Mabry served her with practiced care, cajoling her like a sick child. She let herself be persuaded to try just one bite and then another until her plate was empty and she was ordering seconds. Keilen stared at his food and pushed it around on his plate. He did not look up when Dulcie's small white hands brought and removed the dishes.

"Dulcie," Cellina ordered. "Tell the cook we will take tea in the parlor."

"Yes, Mother Cellina," the girl said in a scarcely audible voice.

Keilen watched her dainty steps retreat to the kitchen. When he turned his attention back to the dinner table, he caught Mabry's wink a third time, coupled with a smile of approval.

Lady Cellina's chair creaked as it rolled back from the table. Mabry brushed a kiss to her temple as he reached to retrieve her fallen napkin. She blushed like a maid, and for the first time that evening sighed with contentment. When Mabry had stirred up the parlor fire and adjusted the fans to draw away the smoke he said, "Now what is this important matter…?"

"Yes, yes," said Cellina leaning forward in her chair. "Tell me what is so important that you burst in on me unannounced."

Keilen started to explain the plan for High Prince Allar's majority rite and his part in it.

"That is not only appropriate, it will be glorious!" she interrupted. "You and Jasenth are his only male relatives. Yes, yes, two kings to initiate…"

"I know. I know. That's not the problem," said Keilen. "I'm glad Jay and I will dunk our cousin and that Jareth and Mabry will receive him…"

"My Mabry to receive him! How wonderful and how appropriate! Yes, since Jareth stood in for Jasenth's father and Mabry for yours…"

"I know. I know," said Keilen impatiently. "I said that's not the problem. The place is the problem."

"Place?"

"It's to be at Star Castle Pool."

"The Star Pool! I forbid it. I completely forbid it!" Cellina bellowed. "Neither you nor my Mabry will ever go near that cursed place." She gasped for breath.

"Now dear, it's just a pool of water," said Mabry with a look of concern at his wife's reddening face.

"Just water! It's evil! It's magic! Kylie it has already claimed the life of your mother, rest her soul. I'll not have either of you come home dead or what's worse come home babbling idiots like poor Varen."

"Now, now, dearest Cellina, now, now," said Mabry fanning her. "Kylie was right to come to us with this problem. We are all safe now and we will be safe. We must just work this problem out calmly and carefully."

"Calmly and carefully! Your life, our life is in danger!"

"Let's have our tea first," suggested Mabry. "A wise solution takes time."

"Dulcie! Dulcie, come pour His Majesty's tea," Cellina called.

The girl stepped out of the doorway where she had been waiting. The rose-painted cup rattled as she poured but she did not spill a drop. With downcast eyes she handed the cup to Keilen.

"Did you remember the sugar?" said Cellina. "His Majesty takes sugar in his tea."

Dulcie stopped mid-stride. Her face turned white with terror. She pinched her eyes shut and bit her lip. Keilen did not notice the twinkle of tiny white stars dance into the cup as he reached up. His eyes were only for Dulcie.

"The sugar, girl, did you remember the sugar?" said Cellina breaking the spell.

Keilen took a sip. "The tea is sweet, Aunt Cellina, as sweet as the hand that serves it."

Mabry cleared his throat. Dulcie dropped a blushing curtsy and fled from the room.

"About this problem we were discussing," said Mabry pouring tea for his wife and for himself. "If it is evil magic that we fear, the place is not the problem. Those that do magic will do it where they will. The old pool is no better or no worse for safety. Magic has happened all over the kingdoms at one time or another. I say we have the celebration as planned."

"But Mabry..." Cellina whimpered, her tone suddenly childlike.

"My dearest, you tell me the one thing that is stronger than any magic," he said setting down his cup and moving behind her chair to massage the tension from her shoulders."

"Whatever do you mean?" she said blushing and swatting at his hands.

Mabry stopped rubbing but left his hands firmly on her shoulders. "Love is stronger than any magic. I will come safely back to you, I promise. No love is richer or stronger than ours."

"But what about Kylie?" she argued weakly.

"King Keilen is well loved. And young love is the sweetest of all, not so?" He winked again at Kylie.

"Then you are bound and determined?"

"The High King has commanded," said Mabry. "We have no choice but to obey."

Now it was Keilen's turn to wink at Mabry for his cleverness. He took advantage of the momentary pause to move on. "The good part of all this is that Allar will not ascend to the high throne just yet. He is to go on a journey first."

"A journey! Where?"

"Down the river and beyond the mountains..."

"That's ridiculous!" Cellina exclaimed. "Nobody ever does that. Why would he ever want to do such an unheard of thing?"

"He wants to see the world and search for his lost sisters."

"To search for what is long dead and gone! Gods rest their infant souls."

"He's to be gone a year and then…"

"A whole year! Then he won't be here for Winter Solstice! I'm knitting him such a lovely sweater, all brown and natural tan with a little leaf motif." Cellina's mind raced ahead. "I'll just have to finish it for his manhood gift. But that's only two weeks away! Mabry, Mabry," she gasped in panic. "Fetch me my yarn!"

Jasenth sat on the opposite side of the kitchen table from Lizelle. Anxious to escape the hubbub of Arindon for a few hours at Woodsmeet Farm, he had accepted his aunt and uncle's invitation to dinner. Jareth and Maralinne were often a sounding board for his ideas and problems. They knew when to give advice and when to just listen, until tonight that is. Tonight was his cousin Allar's last dinner before his coming of age festivities. It was traditional for family to gather for such an occasion. Jasenth enjoyed the company of his younger cousin and Queen Avrille, but Lizelle and Janille were also dinner guests. His aunt offered no apology for inviting his troublesome betrothed, and his uncle gave him only the raised eyebrow of a man who knew when not to interfere with his mate. Dinner was delicious but spoiled with tension. Lizelle chattered gaily, smiling and flirting with both Allar and Jasenth. Maralinne busied herself with her duties as hostess. When the dessert dishes were cleared, Jareth stood up to suggest they retire to the comfort of the parlor, but Lizelle begged to help with the dishes. Maralinne and Avrille protested but Lizelle could not be dissuaded.

"I'll wash and Jay can dry," she insisted. "You go ahead with Allar, aunties. We'll join you in no time."

When the dishes were done and put away, instead of heading for the parlor Lizelle sat down at the table. Jasenth waited for her to say something. When she did not, he sat down too. She reached for his hand. He shivered at her touch.

"I wonder what it is like to have a man come courting?" she asked with a sly little smile.

"We don't need to court. Grandfather has already betrothed us."

"Then you already love me?"

"That has nothing to do with it."

"Do you think I'm beautiful? Do you desire me?"

Jasenth looked down. He studied his hands. He shuffled his feet as he fumbled for words.

"Are you afraid of me?"

Jasenth set his jaw and looked her straight in the eye. "I fear your magic. I fear the loss of my kingdom and the cause of the Light if I indulge myself too soon." He touched her hair, letting the pale fluffy curls slip slowly through his fingers. "I am a man, be assured of that, Lizzie, but even though I am young and anxious to prove my manhood, I have some wisdom." He paused, and when she looked demurely away he turned her face back to him. "I promise when the castle is rebuilt…"

"Your stupid castle! You know you're only building it the old way to buy time…"

"Time and good will, Lizzie," Jasenth said with an exasperated shrug. "My people…"

"Your people!" Lizelle exclaimed. "What about us?"

"They're good people," said Jasenth. "It's their love that will build this kingdom, not fear of their king or his witch bride's magic."

"So that's what you think of me?" she answered with an impatient toss of her head. "Waiting for Allar's majority was wise. We both agreed on that. Waiting for the castle to be built is understandable. But after that, what must we wait for?" She snapped her fingers. The air shimmered. A goblet of dark red wine appeared in her hand. "Drink and pledge with me, Jay. Name the day."

"I will not pledge with magic wine," Jasenth stalled. "A true king pledges only with grape grown and pressed by his own people."

"Jayjay…"

"Don't call me that baby name…"

"Well then who are you?" she mocked.

Jasenth stood up and glared straight at her. "I am Jasenth, son of Tobar, prince of Frevaria, and Analinne, princess of Arindon. I am king of Arindon, your king, Lizzie."

Lizelle leaned her chair back, cocked her head and said with a smirk, "And you are also the adopted son of Arindon's gamekeeper and his renegade princess mistress."

Jasenth slammed his fist on the table. "Don't you dare disrespect Uncle Jareth and Aunt Mari! You are nothing but a second child of a pampered Frevarian princess and her bowman paramour."

"I am much more than that, Jayjay," she snapped back. Her eyes narrowed. Her lips pursed in a tight thin line. "I am the ward and pupil of my grandmother the sorceress Janille. We are both more than our birth names. We are the sum of all we have learned." Her face softened a little. "None can change what we are," she quoted the prophecy.

"None can change what we must be," he finished the line. "Alright, Lizzie, I pledge my love to the Light. If you and your magic are of the Light then I also pledge to you." He turned his face away hoping she would not see the burning he felt in his cheeks. "Be patient with me, please..."

The goblet vanished. "Maybe you should go on a quest first like Allar," Lizelle pouted. "Poor Allar, if I were only allowed to help him, just one little clue, but Grandma says no."

"You know where the twins are?"

"Of course," she said reaching for his hands. "I know a lot of things." She pulled him toward her. "Jay, you sweet simpleton, there is so much you just don't understand."

"Oh, like what?" he said trying to pull his hands away but she held on tight.

"Like how much I love you," she purred. "Like how much I want you..."

Jasenth pulled back with alarm.

"Come on Jayjay, we could just disappear for a few minutes and..." She wiggled seductively and blew him an enticing kiss.

"No! No!"

"You know you want me."

Jasenth felt a pulse of desire surge through him. He dug his nails into his clenched fists until they bled. "Stop it Lizzie! Stop it please! This is not love."

"I'm sorry," she said coyly.

"I want you to leave me now," he ordered. "Go home and don't come to me again until you can behave like a mature, responsible woman."

Lizelle's face sobered. "Do you still love me?" she asked with a tremble of fear in her voice.

"Yes, yes, I love you. Now go!" He ran out of the room. Behind him the kitchen fire flared and Lizelle was gone.

Chapter 2

The next day lunch was a simple meal but to Allar it was an important event. He savored each bite of his dark bread and jam. This would be his last meal until noon tomorrow. Custom decreed a twenty-four-hour fast before the manhood rite. The afternoon dragged on. Allar paced. His mother, Queen Avrille tried to sew. Dell, his beloved tutor, sat by the window, scribbling in his notebook. Allar rattled the canister of nuts and fruit his mother kept for her mirror birds, Verity and Jest.

"Very, very good," the plump little female chirped.

"Just a bit, just a bit for Jest," begged her mate.

Allar opened the cage door.

"Little Allie so, so sad," said Verity.

"Tomorrow I won't be Little Allie any more, my friend. Tomorrow I will be a man." He gently stroked the little bird's head.

"Allie going away. Make Mama Avrille cry."

"You must make her happy until I come back," said Allar as he started to fill their treat dishes.

"Allar, don't give them any more," said Avrille. "You'll make Verity sick.'

"Just a bit?" Jest begged.

"No, Jest, in her condition, you know…"

Dell put his notebook aside and began to sing.

"A golden egg
In a golden cage,
A golden gift
For the coming of age."

"Pretty egg tomorrow?" asked Jest.

"Soon, hope soon," said round Verity.

Avrille put her arm around her son. "The chick will be yours when it hatches. It's too bad it can't go with you on your trip." She drew him close and let her tears fall.

"The prince will be gone
But it won't be long," Dell continued.
"One way or another,
He'll return to his mother."

Avrille tried to laugh. "Thanks Dell."
As the bard looked up his eye caught a reflection of the royal pair in the mantle mirror. In the darkened image Queen Avrille looked younger, happier than the woman in front of him and Allar looked wiser and more mature. His hair was dark like his father's.

A familiar knock at the door brought them all back to the present. Sir Rogarth, the queen's knight champion, let himself in. "My Lady. My Lord," he said with a formal bow. "And Dell, my friend."

Avrille rushed to Rogarth and took his hands. Without looking at Allar she said, "Go quickly, my sweet son, before I cry again. Go while I have my heart's friend here to comfort me."

The lights of Arindon were cold and faraway. The few farm house lights Allar had passed on his way were winking out one by one behind him. All night long there would be no moon. His grandmother Janille had told him it would rise full just before dawn. She assured him that was good. The stars would have all night to speak to him. He found the corner of the field he had selected for his vigil. It was as far away from home as he could get without crossing the Frevarian border. Nearby he could see the stark wall of the unfinished castle his father had bequeathed him. The grove of ancient trees reaching above the walls was fed by the Star Pool, the place where his mother told him his life began. Tomorrow in that same place he would become a man.

He spread his blanket roll on the damp ground. His stomach already felt the ache of fasting. Noon until noon the ritual decreed. The time was not half over yet. He snuggled down in his blanket, tucking an arm under his head for a pillow and looked up at the sky. Most of the familiar star patterns were already visible. He named The Bear, The Queen and The Twins. A farm dog howled. The wind swept the field, bringing the smell of damp, newly-tilled soil. The dog howled again, answered by the cackle of chickens startled awake. Probably it was a fox, he thought. His stomach rumbled as he thought of eating roast chicken with herbed stuffing and lots of gravy like his Aunt Maralinne made for him last night. That had been a grand dinner, with all the family there. They ate and ate right down to the last apple pie, laughing and talking until late. No one mentioned his leaving. Old stories, old jokes, old songs bound them together denying the future, if but for one night. Allar waited and shivered fighting to keep awake for his vision in the stars.

Queen Avrille rocked by the fire. Rogarth sat beside her. The rain drummed on the roof. "Sing me something, Dell," she said.

"What will it be, Lady Queen," asked the aging bard as he picked up his harp.

"Sing me something of Allar...no sing me something from before that. I want our story from the beginning, when Will and I were just beginning."

Rogarth took her hand. She smiled up at him, but she quickly turned away as her eyes filled up with tears.

"Tomorrow our prince is a man. Tomorrow you are free," he said hoping to cheer her.

"Tomorrow my life is over," she sobbed.

Dell tested a string, buying time until he could find his voice. He still thought of her as the vibrant young queen glittering on King Willarinth's arm. This mature, quiet woman wrapped in a plain green shawl with her hand on the arm of her gray-bearded champion was like a different person. Avrille's hair was still long and thick and dark but now she wore it pulled back with a single braid wound around her head. It had been a long time since she had worn the double crown in public, yet her people worshipped her, never questioning her leadership. Since the disappearance of King Will and her twin daughters, she had held on to her cherished son with desperation, fearing yet another loss. When her nephew Jasenth came of age and assumed his role as King of Arindon she retired from active part in policy making. Instead she busied herself in the village with her healing arts and teaching or spent quiet hours with Rogarth her loyal friend...

"Dell?"

The bard snapped back to the present. He struck a beginning chord. The words and melody entwined, weaving a spell of remembrance. His fingers barely touched the strings. The harp sang and the queen wept.

"Banished children of the light
United here their troth to plight;
On snow white steeds they pass the throngs,
Wreathed with flowers and joyous songs.
One crown of silver,
One crown of gold,
One star risen..."

The fire leaped. A shower of sparks swirled and took form.
"Don't surprise me like that, Lizzie," Avrille exclaimed.
"Oh Auntie, now you sound like Jay."
"I'm just getting too old for unexpected things."
"You're not old. You're just beginning," said Lizelle dancing in the firelight.
Avrille looked at her niece. With her gold hair shining and her wraith-thin body wrapped in a loose white gown Lizelle looked more like a child of ten or eleven than a woman of almost twenty.
"Grandma says I can give a gift to Allar tomorrow."
Avrille shivered. Cold fear held her, belying the fire's warmth. "What will it be?" she asked.
"Just wait and see," Lizelle beamed. "It's a star of course, but that's all I'll say."
Dell laid down his harp, relieved that his performance had been interrupted. Avrille idly entwined her fingers with Rogarth's. She wished Lizelle had not come. Usually she enjoyed her niece's buoyant if unpredictable company, but not tonight. Now she needed Rogarth's calm and Dell's wisdom. Tonight her son's future would be read in the stars. She wondered what future was left for her. Dell sang softly.

"Allar lies in the starlight,
On the ground cold,
Awaiting the dawn,
That his future be told.

His mother weeps,
For the memory to hold,
But the star waif denies
Her that solace gold."

Lizelle laughed. "Dell, if Auntie Avrille wants me to leave her alone, she will say so herself, though that's a pretty verse. Star waif, I like that."

"Dell is right, Lizzie," said Avrille. "Tonight I need quiet. Do you mind?"

"Don't worry, Auntie, Allar will come back. He will come back with your daughters and much, much more." Lizelle's laughter filled the room. In a shower of golden sparks she was gone.

Dell looked at his queen and her champion. He knew his company was also no longer needed. "If My Lady Queen allows, I think it is time for an old man to retire."

"Goodnight then, dear friend."

Rogarth and Avrille sat quietly a long, long time. At last she said. "You are all I have left. Promise you will never leave me. Without you I would be totally lost."

"I wait upon my queen. That service is my whole life. I cannot leave without your command," her knight replied.

"Well said, my servant, my champion," she said without trying to hide the quiver in her voice. "But it is Rogarth, my friend, whose company I need tonight.'

"Then little Avrille, I promise I will stay because I love you. Ask your cards. They will tell you what I say is true."

She shuffled the cards with a practiced hand. "Five for the future," she said. The deck glowed with a soft, silver light. Carefully she turned the first card saying, "My son, what will become of him?"

The fountain card played in her hand. Three youths danced in the pool before the crystal castle.

"See, it is as Lizzie said," Rogarth assured her.

"You draw the next card for my twins," she answered, accepting but not quite believing his interpretation. He handed her the Dark King.

"Will? The twins are with Will? I can't believe that. The cards never said that before. They have always drawn the Water

19

card until now." She glanced at the mantle mirror but it was dark. "Turn another card, for Allar's journey this time."

"Earth! That's a woman's card," she exclaimed staring at the image of a strong, sturdy woman obviously with child.

Rogarth laughed. "Not entirely so," he said. "This is his manhood journey after all…"

"But Allar has no interest in girls."

"Tomorrow when he becomes a man I am sure that will change. It seems that the cards tell us that in the next time turn there will not be a lack of heirs to the Star Throne."

"This is no time to tease, Rogarth."

"Then draw your own cards, My Lady Queen," he said settling back in his chair with a knowing smile on his lips.

"Alright I will," she challenged. "What future for my champion rogue?" She turned the fourth card with a flourish. "The Black Dragon. That at least is no surprise," she said watching as the black, winged beast hovered above a pair of figures. A knight battled valiantly for his lady's virtue, but the dragon swooped down, grasped her in his talons and carried her off. The bleeding knight lay helpless where he had fallen.

"So my future shall be no different from my past," said Rogarth, all mirth put aside.

Avrille laid her head on his shoulder. After a long silence she said, "In the future I will treasure your friendship as I have in the past. That will never be different. Oh Rogarth, how I wish we were free to choose, to be what our hearts tell us is right. But none can change…" She accepted his gentle kiss then she sat up with a sigh. "There is one more card…" With her movement the top card slid to the floor. The Time card looked up at them. "Another circle, or is this the fifth and last?" she asked.

Rogarth took the cards from her and laid them aside. "Tonight we have this peace. Let us treasure it. None can change what we are now."

Allar huddled beneath his sodden blanket. He had not counted on rain. How could the stars speak to him through black clouds? Did that mean he had no future, that he would die of cold or of starvation? How his stomach growled! So this is what it took to be a man? He could not go home. He could not complain.

He could not seek shelter from the cursed elements. The fast night before the manhood ritual had to be observed exactly as tradition decreed. But tomorrow there would be fun and games and feasting, yes feasting. He had never been so hungry. He had never been so lonely or so cold.

The miserable hours dragged on and on. The wind whipped up just as the songbirds began to stir in the fence rows. Allar drifted in and out of sleep, watching the east for the first ray of warmth. With a jerk he was awake to light in his eyes. The dark clouds were separating and racing to the west. The moon slid out of the trees to shine full in his face. Had he missed his vision? He panicked. Had he slept through the sign of his future? His eyes scoured the emerging stars for answers as he watched them assume their familiar patterns.

A cock crowed from a nearby farm. It was almost dawn. He sat up and tried to wring out his blanket, keeping one eye on the stars. The moon shone brighter. The stars began to pale. The "W" of stars in the north, the Great Queen, sank slowly as the Dragon stars loomed higher and higher overhead. From its triangular jaw a brilliant star exploded. It streaked across the sky to the west leaving a sizzling orange tail of fire in its wake. Straight toward the Scales it fell and vanished below the horizon.

"I have seen my future in the stars!" Allar exclaimed. "I have seen a real vision in the sky! I am the Dragon spawn and it is I who will journey to the west. I will set the balance between Light and Dark in this age," he told himself. His stomach growled in protest. "Six more hours," he sighed. "Then I can eat." As the sun broke free from the clutch of the hills, he picked up his bedroll and headed back to Arindon.

Chapter 3

The Star Castle walls rang with shouts and laughter as Jasenth and Keilen, stripped to the waist and armed with long-handled brushes, battled their younger cousin in the ritual cleansing bath. Allar splashed and spat and gasped for breath. The courtyard pool churned with the frolic.

"Don't drown me you bullies!" Allar pleaded as he surfaced between his assailants.

"Listen to the baby squeal," sang Jasenth. "Get him again! Get him again!"

Keilen held Allar under. The royal head of dark red curls was scrubbed with a vengeance. Keilen yelped and lost his footing. "Damn you royal bastard!" he shouted.

Allar emerged in a triumphant splash with Keilen's ankle in his grasp like a prize. Jasenth leaped to the rescue. The three rolled over and over, splashing and thrashing amid gulps for air and teasing curses.

Queen Avrille who just moments before had tearfully led her only son to this manhood rite now held her sides with laughter. She removed her crown and laid it behind her on her chair. She did not want to lose what royal dignity remained by having it roll off her head.

Dell joined in the fun with a merry song.

"The royal nurse did scream and curse,
The royal son did flail and wail.
The time had come to get the tub,
The royal bum to suds and scrub.
She chased him around the nursery,
In royal arse perversity..."

Howls of laughter drowned out the song. "I got 'em! I got 'em!" Keilen shouted waving a pair of breeches. Allar broke free wielding one of the brushes. The spectators cheered louder and louder.

The ground trembled just a little. No one noticed at first. The pool bubbled warmer around the bathers but they were already overheated from their joyous exercise. The earth shook again, this time in earnest. The center of the pool gushed skyward. Jasenth and Keilen leaped back with alarm. Allar rose in nude triumph on a rainbow column of water. He stepped out onto the surface of the churning water and walked to the edge of the pool to where Mabry and Jareth stood petrified on the rim holding the towels and robes. Their jaws dropped in awe. At Allar's bidding, reverently they dried and wrapped him with trembling hands. Allar turned to his cousins. As if in a trance, the kings of Arindon and Frevaria climbed out of the now quiet pool. They knelt at Allar's feet and kissed his outstretched hands. Queen Avrille picked up her crown. The entwined silver and gold of the circlet gleamed in the noonday sun. The air filled with a hypnotic humming as the two great diamonds sang in the Light.

Allar received the crown but he did not put it on. He fingered first the diamond sun and then the cusp of the moon that cradled it. "I acknowledge my birthright," he said. "But my time to rule has not yet come. I return this symbol of power to my mother's safe keeping for yet another year. My first duty is to seek my sisters, the Princesses Arinda and Arielle, for they should share the honor of my throne."

King Keilen and King Jasenth shivered beneath their towels from more than cold as the new High King again turned to them.

"And now Keilen of Frevaria and Jasenth of Arindon, I charge you to be good stewards of my lands in my absence."

Queen Avrille took her son's arm. Today she wore a simple but elegant gown of brown velvet embroidered with pink and green spring blossoms. She wore her wedding bracelets and the diamond necklace King Will had given her. The thick dark braids that wound around her head were interlaced with pearls.

Allar kissed his mother's cheek. "I also charge you," he continued to address his cousins. "To care for my mother as your own."

Tears rolled down Avrille's cheeks. She was proud to have reared such a son. She prayed Will was watching now. As Keilen and Jasenth knelt before her to renew their fealty, Dell sang a refrain.

"In the light of the noonday star,
The Sun and the Moon know who they are.
They will rise and till the Star King's land,
And tithe their due by his command."

While the young men retired to the dressing tents, the people prepared the feast. Frevaria's royal cook took charge. The tables were soon laden with the best food a late winter larder could offer. There were spiced sausages, herbed potatoes, stuffed onions, sweet breads, dried fruit tarts and aged cheese, all to be washed down with large jugs of cider. Multicolored pennants waved above the striped tents and canopies. Every noble, merchant and landlord in the Twin Kingdoms had been invited. The townspeople and farm peasants pressed in behind them and were not turned away.

Soon Allar emerged from his tent dressed in plain brown breeches and a tan homespun shirt. He waved and shouted to the crowd, "Let's eat!" He reveled in the attention as any fifteen-year-old, moving with new authority through the merry crowd, balancing his laden plate in one hand and his mug in the other. The terror and the tension caused by the magical conclusion to the ritual were masked in celebration.

Janille kept in the background with Lizelle tightly reigned beside her until the feasting was done and the time for gift giving had come. Queen Avrille gave her son a change of clothes she had sewn for him and a bag of healing herbs. Jareth gave him a leather knapsack which Maralinne had lovingly provisioned with journey cakes, cheeses and dried fruit. His cousin Keilen presented him with a small dagger with a hilt shaped like a Frevarian sunburst and blade engraved with the letter "A". "To protect your royal person and the future of the Twin Kingdoms" said Keilen with a formal bow. Jasenth gave him a beautifully tooled, leather bound journal. "That the wisdom gained from your journey may be preserved for future generations," he said with an equally formal bow.

Mabry the miller stepped forward with shy Dulcie on his arm. The girl carried an elaborately wrapped package. With a nudge of encouragement from her father she knelt before Allar. "The Lady Cellina regrets that her failing health does not permit her to attend the festivities today," she said in a scarcely audible whisper. "She has knit this sweater to keep you warm on your journey."

Allar took her hand and smiled at her as he accepted the gift. "Tell Aunt Cellina that I will wear her gift proudly and that I wish her improved health and...and I appreciated the lovely emissary she has sent with her gift." He paused then kissed Dulcie's cheek before he handed her back to her father. Mabry dared a glance at Keilen and was rewarded to see the grim set of the Frevarian royal jaw.

Allar thrust the dagger into his belt and tucked the remainder of his gifts into the knapsack. He was ready to go. He looked up to see his grandmother Janille making her way toward him. A hush fell as the sorceress's black skirts rustled as she made her way through the crowd. Lizelle, dressed in her perpetual white, bobbed demurely in her wake.

"Grandson," she addressed him to set the people at ease. "I place on you the calling. Listen well and heed its voice. It will lead you to what you seek."

Allar's ears suddenly rang with a thousand voices but in a moment they subsided to a steady hum. His feet stirred. He was anxious, very anxious to get going. Janille reached out to touch his eyes. "These kingdoms are but a small part of your inheritance. Go now and see what you are and what you are to be."

His vision blurred with racing colors. When his eyes cleared, he looked around. Everything looked the same but somewhat smaller than it had seemed to him just moments before. Again his feet stirred to be gone.

"My turn," said Lizelle beaming up at him. In a childish sing-song voice she chanted.

"With this star you will know death but will not die.
You will see one bird but hear the song of two.
You will soar to winged heights but never fly.
You will plant a seed but never pluck a flower.
You will know the Dark but come home to Love.
With this star..." she said touching his heart with delicate white fingers.

A searing pain stabbed through Allar's chest. He clamped his jaw for fear he would cry out. Lizelle's touch burned a star sign through his shirt, blistering into his flesh.

"Sorry it had to hurt so much," whispered Lizelle. Then her voice pealed like a bell to the crowd. "Behold Allarinth the Star King, the first and last hope of All Light in this age."

In the awed silence that followed, Allar picked up his pack, kissed his mother and headed for the gate. The people fell in step behind him. Dell struck up a jaunty song and soon they were all singing down the river road to the south. One by one his followers dropped out of the parade, first the Arindians, and then when Allar reached the walls of Frevaria Keilen's entourage stopped and waved goodbye. He skirted the walls with only a handful of farm boys cheering him on and soon he was alone.

The road pulled. The river pulled. The mountain heights pulled. He walked faster. He did not look back. He knew his cousin Keilen, relieved of his competition, was rejoicing in Frevaria. His cousin Jasenth in Arindon had wished him well but had not begged him to stay. There was no place for him in the twin Kingdoms. That was what had made his mother weep at his leaving. His place had been with her, sheltered, protected, cherished, the only part of his father she had left. But now he was fifteen, a man, and the calling was upon him. He had a blanket roll, his knapsack and a few silver coins Jasenth had pressed in his hand with his farewell embrace. He was armed with a dagger and a strange mark. He touched his chest. The place still burned. He pulled his shirt away from the sting. What did it mean? Why had Lizelle placed a star mark on him? Why had his grandmother's eyes held so much pain as she watched him walk away?

The Frevarian farms fell behind him. From here on there was no path. There was only the river to guide him. No one would follow him.

VE, 1 the first day after the Vernal Equinox
Year 5 of the reign of King Jasenth of Arindon
Year 8 of the reign of King Keilen of Frevaria

This is the story of my quest written in the journal my cousin Jasenth gave me as a parting gift. I am certain the events of my coming of age festivities and the official purpose of my quest will be chronicled elsewhere in the history of the twin Kingdoms. Let it be enough to say that I am glad to have the event done with and to be away on my own. Though to find my long lost sisters is my primary goal, there is much more that I want to accomplish now that I am fifteen and a man. The freedom and independence feels exhilarating.

First I must try to describe this feeling, this compulsion that has governed my every breath since my grandmother Janille put this quest upon me. It is like a taunt thread drawing me to the south and west. When I am tired it allows me to rest but no longer. It is like an unheard voice calling me from afar. For now I choose to follow it.

My legs are tired. I am sure I walked more than fifteen miles yet I am officially still in Frevaria. Tomorrow I will tackle the hills. The riverbank is too difficult to follow here. The brush is thick and there is no longer a trail. I am beyond the farms. The forest here is old and undisturbed. I made a small meal from the supplies Aunt Maralinne packed for me. I must conserve my resources until I know more of what is ahead.

 Allarinth

Vernal Equinox day 2
The Hills south of Frevaria
 I made only a little headway today. I encountered a stream and extensive boggy area at the foot of the hills. It took most of the morning and I'll admit several dunkings to reach higher ground. My boots are still wet and my breeches are stained, not that it should matter, my mother is not here. I am a traveler, not a prince, while I am on this quest. I am very tired. After I began my ascent of the hills the terrain became quite rocky. I slid back on loose shale with every step, sometimes farther than I had gone up. At last I gained a rocky ledge with a small cave beneath a boulder that had been split by a gnarled pine. I collected a few cones, a dozen in all, and lit my fire. My legs ache and the star brand Lizzie put on my chest still stings. It is almost dark. Fog has risen from the bog. There is but a faint glow overhead.

 Allarinth

Allar tried to stretch his legs. They refused to move. His blanket roll was damp. His clothes were damp and he ached everywhere. His campfire was long dead and the pale pink of the eastern sky did not promise warmth for at least a few more hours. He tried again to move his legs. The muscles woke with a painful protest. He sat up and rummaged through his knapsack for something for breakfast. The flat cakes Maralinne had made for him were hard now but he was so hungry he did not care. He cut a thin slice of cheese and tried to roll a cake around it but it crumbled. He caught the pieces with a quick reflex and laughed. Who cares about manners? He ate with his fingers and sucked each crumb from the brown paper wrapping. He took a swig of water from his jug and contemplated on how far he had come. From his rocky vantage he could see Frevaria like a golden toy boat riding on the of silver morning mist. It had taken him two days to get this far. When he resumed his trek today he would be out of sight of home and all he knew. There was no surge of adventure pulsing through his veins. Neither was there a fear of the unknown holding him back. Only the pull to follow the river made him roll and tie his damp blanket and hoist his pack once again to his shoulders.

The roar of the river below increased. The vice of the canyon walls compressed the flow to a deep green rage. Allar picked his way down from rock to rock. There was no trail here, only the frothy surge of water. The river roared louder and louder, reverberating against the sheer cliffs above. He scrambled up one rock and leaped to another, all the while trying not to look down. The river ran thick and emerald beneath a crest of foam. The canyon deepened. Footing was more difficult now that the rocks were farther apart and often wet with spray. He dropped to all fours and inched his way along precarious ledges. He stretched across the dashing torrent to grasp for slippery toeholds. The drumming river beat out of synch with his labored breaths. There was no time to be scared.

The rainbow spray swirled above him with a sinister beauty. He was mesmerized by the voice of the river as it pulsed over the rocks where he clutched for life. The water rushed into the maw of the canyon. He could not see beyond the rock where he crouched. He edged closer to the face of the sheer canyon wall in hope that the water would not be so angry there. His body shook from the unaccustomed exertion and the pounding rhythm around him. He had to rest if just for a moment. A small overhang jutted out at the base of the wall. Slowly he crawled along the slippery rocks to the short, splintered stretch of beach. He rolled across the jagged rubble to the comfort of wet moss. With one last effort he dragged himself under the sheltering rock and before he finished a sigh, he was fast asleep.

Vernal Equinox day 4
At the top of a falls overlooking the sea

When I awoke the sky was morning pale. In spite of my aching body I was anxious to get going. The pull was strong. My pack was still on my back and my boots were still on my feet. I stopped only long enough to splash my face in the eddy before I stepped out onto the rocks to challenge the river again. I was totally unprepared for what I saw. Not more than a few body lengths from the ledge where I had slept the torrent plunges over a brink into nothingness.

Now I am sitting on the cliff with my breakfast. Below the falls is a deep green pool amid a tumble of rocks and debris. Beyond that the river snakes placidly through lush vegetation until it reaches a wide lagoon. On the far side is a wall which appears to be a natural barrier of rock and sand piled high to hold the water flow except for one break at the far end. There the river has broken through to empty into an expanse of water that is greater than I could ever have imagined. It is more water than a hundred rivers, stretching farther than the eye can see. A line from the Song of Life comes to mind, "In the Air we fly free, to our birth in the Sea". Is this what it means?

Something has moved out from the trees below. Now it has vanished. Water glints between the trees and grasses. The whole area must be a marsh. I see the movement again. Now I can discern a figure on what seems to be a swinging bridge. I am anxious to explore this strange new land and meet these people. With a little luck I think I can climb down.

Allar

Chapter 4

Fallsveil opened her eyes. It was still dark, too early to get up. There was no smell of cooking fires, no squall of hungry babies, no sound of wind or storm, yet her senses strained alert. She crept out from under her blanket, groping for her sandals. Her grandmother's snores never broke rhythm. She pulled her shift over her head with a shiver and quietly crept out of the house.

Dawn was coming. She could feel the chill. She could see the faint pink light but the village was still wrapped in sleep. She followed her feet out of the circle of thatched houses, irresistibly pulled toward the falls. The thunder of falling water was so much part of her world that she was hardly aware of it. The sound grew louder. She padded along the swinging bridges, past the farm mats, green with new sprouts, onward and upward toward the tumbling water and the emerald pool into which it poured. She climbed out onto the rocks and debris of logs. It was wet and cold where the morning sea mist met the spray of the falls but she did not stop. The insistent calling was now imperative. She let it lead her to the low flat rock where she and her friends often fished. She stopped. White wings swooped down and landed on the boulder across the lip of the pool from where she stood. The Crane! The Crane had called her!

Fallsveil was both frightened and thrilled. Her grandmother was the Cranecall, the wise woman of their village. But the Crane had called her, the apprentice, not her grandmother. Fallsveil met the bird's gaze. It held her. The mist rose and the sun slid out of the golden sea. Fallsveil stood frozen in the Crane's eye until a cry from above broke the stillness. The bird vanished as the body of a man plunged down into the pool. Fallsveil dived in without thinking. Guided by instinct alone she fought the churning water. Her fingers grabbed thick hair. With strong kicks she towed the man's body to the flat rock. She rolled him on his side to let the water drain out of him. He groaned and retched.

Who was he? She knew every man that came to the village. This pale giant was not one of them. She sat there a moment trying to decide what to do. The Crane had called her to save this man. That was a sure fact. She should tell her grandmother, but she could not leave him here and he was obviously too big to drag or carry. She studied him as he lay there with slack pale features. She touched his wet mat of oddly colored hair. It was red! The man groaned again. She pulled her hand back. What had the Crane given them? She felt herself drifting into the world of mists. She opened her eyes in a strange place with walls of stone. Terror, violence and death were vividly close behind her but she calmly drove a hard bargain with someone with golden hair and a golden crown. Her people were exhausted and homeless. They needed her to do this. There was no other way...

Fallsveil snapped back to reality. It was warmer. The sun was higher in the east. How long had she been sitting there beside the half-drowned stranger? The man coughed and tried to sit up.

"Hi," he said with a weak smile. "Thanks for fishing me out."

"I had better get you to Grandmother," she said quickly as she tried to overcome her fear. She watched him slowly get to his feet, testing his balance for a few steps before he re-shouldered his pack. He combed his wet hair back with his fingers and followed her down the spongy path and across the woven reed bridges to a collection of thatched houses perched on poles above the marsh. A cluster of brown-limbed, wide-eyed children ran out to meet them.

"Where did you find the moon fish, Fallsveil?" asked a boy about seven.

"Watch your tongue, Sandy. The Crane has sent us a guest," she replied.

The children skipped along with them chanting, "Moon fish, moon fish, the Crane has sent a moon fish."

A little girl pulled at Allar's sleeve. "Is your hair on fire, Crane guest?"

"No, missy, my hair is not on fire," said Allar with amusement.

"Then why is it so red?"

"Why is yours so black?"

"Hair is black," she answered staring at Allar with amazement.

"Here it seems so," Allar said looking around at the dark heads surrounding him. "But in my country hair comes in many colors."

"You're funny!"

"Piper," said Fallsveil. "Don't be discourteous to our guest. Run and tell Cranecall that he has arrived."

Women of all ages peered out from the windows and doorways at their procession. In the center of the village they were confronted by an old woman crowned with thin gray braids tied back with a blue silk scarf. She stood tall and straight, a personage of obvious authority.

"Granddaughter," she said. "What have you brought to us?'

Allar stepped forward. "I am Allar. I am pleased to meet you."

The old woman looked at him critically but before she could say anything more the children at the edge of the crowd began shouting, "The beachcombers are back."

Several reed boats paddled up to the dock. The entire village sprang into a flurry of activity. The boating party began unloading nets full of shells and bundles of smooth gray wood. The old woman gave orders concerning the distribution of the cargo before returning her attention to Allar. "You will stay the first watch with us, and then we will decide what to do with you."

"Thank you," he said. "Your hospitality is most generous."

"He needs dry clothes, Grandmother," said Fallsveil.

"There are some man's things in the trunk. Give him what he needs but keep and eye on him."

Inside the reed house Fallsveil laid out a shirt and breeches. Then she left him alone. When Allar had dressed and hung his wet clothes over a chair he went back outside to look for her but she was nowhere in sight. Cooking fires had been lit in boxes of sand in front of each doorway. The smell of grilling fish and baking bread filled the air, reminding Allar that he was very hungry. He wandered toward the nearest cook fire. The women ignored him as they went about their meal preparations. He watched them drain some dark brown grain that had been boiling in a pot. With deft hands they shaped it into flat cakes and baked them on griddles suspended over the fire. Beside them fish were sizzling in a flat wire basket. The smell was tantalizing but before he could he could ask how soon they would eat a loud horn sounded from the direction of the sea. Immediately the women doused the fires and packed their food into baskets while the older children herded the younger ones inside the houses.

"There you are," said Fallsveil running up to him and taking him by the hand. "We must go inside, now. Carinna's conch has sounded the tide turn."

When they arrived back at the house the old woman was unrolling curtains down over the windows although it was bright morning. Fallsveil tied the door latch securely behind them.

"Why must we...?" Allar started to ask but Fallsveil held a finger to her lips signaling him to be silent.

She spread a cloth out on the floor and opened a food basket. "Sit with us," she whispered as she dropped cross-legged on the edge of the cloth.

"Blessed be the Crane," said the old woman.

"Blessed be the Crane," said Fallsveil.

"Mother of the Sea we thank you for this bounty."

"Mother of the Sea hide us from the Westshoren raiders."

"Keep us safe beneath the wings of the Crane until the tide turns and all is well," Fallsveil's grandmother concluded.

Allar sat in respectful silence until they invited him to join their meal. The grilled fish was river trout, one of his favorite dishes. A twinge of homesickness tried to spoil his appetite until Fallsveil handed him a shell bowl of soup. The smell was wonderful. Made of shellfish much sweeter than river clams and flavored with greens and herbs it was truly the best soup Allar had ever tasted. He let the thick steaming broth roll over his tongue and slowly savored the chunks of meat. "This is good," he said. "This is very good."

He dipped his pieces of flat nut-flavored bread into the soup. "What grain is this?" he asked between bites.

Fallsveil looked at him with puzzled surprise.

"What do you call this bread?" said Allar trying to rephrase his question.

"Meenom."

"Meenom? Where does it grow? You must show me."

"Meenom grows everywhere," she said with an expansive gesture. "You are a funny man to ask such a thing."

When they had finished their meal and packed the remains back into the basket, Fallsveil and her grandmother rolled thick woven mats out onto the floor and curled up to sleep. Allar sat on the edge of his mat. His stomach was pleasantly full and he was tired, but sleep did not come easily since it was day outside, not night. The smell of the fish oil lamp was very strong and the soot made his eyes sting. He pinched them shut willing his hands not to rub. His throat was dry. He swallowed slowly trying not to cough. Time dragged. He studied the room. The intricate thatching and weaving of the furnishings were both functional and decorative. He let his mind wander in and out of the roof weavings until excitement of his adventures and new surroundings finally gave way to exhaustion. When the conch horn aroused the village the sun was slanting through the curtains at a different angle.

Allar spent the evening wandering through the village. The women had now set up weaving frames in front of their doorways. When he stopped to admire their work he was met with wary courtesy. He fingered the soft fabric on one young woman's frame. He asked her what she was weaving and what plant the threads came from.

"It's reed fluff for dresses," she told him. "We gather it in autumn when the marsh dries."

Other frames held coarser fabrics like what he had seen used for household furnishings. These they told him were made from the stalks of reeds. He was amazed at the variety of colors and the complexity of designs they produced from such simple materials.

He watched a group of small girls playing with their dolls. He picked up a rag doll and made it dance on his knee. The girls giggled at the dolls antics but when Allar tried to inspect the tiny doll clothes the girls quickly gathered up their things and ran to hide behind their mothers. Allar's friendly questions went unanswered.

On the dock several boys were involved in a board game. Shells and stones marked their plays on concentric circles on their game board. The shells were named "weavers" and the stones were "raiders" they explained. Like most boys' games it was some sort of war play. Allar watched them count out the markers in turn, arguing over the numbers as they placed them on the board. They answered his questions with impatience and when they did not invite him to play he left them to their game and walked along the swinging pathways. The sway of the bridgework made him feel uneasy though the construction seemed sturdy enough. He kept a firm hand on the side rail and tried to match his steps to the rhythm of the span. He wondered how deep the water was beneath him and whether the villagers ever fell in.

The sky darkened. Lamps were lit and the cooking fires were kindled again. Allar's mouth watered at the thought of another delicious meal. Again the conch signal sounded. All activities stopped and everyone went inside just as they had done earlier. Again Fallsveil came looking for him, but this time she took him to a different house. It was sparsely furnished and smelled a bit musty but when the fish oil lamp was lit it looked cheerful enough. Fallsveil unpacked her food basket and set out the cloth for two. The food was both filling and delicious, and when they had finished Fallsveil offered him a warm sweet drink.

"Sleep safe under the wings of the Crane," she said.

"Thank you and good night to you too," he answered. He had so many questions to ask his new friend but soon they seemed unimportant. He curled up on his sleeping mat, barely aware that someone was covering him with a blanket.

"Is the visitor asleep?" asked Cranecall when her granddaughter returned.

"I gave him the dream draught as you told me to do," said Fallsveil.

"Then sleep, the watch is half over already,"

"Will you send the visitor a dream, Grandmother?"

"That is not for you to know. But if you ask, will I be walking with our Mother of the Night Sky, the answer is yes and I will need you to watch over me as always."

"Yes Grandmother."

Allar wrestled with the silvery blanket. He shivered as the blanket billowed like a sail in the cold wind. Gray fluttering probed outside his cocoon. He pushed them aside and nestled deeper. Again and again the fluttering came but the moon-silvered hammock that rocked him held fast and secure.

Cranecall remained in bed long after the waking conch had sounded. Fallsveil kept vigil until her grandmother's slow breaths quickened and her cramped limbs began to stretch beneath the blankets. "Grandmother," she called softly. "Grandmother."

Cranecall's eyes opened slowly. Her hand groped for the cup of antidote Fallsveil held for her.

"Your dream journey was long and difficult this time," said Fallsveil.

Cranecall swallowed the bitter drink. Gradually she felt it counteract the dream draught she had taken the night before. "A long one and all for nothing," she said as she sat up.

"Where did you go?" asked Fallsveil. "To Allar? To his homeland?"

"I found him alright, but the Mother of the Night Sky had him wrapped in her bosom. I could not get in no matter how hard I tried."

"Perhaps it is not right to probe our guest if a Mother protects him?"

"It would be better if it were our Sea Mother that cradled him," said Cranecall as she rubbed the sleep from her eyes.

"Here Grandmother, bathe your face," said Fallsveil offering her a moist cloth and towel. "I will get you some meenom cake and fruit."

"I don't want anything to eat yet," Cranecall answered. "You know how dream walking always affects my stomach."

Vernal Equinox 6
Village of the Reedweavers

I have been in the village of Thatchmeet three days. They have treated me as a royal guest but I cannot put the feeling out of my head that I am in reality a prisoner. This is the first time I have been left alone but even now there is a boy who keeps about twenty paces from me. I suspect he has been told to note my whereabouts.

Let me begin my account of my adventures here from the morning I arrived with a sudden fall from the cliff. The descent seemed easy at first. Had I not been startled by the flight of a gigantic bird, I may not have lost my footing. When I realized I was going to fall I pushed myself away from the cliff and fell toward the pool below. It knocked the wind out of me when I hit the water but lucky for me Fallsveil was there to drag me out before I was swept over the lip of the pool and onto the rocks.

Fallsveil, what a beautiful name for a strange and beautiful girl! She is thin and dark both of skin and hair as are all the people here. She says she is fourteen years old. Everyone is fascinated by my appearance, especially my hair. My short curls and reddish brown color which I always thought as dark compared to the reds and blondes of the Twin Kingdoms, to them is somehow amusing. The children have nicknamed me Moonfish because of my paleness. I have tried to take it in good humor. I told them I was a prince of my land and was on my manhood journey. My appearance and the dagger Kylie gave me seemed to make my story credible to them.

It is very pleasant talking to Fallsveil, comparing our worlds which are so different though they are only the height of the falls apart. The thing that strikes me as most unusual here is that the village is populated entirely by women and children. When I asked the whereabouts of the men, Fallsveil's first reaction was shock, then embarrassment. Finally she said the men hunt seals but refused to say more.

The pull to travel westward which I experienced in the earlier part of my journey is still with me but not nearly so strong. It is as if I am meant to stay here, perhaps so that I can learn something important before I venture on.

Allar

VE 8
Cranesbill, the barrier between the lagoon and the sea

I never tire of listening to the sound of the waves. The rhythm of the surf seems a part of me though I have never set eyes on the sea until now. Fallsveil says it is the heartbeat of our mother, the sound we all hear before we are born, the sound we listen and long for all our days. She said we hear the sea call to us to remind us of our mortality and to promise us that someday we will again be part of her on the last voyage. I did not understand all this until she explained that they do not burn their dead as we do but set them adrift in boats when the tide turns out.

This tide, let me try to explain it. For part of the day the water from the falls flows out into the sea as one would expect. At other times the sea flows back into the lagoon. There seems to be no rational explanation for this. All Fallsveil could tell me was that the tide was the breaths of our mother. The sea is a fascinating thing. These people are caught between the falls and the vast sea itself. They have built their village and live their entire lives in the lagoon where the tides balance the warring forces of water. I am sure there is purpose in all this.

Allar

Fallsveil sat on the edge of the dock sewing with two younger girls. They had brought their dolls and were asking her how to make dresses. Fallsveil showed them how to measure and cut the tiny pieces. She threaded their needles before she returned to her own work.

"Our dolls are going sailing," said Piper.

"Our brother thatched us a boat," said Puffin.

"It's just big enough for dolls," Piper added.

"Your brother is a good boy. He will make a fine seal hunter someday," said Fallsveil.

"Then he will bring mother and us lots of oil and furs for winter."

"If he doesn't take a wife and give it all to her," said Piper.

Puffin laid down her sewing. "If the stranger takes you, Fallsveil, what will he bring you?"

"Allar will be long gone before I am old enough to be taken," Fallsveil replied looking down at her work to hide her blush.

"Our mother says you two are walking and talking like it was the summer moon."

All three of them giggled.

"Hush now you two," said Fallsveil. "Here he comes."

Allar greeted them with a smile but the little girls became shy and quiet.

"Why don't you tadpoles run to get your boat so the dolls can have their ride before tide turn. I'll finish their dresses for you."

The little girls giggled, glancing back at Allar and Fallsveil as they sprinted back along the swinging bridges. When they were out of sight Fallsveil turned to Allar and said, "Blessed be our Mother for little ones like those."

"Are they your sisters?"

"No, we have no common Earth Mother. I have no sisters or brothers, have you?"

Allar sat down on the dock beside her. "I had two sisters but they were stolen by the Darkness before I was born. I am on this journey to find them and bring them home to our mother."

Fallsveil laid a sympathetic hand on his arm. "May the Crane shelter them until they are found unless Our Mother the Sea has drawn them already into her deeps."

"Who is this mother of the sea?" asked Allar. He looked down at her hand on his arm hoping she would not draw it away.

"Carinna, don't your people honor her?" she said with surprise.

"We have Carinna Goddess of Water." He watched with disappointment as she withdrew her hand.

"They are the same I'm sure," she said smiling up at him. "Tell me of your Earth Mother."

"Sea mother, earth mother, you have me all confused."

"The mother that bore and nursed you, silly," she laughed slapping him playfully on the knee.

Allar moved his legs uncomfortably. "Oh! My mother is Avrille, High Queen of the Twin Kingdoms. What about your mother?"

"Mine was Murex but she is dead to us," Fallsveil said matter-of-factly.

"I'm sorry," said Allar.

"I have Grandmother to teach me so I am not sorry." She picked up the doll dresses the little girls were sewing and threaded her needle.

Allar watched her knot the end of the thread and begin to hem the tiny garments. "Tell me," he said when the silence seemed a bit too long. "Do your people have any more mothers since you have mentioned two already?"

"We are also children of Marielle, Mother of the Night Sky," she said as she laid one finished doll dress aside and reached for the other.

"My grandmother's name was Marielle!" Allar exclaimed. "And the moon was her symbol."

Fallsveil gave him a startled look then quickly resumed her work. Allar noticed her hand shook as she took another stitch then stopped. "Blessed be the Crane, their eyes and ears in this world," she murmured.

Soon Piper and Puffin returned with their dolls and a tiny reed boat. "Help us sail them, Fallsveil," they begged.

Fallsveil pulled her dress off over her head and slid into the water. The little girls tossed their clothes onto the dock and leaned out over the water to launch their doll-laden boat. They jumped in after it and nearly capsized their toy but Fallsveil grabbed it and held it steady. Allar remained on the dock in embarrassed confusion. Nude children in an aquatic environment he could accept as a practicality but to see a young woman! He was not ignorant of female anatomy, but never having been presented with such a close and uninhibited view he simply stared. The sun sparkled on her smooth dark limbs as she pushed the toy boat ahead of her. The green water rippled and broke over her taunt muscled legs and soft round buttocks.

"Come on in," she called.

"I'll just watch," he said nervously shifting his weight.

Piper and Puffin climbed on Fallsveil's back. "Don't bother with him. Just play with us," they said.

Allar sat down on the dock, envious of the children's closeness to Fallsveil. A feeling of warm discomfort spread over him. When the girls and their toys were far out into the lagoon he eased himself to the edge of the dock and slid into the water's cool relief.

Fallsveil pulled on her dress over her wet skin. She loved to swim in the lagoon as the tide rode out but now it was her turn to hunt for driftwood. As she combed the narrow spit of sand for anything useful she thought of their strange visitor. He was certainly ugly, all pale skinned with hair as red as a cooked crab, but she found herself attracted to his friendly manner. He was as curious as a child, eager to learn and share. Though he was a grown man, he was not loud or harsh or possessive like the seal hunters she knew.

She picked up a twisted gray stick and tossed a length of seaweed aside. The stranger again took over her thoughts. How long would he stay? What did he really want here? Grandmother had tried to probe him and failed. She picked up another stick. "Mother of the Sea," she said looking out over the waves. "Is it right that this man has come to us? Is it right that the Cranecall's chosen daughter looks at him and finds pleasure in his company? Show me a sign."

She stood ankle deep in the water and lifted her face to the salty wind. Something struck her toes. She looked down. A star shell, perfect and unbroken lay in the receding ripple. She picked it up. "I will make this into an amulet," she said to herself. "This is my sign. Blessed be the Crane." She slipped the shell into her bag and continued her search for firewood.

Vernal Equinox Day 14
Thatchmeet

Today there is a flurry of activity. Children are hanging little fish oil lamps made of shells above the doorway to each house and all along the maze of bridgework. They make a game of it but I can sense tension, almost fear, beneath the surface of their actions. No one will answer my questions directly. The small boy who put his lamp over my door said "May the eyes of Our Mother of the Night Sky protect you," before he ran away. Fallsveil calls the moon the Mother of the Night Sky. I have counted the days. I have been traveling two weeks, two weeks since the full moon. Tonight is the dark of the moon. To these people the event must have fearsome significance. I tried to find Fallsveil to ask more but only saw her briefly. She told me to remain inside my house after nightfall. To my questions all she would say before she rushed off was that the women of the Crane's Nest, the ruling council, meet tonight and they wanted her to be there too. So I wait for the dark of the moon. The smell of burning fish oil is almost overwhelming.

Allar

Fallsveil brushed back her hair and twisted it into a knot. With shaking hands she carefully inserted two shell pins to hold it in place. Tonight she would be sitting in the Crane's Nest with her grandmother though she was still only fourteen, a child. Her grandmother turned her around and looked at her critically. Then she smiled.

"You are to be honored tonight, granddaughter, but your face is as if you were to be judged."

"I'm just nervous," Fallsveil replied.

"Don't be. The Crane's Nest, for those who sit in it, is no more fearsome than the gossips fishing at Falls Cup Pool. We talk women talk. We plan for the good of the village. And when the time is right, we weave the story. That is all. Now smile and make me proud."

"Alright, I am ready to be the Cranecall's pride," said Fallsveil.

They left the house together and walked along the spiraling paths to the center of the village. The Crane's Nest meeting hall was open to the sky. The roof and ceiling curtains had been folded aside. A low fire glowed red in the brazier. Fallsveil's eyes adjusted to the dim light. Around the fire was a circle of solemn half-lit faces. She knew these women. She worked with them and talked with them every day, but tonight they were fearsome strangers. The five women of the Crane's Nest spoke with the gods and meted out divine will to the village.

"Sit here by me, granddaughter," said Cranecall.

Fallsveil obeyed. She was glad to sit and be less conspicuous to the circle of fire-red eyes.

"Dark," said a voice.

"Dark," said another.

"Dark of the Moon," said Cranecall.

"We are but children," said the first voice.

"We are helpless and afraid," said the second.

"We cry in the dark," said a third.

"Dark. Dark. Dark," wailed the circle of voices.

"Dark of the Moon," said Cranecall. "Hear us Mother of the Night Sky. Return to us."

There was a rustle. The air began to vibrate with the beat of gigantic wings. The fire blazed bright.

"The Crane! The Crane!" the voices rose in praise. "The Crane! The Crane! Blessed be the Crane."

"Shelter us with your wings," said Cranecall.

Again the hall was filled with rustling. Fallsveil looked around at the faces. Now they were smiling and familiar. Beside her she saw Willow, her neighbor, tucking a feathered wand back into its case.

"What business have we?" said Cranecall.

"My son has returned with a message from the men's camp," said Willow. "The hunt has been good and we are to prepare for their return just after full moon."

"Blessed be the Crane," they all sang.

Cranecall laughed. "Yes, blessed be! It has been a long season of sleeping alone." They all joined her laughter. "Speaking of babies," Cranecall continued as she turned to her neighbor. "Lilly, what shall we name that new grandson of yours?"

"The shadow child was put to the tide already," Lilly answered. "But my daughter wishes to wait until the child's father returns to name him."

"It's a love match child then?" said Cranecall.

Fallsveil shivered. She knew she had been a twin. Every dark of the moon she hung her lamp to keep its severed soul from finding its way back to haunt her. Only the first born could be sheltered beneath the wing of the Crane. The shadow child had to be set adrift as an offering to the seals to insure a bountiful harvest.

The circle of laugher brought Fallsveil back to reality. Tidesong was saying, "...and I found myself hanging by one arm. I didn't know whether to drop the fish basket or my son Skeeter."

"I would have dropped Skeeter. Never have I seen such a troublesome love gift from a seal hunter as that child."

"We will fix the bridge," said Cranecall. "Springbud, you take your girls out there first thing in the morning. Now are there any other matters of business?"

The chatter went on and on. Fallsveil's eyes scanned the room. The sacred weavings on the walls were alive in the firelight. The tiny figures seamed to dance through the stories of their history up one panel and down the other until they joined the giant loom frame that waited in the corner.

"Granddaughter!"

Fallsveil snapped her attention back to the circle."

"Now tell us all there is to know about our guest."

"From the very beginning?" said Fallsveil suddenly fearful and shy again.

"Yes, from the beginning," said Cranecall with an encouraging smile.

"Even what everyone knows?"

"Yes, everything. You are our best witness."

Fallsveil told the story from the first early call of the Crane. The circle sat in respectful silence. "...and so then I brought him to the village." She paused to look at her grandmother.

"Tell us who he says he is," prompted Cranecall.

"He is named Allarinth, but he is called only Allar. The ending of the name is part of his father's and grandfather's name, a tradition of his people."

"Who are his people?" asked Willow.

"He comes from the land above the falls. He says there are two villages there. Each one is ruled by a cousin of his. Both are young men not much older than he is."

"Can you imagine that? Men ruling! And young ones at that!" exclaimed Lilly.

"But his mother," Fallsveil was quick to add in her friend's defense. "Avrille he calls her, she is High Queen and rules over both villages until he returns from his journey."

"As it should be," said Willow. "Does he say why he journeys so far from his people?"

"Allar says his sisters were abducted by the Dark and he means to find and rescue them. He also says he journeys to seek his place in the world."

"Tell us more," said Springbud leaning closer to Fallsveil.

Fallsveil retold Allar's stories of riches and knowledge and magical wonders far beyond anything their simple lives could imagine.

"Then it must be true," said Willow.

"The symbol on his dagger tells us it is true," said Cranecall.

Fallsveil had seen Allar's dagger with a blazing sun on its hilt. He had told her it was a parting gift from his cousin. Cranecall led her granddaughter to the sacred tapestry on the wall. The circle parted for them to pass then crowded in behind them. She pointed to a section woven near the top of a panel. "This story is two years before you were born."

Fallsveil followed her grandmother's finger to where a picture of the falls was woven into the tapestry. A strange boat hovered over the pool as if it had just glided over the brink. The image of the Crane, barely visible beneath the boat, stretched its wings as if to cushion the vessel's fall. Tiny dried flowers were woven into the picture to adorn the boat, and on the side of its high curved prow was a golden sun.

"Has he told you anything of this?" asked Cranecall.

"No, but I will ask him if you wish. We talk mostly of current things. This event would have been before he was born. He is just fifteen, just this equinox a man. Was someone in the boat?" Fallsveil asked. Her curiosity was now aroused by the picture and its possible connection to her friend.

"The boat was empty except for this," said Cranecall patting the blue scarf she always wore. "There is one more thing," she said leading Fallsveil to the place where the weaving joined the loom. Next to the silent shuttle was another picture of the falls with the village woven beneath. The sky was full of dark pointed clouds in the shape of a starfish. "This was woven last dark of the moon," she said with a catch of fear in her voice.

"You think Allar is the starfish?" Fallsveil exclaimed with disbelief.

"We have all seen the new scar on his chest," said Willow.

Fallsveil looked anxiously from one face to another. What were these women thinking? What were they planning? She had known them all her life but now they were frightening, threatening, plotting against her and her new friend.

"Tell us," said Cranecall kindly, sensing Fallsveil's distress. "Did he say how he got the scar?"

"His cousin gave it to him at his manhood rite."

"It seems he has got a lot of cousins," observed Lilly.

"This one is a girl, an apprentice wise woman like me…" Fallsveil's voice failed her. She was afraid to say anything more. The fire in the brazier spat and flared. Fallsveil felt uneasy, as if she were being watched. The unease crept inside her, gently pushing at her thoughts. Soothing, reassuring fingers probed for contact. The fire-lit circle of eyes around her did not move. Her grandmother held her hands out, frozen in time. Gently, very gently the otherness pushed Fallsveil's self aside, flooding her with calm and submission. She did not fight the feeling as the otherness slid down inside her body. Her legs quivered. Her feet started walking toward the loom. Her hands tingled. She picked up the shuttle and wove. The women of the Crane's Nest stood like statues behind her. Faster and faster her fingers flew. The fire blazed high. It swirled and took the form of a woman.

"Well done!" sang a voice like liquid silver light. "Heed my message and my messenger."

The image vanished and Fallsveil collapsed over the loom.

"Blessed be the Crane!" chorused the circle of women.

Fallsveil awoke to concerned faces peering down at her. Sharp-spoken Willow, light-hearted Tidesong, inquisitive Lilly and quiet, patient Springbud, they were all her neighbors, all her grandmother's friends. "What happened?" she said looking up at them, half expecting them to vanish into something sinister again.

"Come see," said Cranecall helping her to her feet.

There was a new picture on the loom. A young woman sat on rock. In her hand was a starfish. By her feet was a tidal pool in which was woven a miniature scene of the falls and the village."

"The future is in my hands?" said Fallsveil.

"I think we should send him away," said Lilly.

"I think we should drown him before he drowns us," said Willow.

"Willow, we can't kill the man!" Springbud exclaimed.

"We will wait and think on these things," said Cranecall. "Then we will meet and decide."

Tidesong gave a nervous little laugh. "We had better be rid of him before the men come home."

"Yes, all must be decided and done before then," said Cranecall with finality. "Blessed be the Crane."

"Blessed be the Crane," the circle answered.

The meeting adjourned. Cranecall put her arm around her granddaughter. Together they walked out into the lantern-studded night.

Chapter 5

Vernal Equinox Day 18

It has been three days since the dark of the moon. I have not spoken to Fallsveil though I have dreamed of her every night. The painful difference between these dreams and reality is almost unbearable. Today I saw her at a distance. I am sure she saw me too, but she kept her head turned. What is wrong? Have I offended her somehow? These people have treated me well. Their way of life is fascinating yet I have thoughts to move on. The pull that I felt at the beginning of my journey is still with me. Here at Thatchmeet it has been only a subtle reminder but increasingly these last three days it has been intruding into my thoughts. I must get some answers. I sense danger, but from a village of women and children? Or is the danger in me and in the new feelings Fallsveil has awakened?

Allar

VE 20

Today I went alone to the farm mats. The village cultivates grain and herbs in the middle of the marsh by tying woven reed mats between the trees. The seed is sown onto the mat and the seedlings attach themselves to and become part of this floating field. Today there was no work being done. Only two little boys were there with sticks tied with colored ribbons which they waved to scare the birds from the mats. Occasionally they would wade out to stir the water beneath the mats to discourage any creature that would dare nibble at the dangling roots. I tried to talk to the boys but got only reluctant one-word answers. Why won't people talk to me anymore? Are they angry with me? Are they afraid of me? Why? Are they hiding something they are afraid I might discover?

Allar

Fallsveil watched for Allar to come out of his house. The Crane's Nest had decided to find out all they could about their strange visitor before sending him on his way. Cranecall insisted that Fallsveil be the one to question him. For that Fallsveil was glad but she did not know how to ask for the information they wanted without deceiving her friend.

Was that his face in the window? Should she step out on the walkway now? Her heart fluttered. She did not want Allar to leave, but she understood why he could not be there when the seal hunters returned. Duty to her village warred with the emotions that were stiring inside her. She smoothed back her hair and stepped out onto the walkway. Before she was halfway to Allar's house the door opened.

"Fallsveil!"

"Hello, Allar. It's a good day to take a boat out to Crane's Beak. Would you like to come?"

They raced hand in hand to the dock. There Fallsveil untied a small reed boat. Allar tumbled awkwardly into the bottom. Fallsveil laughed as she agilely balanced one knee on each side of the rocking craft. With strong, swift strokes she paddled out into the lagoon. As anxious as he was to have his many questions answered, Allar was so relieved that Fallsveil's silence was finally broken, that he held back. He did not want to spoil the moment. The sun was warm in the gently rocking boat. The bundled reeds prickled his legs and the smell of pitch waterproofing seeped up from the bottom. He watched her brown arms dip the paddle in a rhythmic arc. Fallsveil kept her gaze out over the water. She was too shy and confused by her new feelings and too worried by the weight of her duty to the Crane's Nest to meet his eyes. To ease the awkwardness, she hummed a little tune. Allar joined her with a counter melody.

"It is both beautiful and curious," she said when they had finished. "Two songs can merge and weave yet stand alone."

"It is a music technique I learned from my tutor, Dell. He is our court bard."

"A court bard? We have no court bards here," said Fallsveil.

"A bard sings old songs to entertain and educate the people. He also makes up new songs about things that happen now so that our children will remember them."

"Oh, like our moon weavers..." Fallsveil stopped in mid sentence. Had she said too much?

"What do moon weavers do?" asked Allar.

"I cannot say. It...it's a sacred thing...not meant for strangers..."

The boat glided through a shallow patch of reeds. There was a rustle in the vegetation. Giant white wings swooped over head. "Blessed be the Crane," Fallsveil gasped.

The bird soared, circling their boat. Fallsveil opened her arms and lifted her face to the messenger of her goddess. The bird dipped low ahead of them, skimming the surface of the water toward the far end of the seawall. There it hovered, with its long legs dangling, lazily floating down until its feet touched the rocks. It folded its wings, cocked its head and waited.

Fallsveil paddled straight toward the crane. "Be quiet and listen," she breathed.

Allar obeyed. The bird marked their approach. When the boat grated against the rock wall, Fallsveil hopped ashore and tied the line. Allar clambered after her. The crane was standing a few yards away. It shifted uneasily from one foot to the other. Fallsveil knelt and waited. Allar dropped down beside her. The crane turned away from them and began picking about in the tiny pools of water among the rocks. There was a sudden splash and the bird took flight.

"Look!" cried Fallsveil. The bird was carrying something in its beak. "A starfish!" The bird winged out over the breakers and with a sudden cry dropped the starfish into the sea. "So be it," said Fallsveil. She turned to Allar. "There are things Grandmother told me to ask you today. Answer me truly for on your words hang the future of our village and your own future as well."

Allar was more than puzzled by all that happened on their outing. He knew that the crane played the role of emissary between these people and their goddess and that what he had just witnessed was a religious experience for his friend. But how did he fit into all this? What questions did she need to ask him? He had been open and honest with her as to his origins and the purpose of his journey.

Fallsveil climbed to the pool from which the crane had plucked the starfish. Allar crouched beside her to look into the tiny world beneath the surface of the water. He was drawn to the gently undulating seaweeds that forested the slope of rock. Wedged along a crevice anemone tentacles waved. Hermit crabs scuttled across the bottom. "It's beautiful!" he exclaimed as he watched a minnow dart through a sparkle of sunlight. He rubbed his hand over the barnacled rock, squinting to watch their feeding fingers reach for infinitesimal bits of nourishment.

"Grandmother says these worlds are here to mirror ours, to teach us to live our lives as we would have the gods see us in their mirrors." She stirred the water with a finger. "We are the gods to these worlds. See, I can tip their balance. I can pick them up and transport them to a different world. I can watch them mate and grow and change. Or I could throw in a starfish to devour them."

"The crane plucked out the starfish," said Allar beginning to understand her allegory.

"Yes it did, and that is what we must do when our way of life is threatened."

"What, who is threatening you?'

"I will explain but first I must ask you the questions Grandmother told me to ask,"

Allar nodded.

"Two years before I was born there was a boat, a very strange and beautiful boat made of wood, not reeds like ours..."

"Where did it come from?"

"From over the falls just like you did. The story is woven into the sacred tapestries in the Crane's Nest house. I am to ask you if you know who sent that boat."

Allar tried to think...a boat...from above the falls...from the Twin Kingdoms? The sun beat down on his back. "When did you say it came?"

"Midsummer, sixteen years ago."

Allar took off his shirt. The sun felt good on his shoulders. "Who was on the boat?"

"It was empty," Fallsveil replied.

"I doubt anyone would have survived the fall."

"The story tells that the boat did not fall, rather it floated down to the lagoon on the wings of the crane."

Allar thought out loud, "The year before I was born...midsummer...what happened then? Who could have...? Grandmother Marielle and Gil! That must be it. My grandmother Queen Marielle died midsummer before I was born. I was told that Gil, her consort, took her on her last journey down the river in the Frevarian royal barge."

"Barge? Frevarian royal barge?" Fallsveil rolled the unfamiliar words over her tongue.

"Yes, Frevaria is one of the two kingdoms, or villages, in my land. The royalty of both kingdoms were living there because the castle at Arindon had just burned. If the barge came down here why did no one find the bodies?"

"The boat was truly empty. It contained only flowers and a banner of such a beautiful blue cloth that…"

"Blue banner! My grandmother's banner was blue."

"Now my grandmother wears it."

"Where is the boat now?" asked Allar.

Fallsveil waited a moment before she answered. "It's hidden and I may not tell you where. They fear you would claim it and take it from us."

"Why do they think I would do that?"

"The picture of the sun on the prow of the boat and the one on your dagger are the same," said Fallsveil with a note of sadness creeping into her voice.

"Of course it is. My cousin Kylie who gave me my dagger is king of Frevaria. All things Frevarian bear the mark of the sun. I am high king over both Frevaria and Arindon so by rights the boat would be mine. And if I am to continue my travels someday I will need a boat."

Fallsveil looked down into the tidal pool. Allar waited for her to say something more and when she did not, he touched her cheek. "Have I said something wrong?"

"You want to leave?"

Understanding her change of mood, he was both pleased and saddened. "I have no place here in your village," he began to say. "I am a grown man among women and children. Except for you, my sweet friend, I have no reason to remain longer than I am welcome."

"They…the Crane's Nest…even Grandmother all want you to leave, but I don't want you to…" She looked up at him with imploring eyes. "You are in danger here. Some of them even wanted to have you killed, but Grandmother said you only had to leave before the seal hunters come home."

"Kill me! Why?" Allar was suddenly very much afraid.

She touched the star brand on his chest. "You are the starfish to our world. They fear you will devour our way of life."

Allar took her hands. "Are you afraid of me?"

"No, I'm...yes I am. I like you. I want to know about you and your strange land but I cannot. Your ways are not ours..."

"To me your village is strange with all women and babies and no men. In my land we live together and work side by side. I want to know you and share our different lives so we can learn from each other. Tell me why it is so important that I am gone when your men come home."

"Our men hunt the seal and live in camps along the shore. In summer when the seal harvest is done they come here to Thatchmeet to take wives and celebrate with us until autumn. When they leave to hunt again they take the boys who have come of age with them."

"Aren't they afraid to leave their families alone for half a year?" said Allar.

"Thatchmeet is safe beneath the wings of the Crane. It cannot be seen from the open sea. No Westshoren raider eye can see what the Crane protects."

"You mentioned these raiders before, in your prayers if I recall. Who are they?" Allar slid an inch closer to Fallsveil. She didn't seem to notice so he boldly moved beside her. Then he shielded his eyes as if the move was to avoid the glare.

Fallsveil leaned back on her elbows. Allar's eyes traced the curves beneath her dress.

"I have never seen the Westshoren raiders, blessed be the Crane, but the weavings tell that they are cruel and ruthless. Their hair is dark like ours but their skin is pale like yours. They fish the open sea in boats made of cut trees and cloth sheets that blow in the wind. We fear them because long ago when the village displeased the Mother of the Sea she withdrew the Crane's protection. The raiders came and carried off our women and burned the village. Only a few survived.

"They don't think I'm a raider do they?"

"No, you are the starfish. The Crane has showed us that you must be plucked out of our tidal pool and cast into the sea. You must leave, though it hurts me to think of losing you."

"Then come with me," said Allar with all his newly-found emotions rising in vain hope.

"No, no," she said as she blushed and turned away. "I cannot..."

"You don't have someone, some lover, some husband coming back do you?" he said in sudden panic.

"No," she said turning her head away from him. "I am not of age until next year."

Allar grabbed her hands. "Can you make promises now, for next year?"

"Some do but I cannot. I have been called by the Crane. I am to lead my people when my grandmother is no longer with us. I cannot make promises."

She tried to pull her hands away but Allar held fast. "My dear sweet friend, when I have completed my journey and return to my kingdom I will send for you."

"You say so now, but I know you won't."

"I swear..."

Fallsveil stood up. "I will tell Grandmother what the Crane showed us and I will try to persuade her that you should be given the boat that you may journey safely away from us. What I want for myself I cannot have at the peril of my people. When I am Cranecall someday I will be wiser because we have shared this friendship. Perhaps then..."

Together they knelt and looked into the infinity of the tidal pool. Their faces reflected godlike in the miniature kingdom below. Allar kissed Fallsveil's cheek. He felt the pulse of the journey surge with fierce resolve. The pool rippled slightly. He watched their faces move closer and apart. The reflection quieted and grew dark. The faces changed. His looked familiar but older. Hers was hard and lined with pain. A voice inside of him spoke of love and betrayal, of duty and regrets. Allar looked up at Fallsveil. The sun was sparkling on her tears.

VE 28

My house at Thatchmeet

I was awakened by a flurry of activity today. The boy who brought my breakfast was obviously anxious to be done with serving me but I insisted that he tell me what was going on. All I could get him to say was that they were diving for the boat.

All day I watched the older boys and girls dive repeatedly into the center of the lagoon while Cranecall and her cronies stood on the dock shouting directions. By late afternoon the enthusiasm had died down but still Cranecall urged them to hurry so that they would be finished before the tide turned. At last something large broke the surface of the water. Slowly the object rose. Muddy and covered with a tangle of lily pads and seaweed, a boat with a high jutting prow and arched canopied aft emerged. The boys hacked at the vegetation until the boat bobbed free. One of the girls threw a knotted rope over the ornate prow. When the loop caught, the entire team cheered as they towed their prize to the dock.

    Allar

VE 31
Thatchmeet

It has been three days since the raising of the boat. They have bailed it out and scrubbed it until the blue paint and yellow sunburst motifs gleam. There is no doubt this is the royal Frevarian barge that my grandmother and Gil took on their last voyage.

Fallsveil and I have been spending pleasant afternoons watching the work. Sometimes Piper and Puffin join us. Fallsveil sits with her weaving. She is making a new fishing basket. Today as I sit with my journal the little girls are curious about my writing but the concept of written language is alien to them. I sketched the boat and that made sense to them but when I wrote the word beneath the picture they just laughed. There is so much we can share with these people.

    Allar

Vernal Equinox Day 32

Today Cranecall inspected the boat. It seems now that they have readied it there is some disagreement as to what to do. I will have to ask Fallsveil. The urge to travel is strong in me and I am beginning to get tired of eating only fish. I am restless to be gone yet when I am with Fallsveil I could stay forever. She has been a true friend. I am very sad to think of a day without her tender smile. She is beautiful in a way very strange to Twin Kingdom standards. She is like polished dark wood compared to the marbles and ivories of my kinswomen. Dear Dell, how is that for a poetic phrase? How I miss your guidance and companionship.

    Allar

Fallsveil waited until her grandmother's breathing had slowed to muffled snores. She carefully pushed back the bedroom curtain and tiptoed to the main room. How could she leave undetected? By way of the squeaky reed door was out of the question. She looked out the window. It was very dark. The moon had not yet risen and the fog diffused the dim reflections of the night fires. She knew there was only one way. She picked up her new fishing basket and strapped it to her waist. She sucked in a deep breath and untied the window latch. She had not window tumbled since she was a small girl. With a deep breath she summoned her courage, gripped the window frame, tucked her chin and somersaulted into the dark.

When she remembered to breathe again she was hanging from the window frame by her fingertips. Her toes dangled only inches above the water. Her back scratched against the house thatch. She counted, then counted again. When she dared to let go she dropped with a clean swift motion. The water where she landed was only knee deep but she knew the marsh. To walk anywhere alone, especially at night was foolhardy at best and deadly if the Crane did not guide every step. Holding her nightdress high she breathed a prayer and took a step toward the nearest walkway. The few feet to the swinging platform seemed like miles but she made it and climbed up. She darted like a shadow along the walkways toward the light in Allar's house.

Allar dragged his knapsack out of the corner. He rolled out his blanket on top of his sleeping mat. Then he rolled the two back up together. He folded his change of clothes and tucked them inside the sack. He checked the bag of herbs and teas his mother had given him. Everything was still dry and usable. The food wallet was next. He had eaten all the cheese and apples but there was still some dried meat and two very stale journey cakes. He wrapped them up again and added the meenom cakes he had been hoarding the last few days. Tomorrow, so they told him, there would be one last feast at mid afternoon. Then they would say their farewells and set him and his boat to catch the outgoing tide. It sounded so grand. He was sure they would provision the boat. He had seen them loading things onto it yet the same force that drew him to the west also told him to be cautious. He tucked his dagger into his belt and tied his pouch of coins inside his shirt. He wound the colored band around his hair that Fallsveil had woven for him and pulled on his socks and boots. Why was he getting ready now he asked himself? It could not be much past midnight. He rolled up his sweater and stuffed it into his knapsack. He knew he was too excited to sleep, so he picked up his journal to write one more entry to pass the time.

Vernal Equinox Day 38
Thatchmeet the night before my departure

    I have been away from home a little more than a month but already I have learned so much. I could fill this journal and more. But I have also learned thrift so I will summarize. First, I have learned the meaning of loneliness. My mother's watchful care, how could I ever have felt it smothering? Dell's gentle wisdom and beautiful music, Rogarth's strong and quiet devotion, even the hearty competition of my cousins Kylie and Jay, I sorely miss them all.
    Second, I have learned there are many ways to structure a family and a kingdom. Any system will work as long as the people agree and help each other.
    Third, I have learned that people can be beautiful even if they look different from myself. Fallsveil's dark eyes will haunt me for a lifetime. No blues or greens of the Twin Kingdoms have ever spoken to me with such significance. And hair color which to us is a way to discriminate between human and Allarian, here is uniformly dark to match their dark skin.
    Fourth, I have learned that art and beauty can be simple utilitarian things like a woven mat, a shell bowl or the rhythmic stroke of a paddle. These people have no written language yet they have a history, a religion and a culture as rich and complex as ours. In many ways they are more aware of the balance of all things than we who shut ourselves inside solid walls. Here the wind and tide sway the houses and the hanging walkways which serve as streets. They are more surefooted than we are, having the daily experience of observing and keeping the balance in nature.
    Fifth and last, I am beginning to learn much about myself. I have always been surrounded by doting, protective kin. I am the

Star Prince, a fact I took for granted. Here I am the least important, unwanted guest. Fallsveil is the only exception. The pain I feel at leaving her was quite unexpected. I never thought much of girls at home. They were pretty to look at but boring to talk to. Now I am beginning to...

"Allar! Allar!"
"Who? What?" Allar dropped his pen.
"Allar let me in."
Fallsveil slipped quickly through the door.
"You're all wet," he exclaimed.
"Let me be quick and brief," she said. "You are in danger. You must leave now, tonight."
"But tomorrow, the feast, my boat?" Allar babbled in disbelief.
"Tomorrow they will celebrate your death rite. The Crane's Nest met and decided today"
"Are you sure? Were you there?"
"They met in our house. I heard all that was said. They want you dead," said Fallsveil grabbing his hands and urging him to the door.
"But they were provisioning my boat and..."
"With ritual funerary baskets and festival sweets, nothing substantial and no water. Grandmother spoke against oiling and firing the boat. She said it were better that you just be set adrift for the Sea Mother to do with as she will, but a four against one vote overruled her even though she is the Cranecall."
Allar's face drained of all color as the cold fear of reality washed over him. Set adrift...a burning boat... no water...what should he...what could he do?"
Fallsveil thrust her new fish basket into his hands. "Here is dried fish and meenom cake. I wrapped it in leaves so it should keep."
"Won't the food be missed and you be blamed?" Allar said awkwardly holding the basket.
"I don't think so. Grandmother baked a double batch of cakes tonight, something she rarely does. She also went to bed early. She wants you to live but she is bound to the will of the Crane's Nest."
Allar began to tie the basket underneath his knapsack.

"I also want to give you this," said Fallsveil handing him a flat white shell hung on a braided thong. The chalky disk bore the sign of the starfish.

"This is beautiful. Did you carve it?" said Allar holding the shell up to the lantern to examine it more closely.

"No, the Sea Mother sends them to us just as you see it. Wear it for me, will you?"

"Every time I look at it I will think of you," he said searching the room for something he could give her in return. His journal lay open on the table. He tore out the last page and on it he drew a large heart. "This is my heart," he said. "In it I shall place my name and yours." She watched him with the quizzical look she always had when she watched him write, admiring but not quite understanding. He handed her the page. "Keep this as a memory of me, and if you are ever in need, send it with a runner up over the falls and I will come to you."

"You will never come again," she sad sadly. "This I know, but that I will someday have need of you, that I also know," she said recalling her vision on the morning he arrived. She folded the page and tucked it into the tiny sealskin pouch she wore at her waist. "Come. We must hurry. Leave the lamp burning so it will seem that you are still here."

Allar blindly followed her along the dark swinging walkways spiraling outward to the forest. At the edge of the village Fallsveil leaped off the bridge to spongy ground. Allar jumped after her. He slipped and slid through the thick brush and soggy but solid hummocks to the rocky shore of the Crane's Mouth where the river cut through the seawall and emptied into the sea. There they stopped in the shadows. Fallsveil reached behind a rock to produce two water jugs.

"This is all I could get. It won't be nearly enough. You must ration it a drop at a time if you are to live. And never, even when your need is greatest must you drink sea water. It is poisoned with salt."

Allar took the jugs and tied their handles to his already overburdened belt. Fallsveil looked up at the moon then out at the glassy water of the lagoon. It neither flowed out nor flowed into the narrow strait where they stood. "The tide balances at this hour but soon it will turn toward the sea and you must ride it."

"What about my boat?" said Allar desperate in his confusion.

"I will swim out and cut the rope. You must catch it when it comes through here."

"Will it come fast? I can't jump far with all this gear," he said starting to panic.

"No, no, it will come with a gentle drift, so slowly that the village will neither hear nor see, by the will of the Crane."

He took her hands. "Then this is goodbye?"

She lifted her face to him. "Kiss me and let it be done quickly."

Allar melted into the soft warmth of the moment then jerked back to the danger of reality. Fallsveil slipped out of her clothes and dived into the water with a clean cut. He strained his eyes but caught no more sight of her. Not knowing what else to do he settled down on the shadow side of a rock where he could see the boat moored across the lagoon. The moonlight gleamed on the silent water. Just as the first morning birds began to call the lagoon rippled. Allar looked at the boat. Had it moved? He watched as the ripples came faster and deeper. The dark prow of the boat bobbed merrily as it drifted nearer. He waded out into the turning tide flow and crouched, ready to leap as the boat passed.

Chapter 6

Vernal Equinox Day 39
My first day on the sea

    The sea has calmed a bit. I am no longer in immediate danger. I have assessed my stores and have tried to determine my direction. Of the baskets stowed on board those on top contain only cakes and flowers, the funeral offerings Fallsveil mentioned. Beneath these however, disguised in double containers, I found dried fish, dried fruit and two more jugs of water. Blessed be the Crane or rather Fallsveil's grandmother. I am sure it was she to whom I am in debt. With these things and what I have in my sack my chances of surviving are good. That is if I can master this boat.
    The ride on the tide through the breakers was a matter of hanging on. I was completely helpless. Waves crashed over the sides tossing me like a toy. The experience was so frightening, so intense, yet now only hours behind me it all seems unreal. Out here on the sea the waves roll powerfully beneath me but I stay afloat. The bad thing is the wretched nausea in my stomach.
    I experimented with the oars. I have pulled in two of the three pairs and have been able to propel myself a little with the set closest to the rear of the boat but it is hard work. My muscles are not used to such strain. The pole is nonfunctional. I tried to reach bottom with it but touched nothing. I can see land behind me to my right. It is all high rocky cliffs. At only one place does the vegetation reach down to the beach. I assume that is where Thatchmeet lies but I can not see the falls from this distance. By the sun I estimate I am traveling southwest. The pull of the journey in my chest is strong now. The need to obey the pull wars with my helplessness to direct this clumsy boat.
    Allar

VE 40

My second day on the open sea

I have definitely decided I am not a sailor though I have been on the sea not yet two days. I have continuously felt sick and disoriented. My stomach is queasy at best. I tried to eat but that made me feel worse. Perhaps I should not have eaten the sweet cakes first but I thought they would not keep well in this heat. Already I am red from the sun. I wish I had a hat. I did not sleep much last night. A fog drifted over me for much of the time. Eerie sounds floated on it. I could hear barking like a whole kennel of dogs, yet I am far from shore.

Now it is late afternoon. The land is but a thin gray line. A chain of small islands extends out from the cliffs along the shore. At first I was afraid I would be dashed into them but as the day progresses I am drifting past them and farther out to sea. The barking I heard in the night has increased. I see movement of what appears to be gigantic fish lying about on the rocks. Are these Fallsveil's seals?

This is such a glorious adventure but I am so lonely. I wish I had someone, anyone to share my existence. I miss you, Dell. I always think of you when I write. Such songs you could make here! And Rogarth, I could use your strength of body and spirit to control this unruly boat.

Allar

Armon Beck filled the mugs himself. Not one but two kings were seated in his tavern this afternoon. He carried the foaming mugs to the table by the fire.

"Will there be anything else, Your Majesties? Some bread or cheese or cold meat?"

"Are you hungry, Kylie?" said Jasenth.

"Yes, let's eat first," said Keilen. "I can't think on an empty stomach."

"Give us a loaf of that dark stuff," Jasenth ordered. "And do you have any of your potato soup today?"

"But sire, that's peasant fare," the tavern keeper protested.

"It is good soup, Armon. Bring us each a bowl."

"As you wish, sire, but allow me to fix a platter of meat and cheese and..."

"Bring whatever else you want, good man," said Jasenth and turned his attention back to Keilen. "Where should we begin?"

"I'm not sponsoring a Midsummer ball no matter how much the ladies whine and beg," Keilen declared.

"And I'm not going to compete in another stupid tournament," said Jasenth with equal emphasis.

"Tired of losing?" Keilen said with a sly grin.

"I'm tired of wasting my kingdom's energy on worthless military games."

"The tournament is not worthless!" Keilen exclaimed. "It prepares men for battle. It hones their skills, tests their endurance, it…"

"Who are we battling? There have been no Delven seen in the kingdoms for almost twenty years," replied Jasenth. "Do you and I have to start a war so our military skills don't get rusty?"

Keilen pushed his chair back from the table with a nerve-grating scrape and folded his arms across his chest. "Well at least we agree on one thing. We are not sponsoring any ball."

"Agreed!" Jasenth thumped his fist on the table. "Let's enjoy our bachelor years. Someday, too soon I'm afraid, we won't have a choice about balls."

Keilen laughed. "Now tell me about this new idea for a Midsummer fest that I have ridden all the way from Frevaria to hear."

Jasenth pulled his chair closer to the table. "First," he said "The celebration should be for everyone in the kingdoms, nobles down to the simplest peasant, with games and contests that all could join, like foot and cart races on the road, swimming and boat races on the river, and contests of common skills."

"Like wood chopping?" said Keilen with more than a touch of sarcasm.

"And trench digging," Jasenth continued, oblivious to Keilen's remark. "And women things like pie baking and husband calling and…"

"You're serious about this, really serious?" said Keilen.

"Of course I am," answered Jasenth. "We could have a grand picnic and afterward if the ladies must dance let them kick off their shoes and reel on the grass with the village girls."

Keilen shook his head. "This fraternizing with the peasantry is an important thing to you, Jay, isn't it?"

"Don't be such a royal bore, Kylie. We could have barges on the river and tents and carriages along the road to accommodate you Frevarians if you are too 'traditional' to join in the fun." He cuffed his cousin's shoulder. Keilen cuffed him back. "Kylie, just think of the food. Your illustrious cook can plan the food as long as the peasant's contributions are honored."

Keilen shook his head. This crazy plan just was not how things should be done.

"Come on Kylie, it would be fun."

The tavern keeper arrived with their food. King Jasenth and King Keilen fell silent to the simple goodness of their meal before resuming their conversation.

When Keilen left Beck's tavern he did not return to Frevaria. Jasenth watched his cousin ride toward Mill Manor. Why? Did he still need to consult with his former regent after eight years of kingship? Jasenth did not question the loyalty of his Aunt Cellina or her husband Mabry, but his cousin Keilen he did not fully trust. He would send Ame, his mirror bird. Yes, that would be clever. The bird would be discreet and the information irrefutable. He walked back to the castle whistling.

VE 47

I have not written because there is nothing to write about. I drift farther and farther. I have tried but I can not row this wretched boat against the will of the sea. That I have survived at all so far is a miracle. I am so sick. I still have plenty of food left. I have been too sick to think much of eating. It is the water I am worried about. My supply is more than half gone. My throat is dry and my lips are swollen. Fallsveil was right. The sea is too salty to drink. Even with my improvised basket hat my face burns from the sun and wind. My only pleasure is the seals. I often hear their cheerful barking. They swim around the boat, poking up their moustached muzzles to get a look at me. They are curious and playful creatures. I will admit to talking to them. I am so starved for companionship.

Allar

Queen Avrille leaned her head on Rogarth's shoulder. Since Allar left, proprieties no longer seemed as important. She needed Rogarth now more than ever. Her son had been her sole reason for living, and now he was gone. Her nephews Jasenth and Keilen ruled the kingdoms without any need for direction from her. She was sad, bored and very restless.

"I know!" she said sitting up suddenly. "Let's ride out to Woodsmeet. It's been weeks since I've seen Mother."

"I will ready the carriage," said Rogarth.

"No, my gallant champion, let's ride horseback together like we did long ago."

The gray-haired knight smiled lovingly. "So today you are to be little Avrille, not the High Queen?"

"Today?" Avrille pondered the delightful possibilities. "I think I shall be your little Avrille from now on, my dearest friend." She blew him a quick kiss and danced up the stairs to change into her riding clothes.

Janille looked up from the reflection on the water in the dishpan. "Lizzie! Lizzie! We're getting company. Set two extra plates. Lizzie!"

Lizelle sat cross-legged on the edge of the porch rocking rhythmically. Her eyes were closed and a half smile played on her rosebud lips.

"Lizzie!"

"I heard you, Grandma," she mumbled without opening her eyes. "Must you interrupt me now? I'm having ever so much fun playing with Allar's seals."

"You know you are not to tamper."

"I'm not," said Lizelle dreamily.

"See that you don't," said Janille shaking her granddaughter's shoulders. "I've just seen April and Rogarth riding this way."

"I felt them too and I didn't need to scry them in the dishpan."

"No sass, missy Lizzie, set the table like I told you."

"Yes, Grandma." Lizelle yawned and unfolded her legs. "We really should do something for Auntie Avrille and Rogarth."

"Some things are best left alone, Lizzie," cautioned Janille with a faraway look.

"You never let Jay and I alone."

"Don't get smart with me, Princess Lizelle," said Janille with exasperated ferocity. "You know very well what I mean. Love and obligations rarely coincide."

"When I marry Jay they will."

"The word is 'when'. When you learn the meaning of love you will marry Jasenth, but not until then."

"But I do love him, so much," said Lizelle with a sensuous wiggle.

Janille snapped the dishtowel at her granddaughter. "That's lust, Lizzie. Every farm animal feels that way this time of year."

"How would you know anything about lust, Grandma?" Lizelle teased as she danced just out of reach of the towel.

"I'll have you know I seduced a king when I was young and beautiful," said Janille drawing herself up straight and proud.

"Did you love him?" asked Lizelle with feigned seriousness.

"I thought so at the time," Janille answered wistfully. "But I was wrong, very wrong."

"I though you were never wrong, Granny Love."

"The table is still not set for guests, Lizzie Lou." This time the dishtowel found its mark.

King Keilen was having dinner at Mill Manor again tonight. Although he always came with a subject to discuss with his former regent or her husband, the entire household knew the real reason for his frequent visits.

"Dulcie!" Cellina called. "Where is that girl?"

"Now dear," Mabry said patting her arm. "Just tell me what you want. There is no need to disturb the young people."

"But where is she?" Cellina panted, not so easily distracted.

"I saw Kylie steering her in the direction of the gazebo."

"What on earth are they doing way out there?'

"Dearest, sometimes even we stroll out to the gazebo."

"She'll catch her death of chill out there."

"I'm sure she will be warm enough," said Mabry. "It's a bit chilly in here though. Would you like a shawl? The pink one is here behind your chair."

Mabry kissed her hair as he tenderly wrapped the mountain of her shoulders. "With the young people out of doors we could spend a few moments..." He kissed her again.

"What if they come in and see us?"

"Then they could learn from the experience. This is the first time for both of them. I wonder if Kylie knows how to stroke the back of a woman's ear?"

"Mabry!" She swatted at him playfully. "Push my chair to the window. I want to see what they are doing."

"That would be spying, Cellina."

"Just wheel me to the window. No, back a bit, behind the curtain..."

"Now that is really spying..."

"The future of the kingdoms may be at stake!" Cellina protested.

"I truly hope so," said Mabry as he wrapped his arms around her. "It must be very chilly out there. See he is taking off his cloak..."

"And wrapping her...Oh Mabry," said Cellina laying her cheek on his arm. "Remember our first days in Frevaria when we...?"

Day 10 on the sea

I write this believing I may die before I reach the light. The fog has carried sounds of bells for the past two nights. Dimly I believe I see a light ahead. The sea is shallow here. Rocks protrude though I know I must be far from land. My seal friends are more numerous now. They have surrounded my boat as if guiding me toward the light. Or do I just imagine all this? I am so weak that I can hardly hold on to reality. I have but one sip of water left and then am dead. I have never thought much of dying before now. Just when I thought my life was beginning to have meaning I am stranded out here with no direction, no hope for living much less ever seeing home again. I was born a king. Have I no more purpose than this? I am so lonely. I am not really afraid anymore. I just drift and drift. But as a king facing death I should make a last will and testament. So this is it.

Be it know that if this book survives me, I Allarinth High King over Arindon and Frevaria known as the Star King do bequeath my title and my lands to my sisters Arinda and Arielle and their heirs. If they cannot be found to claim this their inheritance, let my lands continue under the rule of my mother Queen Avrille and the stewardship of my cousins King Keilen of Frevaria and King Jasenth of Arindon.

With this my last sip of water, I salute my short life and put my trust in the Light before me.

Allar

"So that's how it is," said Jasenth looking away from the mirror. "You have done well, my little amethyst spy. This could affect the timing of things in ways only the gods can imagine.'

"Chirp?" said the little bird.

"Eat your fill," said Jasenth. "And rest if you must. Then find Aunt Jane. The king of Frevaria wooing in Mill Manor is something she needs to know about and it is one message I cannot trust to mechanical communication lines."

Chapter 7

A pebble rolled down the embankment. An inquisitive gull cocked his head calculating, but it did not step aside. The pebble missed. Rindelle Twovoice regained her footing. The gull squawked and flew away down the beach.

"What's that?" she said shielding her eyes to look out over the sparkling water. "There's nothing there now." "But there was something, something long and dark." She squinted in the brightness. The gull swooped and screeched. She watched it hover, then followed its flight out to sea. "There it is again." "No there's nothing, really nothing."

Rindelle Twovoice watched from the headland as the speck bobbed and tossed up one rolling wave then disappeared momentarily behind another. Each time it reappeared it was closer, larger.

"Is it a boat?" "It can't be a boat. No boat the like of that ever tied up at Westshoren." "But it is a boat. We just can't see what sort it is yet." "Well then where's it from and who's on it?" "Let's just watch a while and see." "Should we tell Granny?" "No use worrying her when we don't know what it is."

She watched the speck grow until it was unmistakably a boat with a strange flat deck, high, carved prow and a small canopied aft. There were no oars, no sail, no sign of a crew as it bobbed shoreward at the whim of the wind.

Allar's head throbbed. His skin was on fire. His throat was dry beyond speech. He fought toward wakefulness. Liquid pain trickled down his neck from above his left eye. Someone was singing. The voice floated in and out of his consciousness. He was hurt and sick and very frightened. The song was like his mother's voice, like a fragile thread tethering him to the real world.

"...sleep, sleep attend thee,

Peace, peace thy breast,
Until morning wakes thee,
From thy sweet rest..."

No, this was now. The boat...the sun...the sea...? Pain washed over his thoughts. The boat...no water...only the sea... His stomach did a sudden heave. Hands rolled him sideways. Salty vomit stung his swollen lips. Mercifully a clear sweet stream of water trickled down his throat. Coolness, soft wetness bathed him back into unconsciousness. Only the song remained. He clung to it tightly as he rocked on the dark ocean of sleep.

"...sleep, sleep attend thee..."

Time had no relevance. Only the pain and the song had meaning.

"Until morning wakes thee,
From thy sweet rest..."

He fought to open his eyes. Between the light and his pounding skull a woman's face hovered...young fair features framed with thick dark hair...eyes of deepest blue. The face faded back. He blinked to bring it into focus again. The lips moved with the song. He strained to hear, to remember the name of the familiar face. He drifted back. He was a little boy again. His head hurt...everything hurt. Where was his mother?

"Mother! Mother!" The words croaked out, searing his throat.

The singing changed to gentle laughter. "We aren't your mother, but we'll care for y' just the same until you're well."

The face smiled. Allar willed it to stay. No, it was not his mother. He should have felt foolish. A grown man didn't call for his mother, but he was too sick to care. He tried to concentrate on the woman's face. Her dark hair was tied back with a ribbon. Her dress was a simple peasant frock. He studied her face again. This time it was profiled against the light. She was no one he knew, yet the familiarity that had first awakened him would not be entirely silenced. Too tired to ponder the mystery further, he drifted back to sleep.

Allar awoke again. This time he remembered where he was. He thanked the gods he was no longer on the boat. His head still throbbed but the fire on his skin had subsided to a tingling itch. He opened his eyes. He was lying on a low bed covered with a quilt. He traced the neatly stitched patterns of colorful flowers and stars with his finger. Sunlight slanted through a single window. The unbleached muslin curtains were embroidered with seashells and scrolls of blue and green. A woman of considerable skill but modest means had done her best to brighten this corner of her home. He looked up at the rough-planked ceiling. There was probably a storage loft above. The walls were wood that had once been painted green but now were faded and peeled to a dull gray. On a peg by the door hung a woman's dress. Had she given him her own room? Where was she now? The dress was light blue and neatly ironed. The sleeves were long with lace-trimmed wrists, a peasant woman's best. He inspected the room more closely. On a small table was an open box filled with seashells and dried flowers such as a young girl might collect. Beside it lay a comb and several lengths of ribbon. On the other side of the bed was a three-legged stool. How long had she sat there watching him, caring for him? The thought was pleasant but a bit unsettling.

He tried to move. His limbs ached. His head swam. His stomach complained sharply. He was very hungry. "Hello!" he called. "Ho! .Anyone? Hello!"

Quick footsteps brought a face to the curtained doorway.

"So you're up," said a harsh old woman of at least sixty.

Allar tried to conceal his disappointment.

"Y' be wantin' fed?"

"I think so," his voiced croaked.

"I'll fetch y' some soup," she said and dropped the curtain again.

Where was the young woman? Was this her mother or her grandmother? Who else lived here?

The old woman returned with a steaming bowl. "Set yourself up if y' can."

Allar fumbled with the pillows. Then he reached to take the bowl.

"No y' don't," she said holding the bowl out of his reach. "I'll not have y' sloppin' on the quilt."

73

With that she ladled the rich broth gently over his blistered lips. Allar let her feed him. He was too weak and hungry to object. The woman's face was hard. Her jaw was set firm. The gray hair that she had pulled back in a tight knot behind her neck still held a trace of what may have been red. She had been handsome once. The well-crafted cheekbones and gray-green eyes told of what had been lost to years of hard life.

"Mind your business," she scolded him. "Don't go driftin' off if y' want your stomach full." She wiped his chin with the back of her hand. Allar swallowed the last few spoonfuls and lay back again.

"Thank you, my lady. That was very good," he said with a rasping unfamiliar voice.

"At least y' got manners," she grumbled. "Can y' manage some bread?"

"I think so."

She left him again. This time the door curtain remained open. He peered out into a simple but spotless cottage kitchen. Herbs hung drying near the window. Rows of shelves along the wall were filled with jars and pots. A table covered with a checkered cloth held an oil lamp. Out of his vision he could hear a fire crackling and the sound of a knife sawing a loaf of bread. He heard footsteps, light hurried footsteps. Was it the young woman?

"Granny, Granny," Rindelle called as the door swung open. "We just..." She stopped when she saw the curtain pulled back and Allar propped up in bed. "He's awake!"

"And eatin'."

"Let us take it to him," said the young woman dropping the basket she was carrying onto the table.

Allar tried to smile but his cracked lips refused.

"We're glad to see you're comin' around," she said tearing a slice of bread in two for him. Can you manage it yourself?"

Allar nodded.

She gave him the plate but kept a steadying hand on it. The old woman brought in a cup of tea that smelled of mint and chamomile and something else he could not name. "When he's done he'll need more o' this," she said handing his young nurse a pot of green gel. Then she disappeared back into the kitchen.

Allar gratefully let the young woman smooth the cool aloe on his face and lips. Her hands were gentle and warm.

"Tell us shipwrecked sailor, have y' a name?" she said smiling down at him.

"Allar," he answered. His voice seemed far away, not quite part of him. He felt warm and content. Somewhere a voice began to sing.

The next day Allar woke up hungry. "Ho, ladies. Anyone there?" he called out. Cautiously he sat up. A wave of pain and nausea swept over him. He clutched the quilt with a death grip and managed to remain upright. The intensity of the feeling subsided but his stomach still refused to unknot. The delicious smells that had aroused him still filled the room. He slid his legs out from under the quilt. His toes touched the floor. Dare he try to stand? His knees shook but held. Slowly he straightened them. The room reeled wildly. He shut his eyes and groped for the edge of the bed. This was not going to be easy. He forced his eyes open. The room reluctantly stayed still. Step by step he inched toward the curtained doorway and the tantalizing smell. He clung to the wall to keep his balance. When he reached the room beyond the door his strength gave out. He slumped into a chair by the hearth.

When he had caught his breath the growling of his stomach led his eyes to the loaves of newly-baked bread on the table. Where were the two women? Dare he take a slice without asking or would that be an unforgivable breach of hospitality? For the moment the question was irrelevant. He was too weak to cross the room. He sank back into the chair. The warmth of the sunlight pouring in from the open windows made him drowsy and content. This was a good place. The smells of herbs hung up to dry and the rows of jars on the shelves reminded him of home. The spinning wheel and the box of carded wool in the corner could well be his Aunt Maralinne's. And the bread, his eyes hungered again on the cooling loaves. A basket lined with a coarse linen cloth embroidered with flowers cradled the loaves. The bread smell filled his mind. He had to have the bread. He was too exhausted to reach it. Outside he heard women's voices. He would wait to ask them…

VE 52
Westshoren, Armina Weatherwatcher's house
   Again I have been rescued from death by a beautiful woman. This time by one named Rindelle who lives with her grandmother, Armina, in a cottage by the sea. The parallels between my situation here and that which I have recently experienced with the Reedweavers in Thatchmeet are obvious. The difference is that I have the former experience to guide me this time.
   Let me fill in the time gap since my last entry. I was shipwrecked and I am told the remains of my boat were washed out to sea again on the next tide. I have no regrets. Were I never to set foot on another boat again I would be very glad. I suffered quite a blow to the head just above my left eye. The pain is still with me but it is sporadic now and the lump is diminishing. But the color, you should see me! My forehead and eye are all black and blue. My skin is healing too. Armina's salves have eased the sunburn but now I am peeling. Again I am quite a sight. Rindelle calls me her blue-eyed lizard. She likes to tease me. Then she reprimands herself. I enjoy her good humor and am more than grateful for her care and compassion during my convalescence. I feel quite at home here. These people are much like the peasantry of our Twin Kingdoms. They are fair-skinned with light eyes, like us but their hair is mostly brown. I am curious to study them. My dizzy spells have lessened. I think I will be well enough to venture out soon. I hope my battered appearance does not frighten anyone. I know it will be a long time before I am pleasant to look at again.
   Allar

VE 60
Westshoren

   Today I walked outside. Rindelle packed us a lunch to take along. I felt very dizzy and weak at first but the excitement of the outing kept me going. We walked out onto the headland. What a beautiful country this is! We spread our quilt between the patches of sand flowers. I forgot what Rindelle named them but they are pink and yellow with feathery blooms on low chunky-leaved vines that creep like a carpet over the otherwise barren soil.

We chatted almost nonstop. She told me all about the town and its people. Except for the sea and the fishing occupations, they could be my own people. Westshoren is both the name of the town and the surrounding country. Several smaller fishing villages dot the shoreline to the west toward a lighthouse perched on a point that juts out into the sea. Shepherd hamlets cluster on the north and eastern hills interlaced with cart tracks. "Fish and sheep that's about all there is," Rindelle said to me with such sadness that I wished I could give her something more.

Caution learned from my experiences in Thatchmeet kept me from telling her that I am a king, but I did tell her almost everything else about the Twin Kingdoms. Oddly, the one concept she could not understand was what a "king" and a "kingdom" meant. She said that kings were only in children's stories and that no person was above another in Westshoren. All the men worked together in the fishing boats, the eldest teaching the youngest and so on. Women "have the say" in their own homes, she told me. But a good woman must please her man. Ruling or paying homage to any but the Mother of the Sea was alien to her. I was glad that I had not mentioned my status after I learned this. I told her about the people of Thatchmeet. She called them Sealies and seemed surprised that I survived at all in their hands. She believed them to be uncivilized butchers. When I told her about Fallsveil and her Grandmother's kindness and that they also worshipped the Mother of the Sea, she conceded that probably it was only Sealie men that were butchers. "Women" she said "know more of life. Men know only how to begin and end life, not how to live it day by day."

How wise she is for a girl of only seventeen. She is so much like her grandmother. They are both sturdy and independent but full of compassion. I am greatly attracted to Rindelle, not by her beauty, though she is pleasant to look at, but rather by her strength of character. I wish she thought the same of me but I am afraid she thinks I am but a troublesome child and if she were not lonely for company her own age she would not tolerate me. But she is willing to talk to me and does so with a strange turn of phrase. She often poses a question and then answers it herself, or makes a statement then contradicts herself. I think her speech is charming and told her so, but her response was unexpected. She said "We don't care if they call us Twovoice. They're nothin' but ignorant fish spawn. We don't care what they think or say." I sensed her hurt and loneliness and vowed at that moment to forever be her friend.

Allar

It was still early evening but Allar fell asleep over his journal. Their day's outing had been pleasant but exhausting.

"Should we wake him?" Rindelle whispered.

"Supper's gettin' cold," said Armina.

"We hate to wake him but…" She pulled the bedroom door curtain aside. "Allar, supper…"

Allar sat up, rubbed his eyes and slipped his journal back into his knapsack. "I'm coming."

Armina had made a cheese soup flavored with onions. There was a salad of new greens and berries, but best of all, there was honey and scones for dessert. Allar ate with gusto. The day in the fresh sea air had left him famished.

Rindelle toyed with her own food as she watched him eat. "Will y' take a spoonful more of soup or another scone?" she asked when his bowl was empty.

Allar's eyes brightened.

"What's left is for tomorrow," said Armina.

"Then he can have ours," said Rindelle. She pushed her bowl across the table. "We're not hungry."

Armina scowled but said nothing.

After offering a feeble "Are you sure?" Allar ate the soup and the salad and the scone and secretly wished for more.

While they were clearing the dishes there was a knock at the door.

"Come on in, Tessy," Armina called out. "Is Burly worse again?"

"No, it's Pier," said the hollow-eyed woman at the door with a fish basket over her arm. "He's got a cut on his hand. I don't know how he done it but it's all swell up and festerin'. Burly opened 'er up with a razor but it still pains 'im somethin' bad."

"Set down a while, Tessy, Granny will give y' a remedy," said Rindelle.

Allar rose and offered the woman his chair. She looked him up and down before she smoothed her skirts and sat. "So this is what the tide washed in? Pier said the weather watcher fished sumthin' out half dead."

Allar smiled and nodded. "Pleased to meet you, my lady."

"Strange, ain't he?" said the visitor ignoring Allar's greeting.

"Allar's from a faraway land. He's..." Rindelle began to explain.

"Tessy came for a remedy, girl, not gossip," said Armina returning with a pot of salve. "What y' got for trade?" she said handing the woman the medicine. "I don't give nothin' for free."

"My little 'n fetched these in," she said lifting a handful of clams out of her basket. "An' I threw in a jar o' my best pear butter."

"When Pier's back on the boat I'll be expectin' a nice fat fish for my trouble," said Armina. "Now do as I say. Wash out the cut with strong soap and hot water. Have Burly hold him down then pack it with this." She opened the pot of moldy-smelling green paste. Wrap it in clean-washed linen and be wary for fever or red streakin'."

"Thank y', Weatherwatcher, you'll git your fish. I'll tell Pier."

When the woman had gone Armina put the kettle on the fire for dishwater. "In the mornin' you'll be movin' your things to the loft, she said to Allar. "It ain't proper now that you're strong to lay in the girl's bed."

"Really she's just tired of us pokin' her for snorin'," said Rindelle.

"In the morning I will do as you say," said Allar. "I am sorry to have inconvenienced you."

"We'll fix it up nice. Y' can have the extra quilt. We don't need it in summer and there's a crate we can turn into a table and..."

"And dishes to wash," reminded Armina.

Allar sat by the fire until the dishwashing was done and the evening pot of tea had been put on. "You have a cozy house here," he said enjoying the comfort.

"Better 'n a boat?" said Armina with a twist of a grin.

"Much better, thanks to your kindness," said Allar. "But I've been wondering, if I were building a place here I would face the front the opposite way so I could sit on the porch and watch the sea. Why would someone build a house with its back to so much beauty?"

"It was the Captain my Pa that built this house. When he sickened and left the boat he said he best be lookin' to the future not the past."

"Good advice," said Allar. "Good advice for a man on a journey like myself. I will remember that."

"But you'll be staying with us now?" said Rindelle pouring tea in Allar's cup.

"For now," said Allar. "But I must find my sisters. It is my duty."

Armina's eyebrows rose at that.

"Allar says they were spirited away by evil magic when they was but two-year babes," Rindelle explained.

"There ain't no evil but what's in men's hearts," said Armina. "Baby girls y' say? Long lost?"

"They were lost before I was born. I never knew them," said Allar. "Mother has never stopped grieving for them in spite of all the comfort I tried to give her."

Soon afterward Armina announced, "We best be turnin' in," and gathered up their empty tea cups. "Candles ain't for idle talk."

"Then goodnight, ladies."

"Goodnight," said Rindelle handing a candle to Allar. "Y' take it. Granny and us can find our way in the dark."

In the days that followed Allar recovered from his ordeal at sea. He fell easily into the routine of life at the cottage but every day his eyes looked longingly toward the town. He was overjoyed when one day Armina announced she was going to market and that he should go along to "fetch and carry" for her.

Allar hefted Armina's basket to his shoulder. In it were bunches of herbs and teas and salve pots of medicinals. The grass was still wet with dew but the sun was already hot. Women wearing brightly colored, lace trimmed kerchiefs opened their shuttered cottage windows and shooed their children outside to feed chickens and weed gardens.

"Mornin' to y' Weatherwatcher," they called. "Mornin' be a fine day."

Armina responded with a curt nod and kept walking. The thatched cottages gave way to wooden houses built close to one another in rows facing the sea. At last they came to Dock Street.

A boardwalk had been built for several blocks and along it crowded shops and warehouses and taverns. Vendors were set up in tents and stalls all along the thoroughfare in one bright busy marketplace.

Allar followed Armina as she traded for flour, salt, sewing needles and a sack of uncarded wool. He plied her with question after question which she answered in her curt manner when she was not otherwise occupied with her trading. Allar offered her a coin from his bag saying. "I want to pay for my care and keep. Here buy something for yourself or for Rindelle."

Armina examined the coin closely. "Better that y' earn your keep," she said and handed the coin back to him.

"Then name whatever you want me to do."

"Y' can chop wood, fetch and carry and whatever is heavy work like fixin' the shed roofs for as long as you're here," she answered. "Might as well make use of y' for soon I fear you'll be up an' gone."

Taken aback somewhat Allar said, "I'll stay as long as I am welcome and do as you ask. There is much to learn here." After a moment's thought he added. "And much to be grateful for."

"Then show your thanks to Armina who has the say and not so much to the young 'n."

"As you wish, my lady,"

"My lady, yes, y' keep callin' me that," she said with a faint, satisfied smile.

At the end of the market row they turned around and worked their way back. This time instead of buying and trading they stopped at each fishing pier. The captains greeted Armina with forced cordiality and handed her a fish wrapped and tied in cloth.

"A fair fish for a fair day," said the first captain.

"Thank y' for a good catch, Weatherwatcher," said the second.

"A fish a day keeps the storm clouds away," said the third as he emptied a bucket of small squid into her basket.

"Ignorant fish spawn," she muttered when they were scarcely out of earshot. "But a lone woman with a child has got to eat.'

"So you scry the weather for them?"

"So they think at least. Armina does what she knows when she has to."

Allar was reluctant to leave the town but when Armina announced, "We must be gettin' the fish to the kitchen before they stink," he followed her, toting her laden basket toward the house on the headland. Next time, he thought to himself, I want to go to town alone. I want to explore the docks and speak to the men in the shops and in the taverns.

"Good to breathe free again," Armina grunted as they passed the last street. "Dirty squallin' town."

"Good to come and good to go," Allar agreed. His eyes were already looking for Rindelle.

Chapter 8

VE 72
Westshoren

I have previously noted similarities between Westshoren and the Twin Kingdoms which have made me feel at home, lulling me into a false sense of permanence though I know I am on a journey. I have spent the day alone thinking seriously. I have been considering my role as the adventurer-explorer, the ambassador who will return to be High King. I am bound to seek knowledge in these new lands, to discover new resources and to make new friends and political alliances so that I may return to rule wisely and in peace. Yet there is something that nags at the back of my mind.

I sense the present simple life both here and at home is not how it has always been. There are remnants of past glories and hints of lost learning and perhaps a common heritage. Rindelle mentions no trade, no other folks except the Sealies or Reedweavers that I have already met. Yet Armina tells of her father, a merchant sea captain, dealing in fine textiles and metalwork. The cloths produced by the women here are well-crafted but practical, not fine. Their laces are works of true art but they are made with coarse local threads, not silk. As for metalwork, I have seen objects of both practical and ornamental nature as well as coins, but all of these seem old. Their smiths produce only the crudest of necessities. Rindelle knows of no mining or trade caravans or trade ships coming here.

And there are the books. Armina's mantel holds several volumes which I must ask to read. One looks like a book of poems, another like a child's primer along with several bound journals. I know both Armina and Rindelle can read a bit and do figures in a practical setting. There are no formal schools here. The villagers seem to be limited to simple letters and signs. What past has molded this idyllic yet rugged place?

At home in the Twin Kingdoms there are also mysteries from the past. Many of our finest treasures have come to us from lost Allarion. How can we regain their knowledge and skills? And most of all I wonder who wrote our songs and prophecies? Is it my mission on this journey to find the answers and to restore our heritage so that we may have a more glorious future?

Allar

The hot sun blazed. Allar pulled the stubborn weeds, row after garden row. Rindelle followed with the water buckets swinging from the yoke over her shoulders. She gave each plant a dipperful. It was good to be active and useful. Allar liked the feel of the earth, the sense of purpose and the satisfaction when the plants grew under his hand. When Rindelle asked how a man knew so much about farming, he told her how he had helped his mother and grandmother with their herbs and kitchen gardens.

The chickens were another matter entirely. Try as he would he could not imitate Rindelle's clucking song that drew them to the porch to eat from her hand. When he reached under a brood hen to check for eggs he had been pecked severely and set the henhouse into such a flutter that Armina came running, thinking it was a fox.

Today it was so hot that Rindelle tied up her hair but the perspiration still rolled down her face. At the end of the row she set down the bucket yoke and plopped down beside it. "The next drink is for us," she said. "Do y' want some?"

Allar sat down on the ground beside her.

"Y' be first," she said holding out the dipper.

"No, after you, my lady."

"We're too thirsty to argue," she said and drained the dipper. She refilled it for Allar. "Two more rows and we're done," she said standing up again.

"Let me fill the bucket this time," he offered.

"No, you'll spill the half," she said with a laugh. "We may be but a woman but we've got a steady gait. All muscle and no balance waters only the weeds around the well." She shouldered the yoke again.

Allar accepted her remark with good humor and attacked the weeds again with renewed vigor.

After dinner Allar carried his candle up the ladder to the loft. At his table he carefully dripped a bit of wax into a jelly glass and set the candle in it. The sooty yellow light was barely enough to read by. He opened a book to the place he had marked and began to read. He did not hear Rindelle climb up the ladder until she stepped off onto the creaking loft floor.

"Readin' again?"

"Yes, Armina's book of poems," he said not looking up.

"Y' like songs? We do too," she said dropping to her knees beside him.

"Many are like songs in my land."

"They are? And do they make y' homesick?"

"Yes they do, especially this home spell."

Rindelle glanced at the page then sat back on her heels and recited the verse.

"Five be One
And One be Five.
Love is home.
Come home to Love…"

"Granny tells the women to say that one for their fishers when there's a storm racin' them to port."

"Does it bring them home safe?"

"It keeps the women from worryin' at least."

"Do they set out candles or make a sign with the song?" Allar asked. He closed the book but kept his finger in the page to mark his place.

"Westshoren women are too spare with candles to be usin' them for frivolity. You know how Granny is."

"Do they make signs of any kind?"

"What signs do y' mean?" Rindelle raised her eyebrows and cocked her head looking at him with amused curiosity.

"Like a circle of stars maybe?"

"We haven't got that one but women do make Carinna's sign on their hearts or elsewhere…" Rindelle blushed. "It depends what they be askin' for."

"They work magic with it?"

"Enough of them are always getting' pregnant. But there ain't no magic in that," she said with a nervous laugh.

"Women in my land set out five candles," Allar quickly continued when he noted her embarrassment. "They make a circle and if the spell is said in the center, the home wish is granted."

"Five candles at once! Granny would have a piece to say about that!"

"I'm sure she would," Allar agreed.

"What wish words do your women say in their wasteful circle?" asked Rindelle.

Allar stared out the window at the rising moon.

"Five for One.
One for Five.
Hie thee home,
Home to Love."

"It's the same almost but different. Like a singer can't quite remember the song," said Rindelle.

"There are others here that are the same except for subtle differences," said Allar opening the book again and thumbing back a few pages. "Like the 'Song of Life' that I read last night."

"That one we say at a passin' before the tide takes the body out." Again she rocked back on her heels and said the verse from memory.

"Light and Life be One.
Dark and Death be One.
Truth and Time but move in Love."

She glanced at him, took a breath and went on.

"We're born to be,
From our Mother the Sea,
To live from our birth,
On the bosom of Earth,
When in Fire we die,
We are free to fly
Away to the Sky…"

"Now comes the part that makes a difference," Allar interjected.

"Time can change what e're we be," they read together.

"Our song is not so hopeful," said Allar as he laid the book down again. "We say, 'None can change what we are. None can change what we must be'. People can pass peacefully with your song but not with ours."

"Granny would laugh to hear that," said Rindelle. "She says the singin' is for easin' the heart. Them that's passin' go peaceful so them that's left can get on with life."

"There is no magic here?" Allar said more as a statement than as a question.

"Magic?" Rindelle raised her eyebrows. "There's love here. That be our power of life and death. Spells and signs be for them that's too poor to know better."

Allar smiled at her. "You are a wise woman for one so young," he said.

"Young! We be older than you!"

"How old is that?" Allar asked realizing he had never asked her age.

"We don't know for sure but Granny tells us we were a child of two or so when we came to her. That would make us seventeen, two years a woman. We be much older and wiser than you, that's but one season into manhood."

They laughed and talked together until Armina called up from the kitchen that candles were to use for reading and not for idle chatter.

"Then we wish you goodnight," said Rindelle.

"Goodnight wise old woman."

Rindelle climbed down the ladder. Allar blew out the candle and started to undress in the moonlight. The star brand on his chest began to throb. The last words of Lizelle's farewell ran through his head.

"You will know the Dark
But come home to Love."

Was this a prophecy or part of yet another home spell? Instead of finding answers on his journey he was finding more and more questions.

The next day Allar was mending the fence to the chicken yard. He looked up from his work to see a young woman coming down the path. He laid down his hammer and called into the house. "A visitor is coming."

Rindelle came out to the porch to greet their caller. "Well Felicity, what brings y'? Come on in."

"I be sick to my stomach these last few mornin' so Ma sent me for the weatherwatcher's tonic…"

The two young women entered the house. Allar nailed a few more braces to the sagging fence and returned his tools to the shed. When he came back to the front yard it was Armina's voice that caught his attention.

"So now y' want me to give y' somethin' to bring it off?"

"Ma said that y' gave Rose Burney…"

"Rose Burney had six already and her man beats her…"

"But there is a remedy…?"

"There's a remedy to make him want y'. There's a remedy to make y' want him," said Armina's rough voice. "There's one to bring on a full belly and one to bring it off. The problem ain't the remedy, missy. It's that y' can't make up your mind which you'll have. Armina always gives y' what y' come for. Shame is that y' didn't have the sense not to need it in the first place. No man's worth the trouble they make."

Allar stepped back off the porch and busied himself with cleaning the mud off his boots. He did not look up when Felicity Spinner passed. He knew Armina would be watching him to see if he had heard what was none of his business. He made sure his boots were spotless before he entered the house.

Rindelle was in the kitchen packing the carry baskets.

"Where are you going?" he asked.

"Crabbin' at Gull Point," she said. "We'd like y' to come too, if Granny don't need y' that is."

Armina's large kitchen knife paused above the meat scraps she was chopping. "Two on the rocks backs crabs in the hole," she muttered.

"Does that mean no, my lady?"

"Depends on what y' mean t' catch."

"Only my share of the work and your good will, my lady," said Allar with a bow.

"Oh Granny, can he go with us or no?" Rindelle begged.

"For twice the crabs he can," Armina answered chopping fiercely.

"How many would that be," Allar wanted to know.

Armina's mouth quirked a tight smile. She scraped the chopped meat into a jar and handed it to Rindelle saying, "As many as bite before the tide is too deep for swimming."

"We love y' Granny!" Rindelle gave her a wild hug and grabbed a second basket.

They ran out across the rocky headland. Gulls screeched and spiraled over head. Rindelle waved a stick above her head. "Y' see what a gull stick be for?" she said. "They're bold enough to steal the bait before we get the lines set out."

Allar took the stick and swatted at the gulls. "I'll keep them off while you fish," he said turning this way and that. The birds hovered overhead and screamed.

"Remember Granny said we must get twice as many," said Rindelle.

"Your grandmother may sound tough but she is not unreasonable."

"Just don't y' cross her," Rindelle warned.

"She likes me. You know she does." Allar let his stick drop for a moment. The gulls swooped down again. "Shoo, shoo," he cried waving them off again.

"Y' tread a thin line with Granny. That we know." Rindelle headed for a rocky point at the edge of the water.

"Why do you think that?" Allar asked as he climbed after her.

"You're a man and I be an unmarried woman. That be reason enough," she said as if the reason was obvious.

"But you don't think that I would…?"

"We like y'. That we know," she said turning to face him. "But what's to come of it, that we don't know. Granny's caution is good. She loves us and we love her." She pulled out a wad of strings from her basket, separated a strand and deftly tied a sliver of meat to one end. "All y' do is dangle it," she said. "When he clamps on, pull him up." She dropped the crab line into the water and almost immediately pulled up two crabs hanging on to the same bait.

"Twice as many it is!" Allar exclaimed.

"Watch out for the gulls!" she warned as wings swung low over the open basket.

The afternoon passed quickly. Soon both baskets were crawling full of crabs. Rindelle tied the lids tight with double knots. With one last wave of the gull stick she announced. "Now for swimmin'. Bring the baskets. There's a sandy place over there behind them rocks."

Allar followed eagerly but he could not shake the feeling that Armina was watching. Almost before they got to the sheltered cove Rindelle had unbuttoned her dress and pulled it off over her head. Allar stowed the baskets in a cleft between two rocks. He was anxious but almost afraid to turn around.

"Here put these high and dry," she said handing him her dress and petticoat.

Allar took the clothes without looking up and wedged them between the baskets.

"Y' can look," she said laughing. "We're not naked."

Allar pulled off his shirt and rolled up his pants legs before he turned. Rindelle was already in the water up to her knees wearing only her camisole and drawers.

"Come on in," she called.

The next wave splashed over Allar's feet. He jumped back.

"Come on in. It's not cold."

He took a few steps but held his ground as a bigger wave smacked his legs.

"You're nothin' but a land lover," she called from a waist-deep trough. A wave arched behind her. At the last moment she pivoted, dived through the crest to emerge dripping but jubilant between the next two waves.

"Now we'll have to wash our hair. Oh well!" she yelled as she rode the next wave in.

Allar would not let himself be lured out any farther than knee deep, but he did enjoy watching Rindelle frolic in the surf. Her wet undergarments clung to her angular figure. She was definitely an attractive woman but not lithe and sensuous like Fallsveil, he thought. He watched her stroke out beyond the breakers, letting them carry her back time and again.

"You look like a seal," he called out to her.

"Where do y' think we learned?" she called back. She gave a playful bark and dived in again.

At last Rindelle had enough of swimming and waded back to the beach. She climbed up onto a warm rock to dry. Allar put his shirt back on and joined her. The sun was hot. Rindelle unbraided her hair and combed it with her fingers.

"Will we eat the crabs for supper?" Allar asked.

"That or smell them in the morning. Are you hungry? Granny says y' be always hungry. That you're too much for a poor old woman to feed."

"I try to earn my keep," he replied somewhat hurt that Armina would think that of him.

"We know y' do and so does she. Granny don't like to say it but she is getting' up in years. Hard work is killin' her. We do all we can but she still has pains more than she thinks we know. We see her reachin' for a remedy when she thinks we're not lookin'."

"I'll do as much as I can for her," Allar promised.

"You're a good man," Rindelle said looking him straight in the eye. She turned away and added, "We better get back. Fetch my dress then turn your back."

Rindelle slipped her dress on over her head like a tent and wriggled out of her wet underwear. "Alright y' can turn around," she said as she slipped her arms into her sleeves.

Allar rolled down his pants legs. He waited until she had wrung the sea water out of her underclothes and tucked them beneath the handle of one of the baskets. Then he picked up the other basket and climbed up the eroded face of the headland behind her. The gulls followed them swooping and screeching angrily.

Time slipped by quickly in Westshoren. Allar felt at home with the simple folk as they wrested a living from the sea or the soil. He admired Rindelle, obedient to her grandmother yet witty and adventurous. They had learned to work well together, anticipating each other's needs and complimenting each other's skills. He also liked wise, old Armina. Her tough exterior could not entirely hide a softness inside as delicate and beautiful as the lace she knitted by the evening fire. It was a good life and Allar felt glad to be a part of it. Had he not been a king on a quest he would have been tempted to stay and settle down. The restlessness in his heart that had driven his earlier journey was almost stilled here. Only at night when the gleam of Farwest Light cast a white, beckoning path across the bay did he feel the reminding tug.

Tonight he stood on the end of the porch and leaned over the railing. He looked around the corner of the house and out across the dark water toward the light. Rindelle peered over his shoulder. He felt her closeness. It made him feel stronger and bolder.

"Does the light call y'?" she said. "We think it does."

"Sometimes."

"Will y' go there when y' leave us?" she said. Her hand slid down from his shoulder, tracing a line across his back.

"I didn't say I was leaving."

"But y' will someday," she said thrusting her hand into her apron pocket. There was a catch in her voice.

"You and your grandmother are good to me here. Why would I want to leave?"

"Granny says y' aren't for us."

"That is why you think I will leave, because she said that?"

"We don't know."

"Let's not talk of leaving," he said. "Why don't we just make the best of the time we have now?"

"Then you'll take us to the Midsummer Jig?" she asked with sudden enthusiasm.

"Jig, what's that?"

"Dancin'. If Granny says yes that is. You'll look after us." Her face lit up with excitement. "She must say yes."

"She disapproves of this jig?" Allar shot a glance inside the house at Armina dozing by the fire. Her mending lay idle in her lap.

"She took us for the eats and the music ever since we can remember," Rindelle told him. "Then the year we was fifteen, old enough for the dancin' she said flat out 'No, we ain't goin' and that was that. Last year Dylan Breaks was after us and we was only too glad to say Granny wouldn't let us, but now...." She looked up at him with eyes like deep, dark pools above the rosy blush of her cheeks. "You're a good man Allar and you'll take care of us...and we so want to go... Would y' ask her? If y' want to take us that is..."

Allar smiled at her, wondering why his heart was pounding so hard. "I will since you say it would please you."

"You're wonderful! We love y'!" she exclaimed throwing her arms around his neck.

Armina's eyes popped open. Her rocking chair gave a warning creak to the young people on the porch as she sat up.

"You are awake, my lady?" said Allar as he gently disengaged Rindelle's embrace.

Armina grunted something undistinguishable.

Allar and Rindelle went back into the house. The air was hot and stuffy in spite of the open windows. They exchanged a quick look before they turned to face Armina's chair. Allar cleared his throat and said, "Rindelle tells me there is to be a Midsummer Jig and that you have not permitted her to go until now for lack of a proper escort."

"...till now...proper escort..." Armina mumbled.

"I would gladly accompany her and I assure you I will let her come to no harm."

"Y' turn a pretty phrase young man," she said, now fully awake. "Dancin', is that what you're askin' old Armina to do with her?"

"Just dancin', Granny, please," begged Rindelle.

"There be more to the jig than dancin' else Dylan Breaks wouldn't be pesterin' y' to go," said Armina. Her jaw was set hard. Her eyes stared straight at Allar.

"Dylan Breaks disgusts us," Rindelle fumed. "And Tom Netter too. We don't want to dance with them. Y' embarrass us, Granny. What kind of woman do y' think y' raised us to be?"

"Good enough I hope," Armina said with a piercing glare at Allar.

"Can we go then, with Allar?"

Armina sat silently a long time. She picked up her needle and mended the pocket of the apron in her lap with meticulous care. Rindelle and Allar stood and waited.

"Alright," said Armina at last as she laid her needlework down. "Y' can go but young man you'll have her back by midnight, not a breath later, honor intact."

"Granny!"

"Y' think old Armina don't know about the couplin' under the boardwalk?"

Rindelle turned bright red.

"I will have her home before midnight," Allar promised. "And I will protect her honor with my own."

Armina grunted again and resumed her mending.

Rindelle sat hemming her new dress. The flowered calico she had bought with the coin Allar insisted on giving her was the prettiest thing she ever owned. She had altered Armina's regular dress pattern, making puffed sleeves instead of long. She cut the neckline both front and back to a modest yet stylish 'V' and trimmed it with her own tatted lace.

Armina sat sourly at her spinning. Her foot tapped the treadle. Her shoulders swayed rhythmically as her leathered fingers guided the yarn to the spindle. The wooden wheel creaked a tune to the treadle's beat. Often Armina sang with her spinning but not tonight.

"There!" said Rindelle as she bit her thread and twisted it into a knot. "We finished it. Isn't it the prettiest dress y' ever seen?"

"Pretty is as pretty does," said Armina without looking up.

"Oh Granny, what's wrong with it? Y' know y' like it. It's the finest thing we ever sewed. Y' must say it is."

"The dress be fine. It be the vain young girl Armina's worryin' about. Acceptin' money from a man then dressin' to please him. You're no better than a fisher slut."

"Granny! Allar gave us the coin for thanks. He offered y' first. We haven't dishonored ourselves for his gifts nor for his attention. Allar's just bein' good to us as we were to him."

"Can't no good come of it all."

"Granny weren't y' ever young?"

"Young yes, foolish no," said Armina returning to her spinning.

Rindelle pushed aside the bedroom divider curtain. She unbuttoned her plain brown day dress and threw it on the bed. With trembling hands she slipped her new dress over her head. She felt bare, daring, yet wonderfully free as she buttoned the lace-trimmed bodice. She twirled the full, gathered skirt until the floor boards creaked behind her.

"Thought y' might be needin' this," said Armina's voice from the doorway. A twinkle sparked in her eyes though her face was stern and disapproving. She handed Rindelle a small shell-framed mirror.

Rindelle held the mirror at arm's length. Her sunburned, freckled face looked back at her above the pink flowered dress. She cocked her head and smiled at herself. The reflection wavered. The gray-blue eyes that looked back at her were suddenly sad. The hair that framed the reflected face was dark like hers, but woven into the thick, dark coil was a jeweled ribbon. The lips smiled with a familiar curve. It was like her own face, her own smile, but the words they formed were strange. "Rindy! Rella!" they silently called. "Where are you?"

"Well if it ain't vanity in person," Armina's voice broke the spell. "Next you'll be pinchin' your cheeks and dustin' your drawers with lavender."

"Granny, y' know you're proud of us," said Rindelle. She quickly handed back the mirror and started to take off the dress.

Armina left the room. The divider curtain fell behind her. Rindelle sat down on the bed in her chemise. She thought about the fleeting image she had seen in the mirror. It had been her own face, but yet not quite. Was it a trick of the light or a vision of the future? Jewels in her hair! She wondered how many of Allar's coins it would take to buy jewels.

Chapter 9

Lizelle elbowed her way through the crowd to the riverbank. The people stepped back opening a path for her, and when she passed they made warding signs behind her back. Janille did not know whether to be angered or saddened when she saw them, so she chose to remain aloof. She spread her shawl on the ground beneath a tree where she could sit and watch the festivities and keep an eye on her granddaughter. Lizelle reached the water's edge just as the rowers pulled around the curve at Starbend. A red Arindian boat was in the lead with three Frevarian blues in close pursuit.

Varen's face was set with single resolve. His hard muscled arms rhythmically pulled the oars. The boat bucked the current but his pace did not waver. The wild cheers greeting the sight of the red forerunner as it rounded the bend diminished when the people realized who was rowing. Varen Starbelly as they called him behind his back, was not popular in Arindon. Though nothing but praise could be said of his work, the people feared the silent young man from the mill. However, Mabry's voice could be heard cheering loud and clear above the crowd. He was proud of his grandson.

Lizelle was tempted to tamper. A little disturbance in the wind or water would surely be fun but after a glance at her grandmother she sighed. Perhaps the excitement of seeing what the men could do on their own would be almost as much fun as tampering. She had promised not to at any rate.

The boats approached the castle docks where King Jasenth and his man Ben stood with the victory flags. Ben jumped up and down wildly cheering his nephew on. Jasenth waved the flags with even less dignity as the Arindian row boat flashed by a full length ahead of the Frevarian second. The first event of the Midsummer Festival had been won by Arindon! Next there would be a foot race. Jasenth and Ben leaped on their horses to parallel the runners. They waved jubilantly to King Keilen and his man Tam as they galloped past.

The runners lined up at a ribbon stretched across the road at the edge of town. They would run ten miles to the gates of Frevaria. The starting horn sounded and they were off in a cloud of dust.

After the runners and their well-wishers had disappeared down the road Queen Avrille took Rogarth's arm. "This dust makes my throat dry," she said.

"Shall I fetch you some fruit punch or some wine?"

"No, my gallant champion, I will go with you."

They strolled together through the market square greeting villagers and sampling the holiday fare.

"Auntie Avrille! Rogarth!" Lizelle called.

"So you did persuade mother to let you come," said the queen.

"No easy task, but yes," Lizelle replied sipping her cup of punch. "And I am being so, so good." Lizelle scowled first teasingly at Rogarth and then in earnest at passersby as they began to back away from her. "It's fun to be so popular!" she pouted.

"Where is mother by the way?" asked Avrille.

"I don't know. I hope I gave her the slip."

"Then stay with us. Arindon must get used to seeing their queens together."

"Tell that to Jay," said Lizelle.

The royal horses flanked the Frevarian castle gate. King Keilen's massive brown warhorse faced King Jasenth's lithe dappled gray. The cloud of dust stirred up by the runners approached steadily until they could discern the blue of Frevarian armbands unmistakably in front.

"One and one!" shouted Keilen.

"Just to keep things even... Makes it all more interesting!" Jasenth shouted back.

The Frevarian winner dashed between the royal horses and collapsed into the arms of his fellows.

"Well done for Frevaria, man!" declared his king.

"Well done," said Jasenth with equal enthusiasm.

Two farm wagons, one festooned with red ribbons, the other with blue were lined up at the gate. They were drawn by sturdy oxen and laden with kegs of Frevarian ale.

"...and remember," shouted the steward. "You can win only if you don't spill a drop. No stops along the way!"

The drivers and their companions guffawed heartily. "Don't worry. We'll save you a swig."

Jasenth and Keilen trotted their horses to the starting line. "Ready men?" said Keilen as he pulled along side the blue-decked wagon.

"The sooner you get it there the sooner you get to drink it," said Jasenth to the Arindian challengers.

"On you mark then," said Keilen.

"Go!" Jasenth waved them toward Arindon.

The oxen lurched at the crack of the whips. The heavy wagons groaned then rattled away.

"Let's follow," called Keilen to Jasenth.

"Follow? Nonsense!" Jasenth called back.

"Well we can't pass them. The road is too narrow."

"Who said kings must follow the road?' sang Jasenth.

"Across the fields then?"

Jasenth's horse pranced with excitement. "Race you," Jasenth challenged.

"You're on."

The two kings galloped across the fields yelling like young boys, carefree for the moment from the weight of their crowns.

Every boy from both kingdoms under the age of seven was squealing at the top of his lungs. Even louder were the squeals of the greased pig that ran for its life through the village alleys and kitchen gardens. The adults alternately cheered for the boys or for the pig depending on how close the melee approached their own back yards. The chase ran in and out of the stables, across the cobbled streets, through the sheep pens and out to the open fields.

Jasenth and Keilen rode neck and neck, laughing and shouting, leaping fencerows and splashing through the ditches. Suddenly a small pink object darted out of the hedges. Keilen's great warhorse reared then stumbled, taking his rider with him. Jasenth and his mount leaped over the squealing piglet, sidestepped the downed horse and rider, and slid to a halt just as a pack of small boys emerged awestruck in front of him. "Kylie are you OK?" he gasped.

"Damn you, Jay!" said the King of Frevaria splashing in the middle of the irrigation ditch."

"Are you hurt?"

"I don't know."

The gaping boys clustered on the bank. Jasenth pulled off his boots and waded into the ditch "Need a hand?"

"Not from you…you…" sputtered Keilen.

"Let me help you," said Jasenth as he waded out a bit farther.

"Then drown yourself, you bastard,"

"I only offered you my hand." said Jasenth forcing a laugh.

Keilen got to the bank unassisted. His clothes were not only wet but before he climbed out of the ditch they were also muddy. Jasenth stood knee deep in the water with his hand extended but Keilen ignored him. Keilen's horse stood calmly until its master whistled. Gritting his teeth in pain and lost dignity Keilen swung up into the saddle. "I'll get you for this, Jay," he said over his shoulder as he rode sedately back to Frevaria.

Queen Avrille and Rogarth were congratulating the winners of the little girls' jump rope contest just as howls of laughter emerged from the bakery.

"What are we missing?" said Rogarth.

"Nothing you need to know about."

"I want to see."

"Oh Rogarth you won't embarrass me, promise."

"Would I do that, Lady Queen?"

"For all the pie you can eat? I'm sure you would."

"Pie? Did my lady say pie?"

"It's a pie eating contest, for peasants only," said Avrille as she allowed herself to be towed toward the raucous cheering.

"Then you are disqualified, my dearest sovereign, but I on the other hand am only a humble servant and…"

The melee in the bakery centered around six blindfolded contestants. Their hands were bound behind their backs but that did not stop them from devouring the table full of pies in front of them as fast as they could. Before the winner could be declared the street outside flooded with dirty little boys shouting, "Hurray for King Jay!" at the top of their lungs.

The pie contest was forgotten for the moment as Avrille and Rogarth pressed through the boys to discover Jasenth stripped to his waist and soaking wet. He was holding a wiggling, grunting object tied up in his shirt.

"Is the king only seven years old or does Arindon confiscate prizes meant for children?" Avrille called.

"Aunt Avrille, Your Majesty," said Jasenth sweeping a playfully mocking bow. "This is a special pig and therefore only royalty can pardon it from the butcher's knife."

"What makes this pig special?" asked someone from the now bulging crowd of spectators.

Jasenth was beaming just as bright as the little boys surrounding him, "This pig is to be knighted today. Rogarth lend me your blade. On this day, this humble pig has brought the crown of Frevaria to kneel in the mud before us." Jasenth whacked the frantic pig on the head and between fits of laughter he and the boys related the tale of how the royal horse race and the greased pig race both ended in the same ditch.

"Ben, where are you man?" called Jasenth at last. His servant pushed his way through the crowd. "Come help me get cleaned up." To the boys he said, "Give Sir Piglet here back to the farmer who donated it and tell him to raise it well so that I may claim it at Winter Solstice."

The young ladies crowded onto the docked barge blushing and giggling. On the riverbank nearby ten young men were getting ready for the swimmer's relay. Two at a time the men climbed into the waiting boats that would be stationed at intervals upstream. Lizelle took advantage of the other girls' dislike of her. While they chattered and sipped punch, she pushed her way to a choice viewing spot by the railing. She hated the other girls with a hatred only loneliness and envy could arouse. She did not want to join them as they waited demurely for the swimmers, but she did wish she had not promised her grandmother not to tamper. Just a little rock of the barge, just enough to spill punch on their starched, ruffled dresses, how easy it would be. She glanced toward shore. Janille's dark skirts had almost faded into the shadows but Lizelle knew she was watching.

Everyone waited anxiously. At last they all could see the swimmers stroking toward the fourth and final boat just upstream. The tokens were quickly exchanged and the last two swimmers dived in unison. The girls jumped up and down daintily. The swimmers sliced the water with strong arms. Slowly, steadily one man pulled ahead. Varen's heavily-muscled arms ploughed the river toward the finish line. The lighter weight Frevarian second lagged farther and farther behind. The enthusiasm of the ladies diminished noticeably when they were able to identify the lead. "It's Starbelly again," they whispered nervously behind their hands. Lizelle compensated for them with a boisterous, "Go Varen! Go!" as he glided over the finish line and heaved himself up onto the dock. The ladies shrieked.

"Well, what did you expect him to wear, clothes?" remarked Lizelle.

Shrugging away the towel that was handed to him, Varen hauled out his Frevarian competitor and slapped him heartily on the back.

"Well raced!" shouted Lizelle. Behind her the ladies clapped timidly.

By nightfall all the games both scheduled and impromptu were done. The people gathered near the tables set up along the riverbank. All the dishes the peasants contributed to the feast were set out. The roasted meats were removed from the spits. The barrels of wine and ale were broached. Now all they had to do was wait for the arrival of Cook's wagons from Frevaria. Torches were lit along the road and runners sent ahead to greet them. At last they came laden with dish after dish of Cook's prize creations and one sour-faced young king.

Keilen climbed down from the wagon with a wince of pain. Tam assisted his lord to a chair set up for him with Mabry's family. Jasenth kept his distance. He looked for his Aunt Maralinne and Uncle Jareth but he did not see them. Instead he caught Lizelle's flirtatious smile. He quickly looked away.

Janille carried her plate of food to the riverbank to join her granddaughter. "Next year, the gods willing Lizzie, you will preside over this event as queen."

"Tell that to Jay," Lizelle pouted.

"Jasenth knows Arindon well and he will play his cards at the right time."

"I'd rather he played at courting me."

"It's difficult to see others with simpler lives enjoy what we must deny ourselves in the cause of the Light," said Janille with a sigh.

"What fun am I having? Jay can have all the fun he wants. Why must I be the one to deny?" Lizelle complained bitterly.

"Mother! Lizzie!" called Queen Avrille from where she and her champion were standing at the edge of the crowd. "Come join us."

Lizelle set down her plate down and entered the circle of torchlight. The musicians were tuning. The dancing was about to begin. Avrille and Rogarth stepped into the center to announce the first dance. The circle formed and slowly began to move. Lizelle took her aunt's hand. A farmer with rough hands took the other. The circle dipped into the center. It expanded and squeezed in again. Lizelle looked around for Jasenth. She could feel him near but...

"Thank you good fellow for attending my lady in my absence," said a voice behind her.

"Jayjay there you are!"

The startled farmer broke out of the circle with a quick, "Sire! Your pardon!"

With a galloping promenade Lizelle and Jasenth rounded the circle. Then they separated to weave their way through the dancers until they were united once again. Janille tapped her foot in the safety of her shadowed vantage point, watching warily that events did not reel out of control. The dancers frolicked to the lively music well into the night. Gradually the families with small children and farmers with chores to be done took their leave. The young and carefree of both kingdoms stayed and danced and drank until the east was flushed with the dawn. Then two by two they went home or slipped into shadowed bowers along the river. Keilen sat in sullen protest most of the evening but after drinking several mugs of ale he did allow himself to be persuaded to limp through one dance with Dulcie. After that he retired with Mabry's family.

Jasenth and Lizelle were the last couple to stop dancing. "I love you! I love you so much!" Lizelle declared throwing her arms around his neck. Before he could respond Janille appeared.

"Time to go home, Lizzie."

"Not now Grandma," Lizelle wailed.

"Goodnight Jasenth," said Janille.

Jasenth turned without as much as a goodbye. Lizelle stamped her foot in anger. "It was all just magic, nothing but magic," she cried. "I wanted it so much to be real. How could you spell me without my knowing, Grandma?"

"I didn't. The spell or should I say small suggestion I did was on Jasenth not you. I just encouraged him do what he really wanted but was afraid to do."

Lizelle's anger melted. "Thank you, Grandma, thank you," she said and hugged her tight.

"You see, Lizzie, I do know love. Someday I hope we will all know peace as well."

It was already dawn. Cook climbed aboard the last wagon bound for Frevaria hoping for ten miles of rest before the pot washing of last night's festivities overlapped with morning kitchen chores. All the rest of Frevaria would be sleeping in. At least he would be able to work half a day in peace, he thought to himself. They had not gone far when they caught up with a figure walking their direction.

"Need a lift man?" the driver called down.

"If I don't have to sing for my fare," the walker called back.

"Dell!" cried Cook. He scooted his bulk up against an empty barrel to make room for the bard.

"Greetings, old friend," said Dell swinging in beside him.

"I see the High Queen doesn't need a song to put her to sleep."

"None that her champion can't sing to her."

"Still lithe and lovely, the queen," mused Cook.

"Still loyal and loving, her champion," mused the bard.

"There are them in Frevaria that would have them wed now that Prince Allar is grown and gone."

"I would see them happy more than any man," agreed Dell. "But the queen still holds that King Will is her lord and keeps a chaste bed for his return."

"Be that as it may then, there are other beds warming in both kingdoms if what I saw of the dancing tonight is a fair measure."

"King Kylie and Mabry's youngest, yes I saw that," said Dell.

"And the little witch was all sparking for King Jay," said Cook.

"Don't be so hard on Lizzie," said Dell. "She is a sweet girl in spite of it all…"

"None in Frevaria would agree…"

"Not even you Cook?"

"I keep an open eye and a closed mouth to all but you in most matters, friend Dell, but to cross my little king in regards to her, that I will not do."

"She is his sister."

"Not that he claims her…"

"Truth does not need claiming," Dell reminded him.

"But if Arindon does marry her…"

"They've been betrothed since birth."

"Hear me say it," said Cook dropping his voice to a whisper. "If Arindon marries the witch, sister to my kinglet or no, it will mean war. And with two hot-headed and hot-blooded young bucks….."

"Then that is where you and I must step in," said Dell.

"Agreed," said Cook.

The slow wagon rumbled on toward Frevaria as the long, bright golden fingers of dawn reached for the castle walls.

Chapter 10

Armina folded her apron and laid it on the kitchen shelf. The window above the sink mirrored her face. With a little laugh she pulled the combs out of her hair and smoothed back the stray strands with a wet finger. "Not that anybody be lookin' at an old woman," she told her reflection as she replaced the combs. She bent down and blew out the lamp. Then she took her shawl from the hook by the door.

The evening was still warm thought sunset was almost over. Only a thin line of pink separated the sky from the purple sea. Farwest light swept beneath the stars though no fisher was afloat. All were merry in the town tonight. Armina walked the dark path guided by the bonfires on the beach. Soon she heard the music floating up on the sea breeze. She liked music and in a younger day she liked a lively dance step too. Tonight though, her mission was not entirely pleasure. No, she was not spying, she told herself. Yes, she had raised the girl right and Rindelle had been obedient and sensible at least until now. The boy was of good breeding though a bit too clever with words. Trust, no it was not lack of trust. Armina just knew that not far off a storm was brewing.

She kept to the shadows as she made her way through the town until she found a spot near the baker's doorway which gave an unobtrusive view of the festivities on the boardwalk. The shop fronts and signposts were decked with ribbons and wreaths of flowers. The smells of cakes and pies from the bakery filled her with sweet memories. Bright torches lit up ruddy faces near the ale kegs pyramided on the end of the pier. Everywhere there was music. The dance fiddler competed with the liquid tavern songs and the laughter of many voices. Armina searched the scene for Rindelle and Allar.

"Y' dance well for a newcomer," said Rindelle as she leaned against Allar to catch her breath. "We think there must be dancin' where y' come from."

"Yes, there is dancing for most holidays," he answered. "Although my mother complains there is not so much as there used to be."

"Why so?"

"Our kings are both young and single. They're not much interested in dancing."

"But dancin' and courtin' be the same thing in Westshoren. Ain't it the same everywhere?"

"In our lands lovers dance but King Jay and Princess Lizelle have been betrothed since infancy. There is no need for him to think of courting. Do you have young betrothals here too?"

"There sometimes is understandin's between families when there is boats and properties to consider but there ain't no bonds a girl can't break if she has no feelin's for the fella," said Rindelle. "What of your other king?"

"Kylie, he's more interested in horses than women. Frevarian men are like that. All they talk about is racing and bloodlines. I think they must care more for their mares than they do their wives."

"We don't think we'd like horses," Rindelle declared. "We'd rather walk on our own two feet."

Allar laughed. "Riding can be fun," he said. "It's boats that I don't like."

The music struck up again. Allar led her out onto the boardwalk to join the dance set. "That song sounds familiar," he said humming along.

Rindelle sang the words.

"Twos are merry on midsummer night.
Twos will be threes before it is light.
The moon on the land,
And the wind on the sea
Bear witness to the love
That I give to thee."

"Who wrote that song?" asked Allar as he swept her into the dance.

"Nobody and everybody we guess," she answered smiling up at him.

The fiddler drove the dance faster and faster. The couples paired and parted and paired again. Armina's foot tapped in time. She let herself be swept into the mood of the night. The young folks were having such a good time. She watched them from her discreet lookout and smiled to herself, remembering long forgotten times, until a presence shifted in and out of her awareness. The feeling grew stronger.

"Armina," said a voice behind her.

"Lightkeep!" she exclaimed spinning around to greet the gray-haired, gray-clad speaker.

"It's been many a Midsummer since y' said yes to a dance with me," he said.

"These bones be too old for dancin'," she laughed.

"We could show the young folks a turn or two," he said taking her hand. "We both had precious charges, I the light and yourself the child, to keep us from our joy. But tonight, Armina, all is safe without our watch. Come dance with me."

They broke out into a merry jig. The boards of the baker's porch creaked in time beneath them. Heads turned to notice but Armina had eyes only for the light keeper. People whispered, "With the weather watcher and the light keep both jolly, it's good none of us are on the breast of the sea tonight." Armina heard only the music.

When the last note had floated out over the waves she sank back to the shadows of the baker's doorway. The light keeper leaned close and pressed her hand.

"Betwixed the moon, the light and thee," he whispered next to her ear.

"The tale of truth will come from the sea.
Gold and silver now are bound.
What was lost now is found."

As suddenly as he had appeared, the old man was gone. Armina felt a sudden chill. She drew her shawl tight and without as much as a glance back at the dancers, she headed home.

Allar and Rindelle wandered along the boardwalk. "Would you like some cider or a sweet?" he asked her.

"No, just bein' here is already enough. Y' needn't do more for us."

"I'm having a good time too," he said. "What more could a man want than to spend a holiday with a pretty girl on his arm?"

Rindelle's cheeks flushed to match the pink of her new dress.

"Come let me buy you a sweet. Then we will have time for one more dance before we must go home."

"Is it that close to midnight?" she said looking up at the stars.

"It was too close before the night started," he said taking her hand and drawing her toward the confectioners stall.

They danced with carefree abandon until the music slowed and finally stopped. The revelers who were not already paired quickly sought each other. With boisterous banter they pulled down the flower wreaths and garlands from the posts and doorframes. Then they ran down to where the last kegs were being rolled out onto the sand and broached. The laughter and singing turned rowdy and amorous. Rindelle and Allar did not join them. Instead they headed home.

"My lady?" Allar called inside when they reached the porch.

Armina heard him but did not answer.

"Lady Armina, I have kept my word and have brought Rindelle safely home, but she regrets not seeing the casting of the wreaths. So, we want to go to the cliff edge behind the garden to see what we can from there. Do you hear?"

There was only silence inside the cottage.

"She hears us, we know," said Rindelle pulling him back off the porch.

They walked to the cliff. The bonfires danced on the beach below. The tiny flower-laden figures circled like fire flies. Voices floated up to them between the noises of the crashing surf.

"The girls throw the blooms on the tide for Carinna's blessing of getting' husbands and children," Rindelle explained.

"So in Westshoren as well as in Thatchmeet where my reed-weaver friend lives, love and fertility come from the sea."

"So the fishers say, but Granny says it's silly like most women things."

"Do the men believe in it?"

"We don't know if they do or not, but they have their own things like tossin' the first fish of every catch back to Carinna for good luck. Granny laughs at that. She says to best not catch too many if y' want more for next time."

"I won't say good or ill of anyone's beliefs," said Allar. "There is much in our world we do not understand."

"All we know is that we're happy," said Rindelle drawing closer to him. "We're happy now, with y' beside us."

Allar did not answer. The light across the restless water called to him. The pull of it clutched the star brand on his chest like a gigantic fist. He knew in his heart that he would be leaving soon.

Armina pushed back the curtain. She saw them on the black cliff, him standing behind her with his arms wrapped around her shoulders. The songs on the beach did not reach the quiet cottage. Her eyes strayed to the lighthouse. She thought of tonight's jig with the lightkeep and of other nights and other dances long ago. The flame in the lighthouse dimmed as the full moon slid down to set behind it. For a moment the young people were silhouetted against the glow. A faint corona played around the eclipsed pair, first red then blue. The image doubled then merged again as the white lighthouse beacon swept the waking stars. The words of the lightkeeper's parting echoed in her thoughts. "Betwixed the moon, the light and thee…"

"What truth? What truth are we supposed to see?" she asked aloud.

The night gave no answer.

Armina stopped at the doorway with the empty laundry basket resting on her hip. The hot summer sun streamed into the little window. She looked around the loft where Allar slept, from the pile of folded clothes she had just put on his straw tick mattress, to his knapsack in the corner, to the wooden crate by the window that served him for a table. The candle in the jelly glass was burned down to a nubbin. "Wasteful!" she grumbled. "Always he's writin' in that book of his." Allar's journal lay open. No, she shouldn't snoop. It wouldn't be right. But the book lay open for all to see. It still wasn't right to snoop. But for the good of the girl, to know if he wrote his intentions, that wouldn't be snooping. She would read just the open page and touch nothing else, just that one page. She crossed the room to squint over the book.

"I need her strength, her clever wit," Armina read aloud. "I see myself ruling my kingdom with a woman like her by my side. Together we could unite the Twin Kingdoms and build it to a place of beauty in the Light. Someday I must choose a wife. Rindelle would be a worthy queen for my people but I shame to say it, for it is probably a weakness, an immaturity on my part, but it is Fallsveil that I think of at night. It is her long dark limbs, wet from swimming, her lips when we kissed goodbye that send me to sweet but painful dreams. I am drawn on my journey again. I must learn all I can of the world and continue my search for my sisters..."

Armina's thoughts raced. He's a king? He said nothing of being a king, though it was obvious that he was genteel and educated. He thinks the girl would make a good queen but not woman enough for his bed...men! She stomped across the loft and climbed down the ladder. The young ones were coming up the path. The girl was laughing and smiling. He was holding her hand. "Men!" she grunted aloud. She would have to think on this. The girl was too good for a fisher's bed that she knew, but not good enough it seemed for a king's. And that is to say nothing of the girl's feelings when she found out. Not that any man is worth a woman's feelings but that don't shut a woman's heart. Armina's thoughts wandered back to her holiday jig with the lighthouse keeper and sighed. "King or no," she vowed. "He ain't gonna tear the heart from no girl of mine." She set the laundry basket in the corner and turned to the kitchen to make supper.

Allar could not concentrate. The journey pull was almost intolerable now. It was time to leave. Not that things weren't going well, they were going too well. The weeks since Midsummer's Eve had flown delightfully by. Not even Armina's sour silence could mar the joys of that time with Rindelle. He looked over at her as she weeded the garden row next to his. Her hair hung in damp curls plastered to her neck. She smiled back at him. Dirt streaked her cheek. How could he tell her he had to leave? How could he destroy her happiness?

When they got to the last row of lettuces Allar took both hoes and headed for the tool shed. Rindelle gathered up the carrot thinnings into her apron. "Granny will like these for supper," she said. 'New carrots, sweet as a babe,' she always says."

"Child, fetch me some water," Armina called from the porch.

Rindelle looked hopelessly down at her full apron.

"Go on in. I'll get the water," Allar told Rindelle. He took the bucket from Armina's hand.

Instead of going back into the house Armina followed him.

"I'll get the water, my lady. There's no need for you to..." he started to say.

Armina glared at him. Her mouth twitched as if she were about to speak then her lips narrowed into a tight line. Allar had seen that look far too often and wondered what he had done to provoke her this time. As if he didn't have enough on his mind at the moment. When they reached the well Allar set the bucket down on the rim. "I need to ask your advice on an important matter," he said.

She glared at him but said nothing.

"I am forever grateful for your hospitality but recently I feel that I have overstayed my welcome."

Armina grunted something unintelligible.

"Rindelle feels otherwise and wishes me to stay on. I am fond of her and do not want to hurt her by leaving. What should I do? I am on a journey. Westshoren is just a point on the map of my quest."

"Which heart will y' tear then, mine or hers?" Armina snarled. "Your comin' an' goin' be all the same t' me but to the child..." She stopped, pinched her mouth tight and shook her head.

"My lady..."

She looked him straight in the eye. "Old Armina knows more about y' than y' think. Just a point on the map! The poor child's heart just a point on the map!" She twisted her face into a fearful scowl. She let her breath hiss through her teeth and walked purposefully back to the house.

Allar slowly drew the water. He needed time alone, time to think. He set the full bucket on the porch and let his feet carry him down the path away from the cottage. He was hungry but the thought of supper across the table from Armina seemed worse than an empty stomach. He had a pocketful of coins. He could buy supper at the tavern. He was a free man. He did not have to be home for any woman's supper.

The Gull's Breath Tavern was loud. Allar walked in boldly. "A mug and a plate of tonight's fare," he ordered over the din.

The tavern keeper nodded without looking up.

"Better make that a mug o' milk," said Dylan Breaks. "Pretty Boy here still needs t' suck teat..."

"If that's what you're drinking, good man," Allar replied with a pleasant even tone. "Then I'll have the same."

"On second thought 'keep," drawled Dylan. "Make his a double shot of my favorite. Pretty Boy talks like he's had a sudden weanin'. Maybe Twovoice taught him a thing or two late Midsummer's Night. Haw! Haw!"

The sullen tavern keeper placed a plate of fried fish and a mug of dark thick brew on the bar in front of Allar.

"How much for this and a round of refills for my friend's table?" asked Allar.

The tavern keeper shot Dylan a glance and catching a wink he said, "Six coppers."

Allar suspected the price had been at least doubled in that exchange of looks.

"Copper?" he replied feigning puzzlement. "In my homeland we coin only silver and gold. Would one of these do?" he said drawing a small silver coin from his pocket and laying it on the bar.

The tavern keeper's eyes popped. He snatched up the coin and quickly filled all the mugs in the room. "Would y' like a bit of bread with your fish, laddie?" he asked turning a toothless smile to Allar.

"Bread? Yes, please," said Allar as he took a swallow from his mug. The drink was strong and fiery. It burned all the way down his throat and exploded into his stomach. This was no castle wine or peasant ale!

Dylan's roar filled the room. "How do y' like a man's pap, Pretty Boy?"

Allar braved another swallow. "Good!" he said gulping quickly. "What is it made from?"

"Sheep dung and fish guts," Dylan guffawed. "Drink up. Drink up. It'll put some life in your manhood if it don't kill y' first."

Allar finished his meal between careful swallows of brew. His head felt light. His temples throbbed. The room began to spin. His stomach turned inside out and everything went soft and fuzzy. The laughter, the hands dragging him along the floor, his own voice cursing as hands dug into his pocket and relieved him of his coin purse, all seemed unreal. The last thing he remembered was making contact with a hard bench against a hard wall and a gray-bearded face leaning over him.

Rindelle ladled out three bowls of soup. "Where's Allar?"
"Gone."
"Granny, what do y' mean, gone?"
"Off t' town."
"On an errand?"
"No, just gone."
"Granny, y' had words with him? Y' sent him away! Granny, how could y'!"
"I did no such thing. Men come and go as they please."
"What did he say? What did y' say to him?" Rindelle demanded.

Armina remained silent.

"Will he be back? We must know," said Rindelle, this time in desperation.

"Set down an' eat. Supper's getting' cold. No man's worth a cold supper," Armina grumped.

"No we won't"
"Set down I say, girl"

Rindelle fled behind the bedroom curtain. She threw herself onto the bed and sobbed. "Granny can't send him away." She punched the pillow then threw it on the floor. "We must find him and beg him to come back." She jumped to her feet, smeared her tear stained face with her fist. With forced resolve, she put on her Midsummer's Jig dress, washed her face and smoothed back her

115

hair. She pushed the door curtain aside, "Granny," she announced. "We're goin' t' town."

Knowing Allar and knowing that it was past supper time Rindelle stopped first at the bakery but no one there had seen him. All the market venders had gone home. That left only the Gull's Breath. Would Allar go to the tavern? She hoped not. She hadn't believed he was that kind of man, but where else could a man without a family get a meal in Westshoren? With emotions wavering between fear and anger, disgust and disbelief she made her way toward the raucous sounds spilling out from the tavern. What should she say? What should she do? What if he was there? What if he wasn't? She listened outside. Dylan's brawling tone sent a repulsive shudder down her spine. She did not hear Allar. She squinted through the dirty window. Dylan and his mates sprawled over two tables. What was that in Dylan's hand? It looked like Allar's coin purse! Her eyes followed the tavern keeper as he collected the empty mugs from the tables. Then she saw Allar slumped on the corner bench. Was he alright? Was he alive or dead or just drunk?

Knowing she would have to confront Dylan Breaks to get to Allar, she pulled the ribbon from her hair, combed out her braids with her fingers and pinched her cheeks. Granny would never approve, but if it were not for Granny, Allar would be at home right now. She smoothed her skirts and stepped into the open doorway. The laughing and swearing suddenly stopped.

"Kin I help y' missy," said the tavern keeper.

"We're lookin' for a man," said Rindelle reluctant to move from the doorway.

"Y' call Pretty Boy over there a man?" said Dylan gesturing in Allar's direction with a slosh of his mug.

"No, we said a man." Rindelle took one step inside the door.

"Come here Twovoice." Dylan slapped his knee. "Have a seat. I'll show y' a man. Barkeep draw up a ladies' drink on me."

Rindelle's gaze assessed the room, ten fishers, six with Dylan, five sheepherders and the light keeper in the corner with Allar sprawled on the bench beside him. There were no other women besides herself.

"Seems we got our pick tonight," she said walking to the bar. Her skirts flounced, countering the swing of her hips.

"Tom, I thinks it's y' she's eyein'," said Davy Grimm.

"Speak for yourself, Davy. It's your yard arm she's a measurin'."

"Shut up y' bilgers," Dylan ordered sidling up to the bar. "Anybody got a copper coin? Wimmin want copper t' buy pretty buttons and colored ribbons t' tie up such pretty, pretty hair..." He fingered a tress, digging deep into Rindelle's shoulder. "How 'bout a copper t' open one of these here little buttons? His finger traced the neckline of her dress. "What y' say, Twovoice?"

"Let 'er alone, Dylan," said Davy. "Can't y' see the weather watcher sent 'er t' fetch the lad home?"

"Seems she don't want our pukin' pretty boy do y' now?" Your granny won't call up a storm on your friends would she?" His fingers started to work at her top button.

Rindelle took a step back. "Our buttons are worth more than a copper to open," she said leaning her elbows back on the bar.

"Smart lass." said Tom.

"Shut up," said Dylan. "You're interuptin' my conversation with my woman."

"We didn't say we was yours, Dylan Breaks," said Rindelle with a toss of her head toward the others.

"What y' didn't say was your price, Twovoice," said Tom edging his chair closer.

"I said shut up," Dylan ordered.

"Now Dylan," said Davy. "Let the little woman choose."

The other fishermen, who had only been spectators until now, joined in the banter.

"Play for 'er."

"Yeah. Play for 'er, Dylan."

"What y' say?" Tom Netter challenged. "A game a darts for who gets 'er'?"

"None of y' bilgers kin stand up t' me," Dylan declared.

"Keep your britches tied, Dylan. Sharky here plays a mean game of darts, now don't y', Sharky?" said Davy slapping the burly man on the back.

"You're on if y' ain't too drunk t' risk losin'," said Sharky.

"I kin beat any arm Sharky kin throw from the bottom of a keg."

"Prove it! Prove it!" the tavern rang with the challenge.

"Copper on the table then?" said Sharky digging in his pocket.

"Copper? I thought we was playin' for Twovoice," Dylan bawled.

"A woman ain't worth much if she ain't willin'." said Tom.

"An' she ain't willin' t' a man that ain't got copper. Y' said so yourself, Dylan."

"Barkeep, fetch the darts. These here bilgers is angerin' me."

The tavern keeper rummaged under the bar until he produced a box of darts and a piece of rumpled canvas. "No brawlin' now or I ousts y' all." he said smoothing out the target and pinning it to the wall.

Dylan drained his mug, fisted his stomach and let out a belch. He squinted at the target's five concentric circles.

"What y' gonna throw, ten 'er fifty?" Sharky challenged.

"Fifty in your belly button," Dylan challenged back as he picked up a yellow fletched dart. He spat on it and let it fly. "Ram 'er baby!"

"Forty! You're losin' your touch," Sharky drawled. "Let's have 'er fifty between the legs." He spat on the red feathers of his dart.

"Don't drown the poor birdie," said Dylan belching again.

"Jest watch how y' plug 'er." Sharky swung back and threw.

"Twenty! Y' better pour your mug over the side, Sharky. Your too drunk t' play."

"I jest weren't concentratin'. Twovoice here was distractin' me. Your play now."

Dylan picked up a second dart. Rindelle shifted her weight and smiled at him.

"Cut that out woman," said Dylan licking his lips. "Here's t' fifty and all y' got."

"Thirty!" the whole room exclaimed.

"Damn y' Barkeep. There's a wrinkle in the target. Straighten 'er out."

The tavern keeper gave the canvas a tug and resumed his dish washing.

"It's, up an' straight this time," said Sharky blowing on his dart. He threw.

"Forty!"

"I'm still ahead of y'," said Dylan.

"Two out a three, y' know the rules," said Tom.

"Easy port," said Dylan kissing the yellow feathers of his dart. "Sing birdie sing all the way home to bed." He let it fly but the dart went wide.

"Ten! Haw, haw! Your breath must a kilt it."

The whole tavern shook with laughter.

"Y' leave me a mile, Dylan." Sharky grabbed his last dart. "Git ready Twovoice."

Rindelle blew him a kiss. Sharky's arm quivered. The dart landed on twenty.

"A draw," said the tavern keeper.

"Naw it ain't. Weren't a fair game with the woman 'ere and all," said Sharky.

"A fair game it was," the tavern keeper insisted. "You're both too drunk."

"Who's gonna break the draw then?" said Davy.

"Let us," said Rindelle stepping forward.

"Wimmin don't play darts," said Dylan.

"We've been stonin' gulls since we was big enough to go crabbin'. Darts can't be so different."

"Give 'er the darts," said the tavern keeper. "She kin throw one for each a y'. That'll break the draw. Then I kin put the game away and y' kin go back t' your drinkin'."

Rindelle reached in the box and picked out two darts. She weighed one tentatively in her hand, put it back and picked out another. "If we better y' what will y' pay?" she said fingering a third dart.

"No woman can better me," said Dylan planting his feet in a wide stance and swelling up his chest.

"Y' bet your whole purse on it don't y'," said Sharky kicking at Dylan's feet, but his aim was off. Dylan did not topple.

"You're on," said Dylan. He shook out Allar's leather coin purse until a pile of copper and silver gleamed on the table.

In rapid succession Rindelle threw fifty, fifty and fifty again. While the room was still with shock, Rindelle scooped up the coins, daintily knotted them into her handkerchief and tossed them to the gray lighthouse keeper in the corner. "Sober him up and send him home. Granny wants her say with him when he's in a proper mind t' hear and so do we."

The tavern held its dazed tableau until she had vanished out the door.

Chapter 11

Allar woke to the smell of strong tea. His head felt thick and fuzzy.

"Don't move too quick, young fella, or you'll wish yourself still out cold," said a voice.

Allar did not want to move.

"Here drink this," the voice continued. "It'll sober y' up like the light of truth."

Allar drank the cup of tea. Gradually his senses cleared and the throbbing behind his eyes subsided to a dull reminder of the night before. He found himself in a small circular room arranged around a fire glowing in a metal stove. A cool moist breeze blew in from the small round windows. Outside he could hear waves crashing on rocks and the bark of seals.

"You're the light keeper?" said Allar when his eyes finally focused on the wiry-limbed, gray-bearded man.

"I been nobody else these sixty-what years."

"How did I get here?"

"I dragged y' home, no easy task to be sure, but I couldn't see leavin' y' in the street when the tavern keep closed up. Them fisher fellas be a mean lot, especially when the catch been poor and they're drinkin' it off."

"Thank you," said Allar ashamed to meet the old man's eye. "I'm sorry to have caused you so much trouble."

"I figured it were my duty seein' that Armina and the girl took y' in first. Armina she's a sharp judge of men. It were my duty to her."

Allar noticed a softness, a slight change of tone when the man said Armina's name. "You know her well then?" Allar asked with curiosity.

"That I do."

"She never mentioned you. In fact she avoided conversation about this place entirely."

"That she would," said the light keeper and let out a long sigh. "She and I, we were young once but nothin' come of it. Some think the girl be mine but that she was found, a babe cryin' on the foggy moor, that's the truth of it. Many the nights I lay abed wishing it otherwise."

Armina Weatherwatcher young enough to be courted by the lighthouse keeper, Allar found that hard to imagine.

Allar spent six days in the lighthouse tower exploring the keeper's small library and listening to his endless store of tales. Allar helped what he could with the housekeeping and the tending of the fish lines. The view from the rocky point showed him the town from a different angle as well as the outlying fisher cots to the east. He could also see the sheepherder's keeps dotting the upward sloping hills to the north. All these things he had already seen from Armina's cottage and on his several outings, but from Farwest lighthouse he could also see north where the ragged, barren coastline faded in and out of the perpetual fog.

At sunset he accompanied the light keeper up the ladders to light the lamp. Like a huge prism, the beveled lens divided the sun's dying rays into a rainbow of light. The old man sang as he trimmed the wick and refilled the lamp's reservoir with oil.

"Over land and over sea
We watch the wanderers home.
Far from land and far from sea
However west we roam.
Fire the night for our flight
To the sky our home."

He struck his flint and blew to nurse the spark to a steady flame. Afterwards he and Allar climbed down again to spend the evening sitting by the stove. The light keeper puffed on his long-stemmed pipe as they talked. Far into the night he told tales and answered Allar's many questions.

On the sixth night, when the lightkeeper's head began to nod sooner than usual, Allar picked up the book he had been studying. It was a healer's text with curious drawings of a man's insides. He was wondering why a bone needed a name when the fire in the stove suddenly glowed brighter. The room filled with golden light. The fire spat and burst into a shower of sparks. Allar jumped up with alarm. Tinkling laughter played behind him. The light keeper did not stir.

"Blind with two eyes even in a lighthouse," said a familiar voice.

"Lizzie!"

"What have you learned, Star King?"

"You would be surprised how much I have learned, Lizzie."

"But have you learned enough?"

"I am writing everything in my journal," Allar assured her.

"What have you learned about death and dying?" said Lizelle laughing again.

"The Reedweavers wanted me dead and I almost did die out there on the ocean."

"I know, I know. I told you so," she chanted dancing around him. "My gift, my wish if only you knew."

"Yes, your parting wish, 'You will know death, but will not die.' I know the second part too."

"Don't be too sure, silly cousin."

"You said, 'You will see one bird but hear the song of two.' I figured that one out. It's Rindelle and her unique way of speaking. They call her Twovoice."

"You are so near and yet so far, so wise and yet so witless," she sang.

"Why did you come here, Lizzie, just to torment me?"

"I just wanted to speed you on your way."

"How did you know I was planning to leave?" The star brand burned on his chest. "Ouch! Lizzie stop it!"

"Don't be such a ninny. You are a man now. What's a little pain for a good cause? Or would you rather bear the shame of running away from an old woman's ill will?"

"I am going because I want to," Allar insisted.

"Which way will you chose to go?"

"I thought I would go north to the mountains."

"You will soar to winged heights but never fly," she sang.

"Then I am right to go north?"

"North or south, you choose. Flip a coin to win or lose. Journey far by road or trail. Catch a little bear by the tail. That's what I am going to do." The teasing tinkle of her laughter filled the room.

"Stop the riddles and rhymes, Lizzie, and tell me…" he started to say but the fire sparked again and she was gone.

Allar rubbed his chest. The burning was gone but the journey pull was stronger than ever. He knew he would not be able to sleep tonight. He looked over at the light keeper muffling snores in his beard. Allar paced the small room. He stopped at the open doorway and looked out. The lights of the town were dim. The stars hung peacefully overhead, but his heart was as restless as the waves on the rocks below. He walked out into the night taking the path to the edge of the sea point. The fog was rolling in. Soon it would blanket all of Westshoren. He watched its white specter arms raise to blot out the familiar star patterns one by one. He shivered in the dampness but he was reluctant to go back inside. Voices in the wind and sea sang in harmony as the stars turned in their cycle. His eyes were drawn to the pivot point in the north, to the tip of the Little Bear's tail. The Little Bear was his cousin Jasenth's star sign. Lizzie would catch him eventually. Their grandfather Arinth had assured that by betrothing them when they were little, but what did all that have to do with him and his journey? He did not care about Lizzie and her riddles. He would go north because he wanted to go north. The fog swirled over his head and the stars were gone.

In the morning the fog was thick and cold. Allar wrapped himself tighter in the lightkeeper's spare blanket and huddled closer to the stove. Daylight came slowly to the one-room abode. At last the light keeper yawned and stretched. "Y' awake, young fella?"

Allar moved slightly.

"Stir up the coals will y' and set in another log or two. It sure is dark and chill for the middle of summer. No fisher in mind of his wits would be venturin' out on a day like this. What say we head to town?" said the lightkeep.

"I have been thinking of that and farther," said Allar.

"Young and restless, I'm surprised y' stayed so long with such an old solitary as myself."

"I have enjoyed your conversation and your books."

"Where y' be goin' now that your of a mind to go, back to Armina and the girl?"

"I'll go there to say goodbye and get my things, but not to stay," said Allar suddenly overcome with sadness.

"So your not hopin' that y' and the girl can have what we old folks missed?"

Allar started to answer but the burning star underneath his shirt kept him silent.

"Some things ain't right. Some things ain't meant to be. It be the smart man who learns early and leaves before it's too late." The old man paused a moment, his thoughts wandering back in time to his own choices and regrets. "Which way be y' headed then?"

"North," said Allar with conviction.

"There ain't nothin' north but sheep," the light keeper drawled.

Allar laughed. "Then I'll learn all about sheep."

The light keeper started rummaging through the contents of several boxes under his bed. "Must be in the trunk then," he said to himself. He pulled out a leather trunk with dull brass bindings.

Allar hovered behind him peering over his shoulder at the jumbled assortment of books and clothes inside.

"Here it is," said the light keeper when he finally located a rolled up parchment. "The Captain, Armina's Pa, left this to me sayin' it was for our eldest son. Since nothin' come of things when we was young there was none to give it to. I'm thinkin' it might be of some use to a travelin' fella like yourself."

His sharp eyes narrowed. He watched Allar as he unrolled the parchment out on the table and weighted down the corners with the candlestick and the sugar bowl. "What do you think of this here map?"

Allar poured over the elaborately drawn map. A great land mass in the shape of a star was completely surrounded by water. The sea was drawn with grotesque creatures sporting in the waves. Dragons and other fanciful creatures roamed the land. Ornate inscriptions were written on each arm of the star. Allar read them aloud, "Westshoren, Eyeren, Iceshoren, Estcliff, Stellaria." Across the center of the map the name 'Allarion' was lettered in gold and silver characters. "So this is the world," Allar mused. His eyes darted over the map. Did the drawings move or was it just his imagination? His eyes stopped at the bend of a river. Two jeweled cities sparkled along its banks. Halfway between them a blank spot marred the scene. Had some past owner of the map dropped something there blotting out the detail? Allar felt the sudden urge to complete the map. His finger traced a star in the damaged spot. The colors of the map surged with intensity and when they subsided a white star-shaped city remained at the place he had touched.

"Be it of some use to y'?" said the light keeper, watching Allar closely. He poked a gnarled finger at the lower left arm of the star-shaped landmass where a lighthouse was drawn surrounded by mermaids. "This here be where we are now. The rest is beyond my reckoning since I never been anywhere but here."

"Yes, I think it will aid my quest immensely, thank you," said Allar.

"Carinna's breath fill your sails, then boy," said the light keeper as he rolled up the map and gave it to Allar. "All these years I've watched for the Light and waited, first for a ship bearin' a queen, none came but for the captain and his daughter. Then I watched and waited for the Light's promise of a royal son and daughters to ease my burden of years, but no wife would have me and no relief's come to keep the light when my duty is done until now perhaps."

Allar did not understand the meaning of the light keeper's words but he felt the emotions that brought tears to the old man's eyes. "I guess I'll be setting out now," was all Allar could think to say. "Thank you for the map and for your kind hospitality," he added as he tucked the map inside his shirt.

"I was glad for the company," the light keeper answered strapping on his carry basket. "I'll walk y' as far as the Gull's Breath but y' best not come in with me if you're goin' on t' Armina's."

Rindelle saw him coming. She ran to the door but Armina was quicker. She lunged with her face set in her fiercest scowl and braced her arm across the doorway barring Rindelle's way. "Where y' goin' so fast, girl?"

"It's Allar."

"So it is."

"Granny, don't do this."

"Y' stay inside, I'm tellin' y'. I'll do the talkin',"

Allar stopped at the edge of the porch. "Good morning, ladies."

Armina said nothing.

"I am ready to resume my journey, so I have come to fetch my things and thank you again for your kindness."

Armina glared at him. "Girl, fetch his stuff," she said back over her shoulder.

"I know I have lost your respect, my lady. I have in my inexperience done what I least wanted to do. So I will give you no more trouble and be on my way. I am deeply in your debt for all your kindness and leave you with much regret."

Armina still made no answer. Allar stood waiting. The silence was painfully awkward. Rindelle finally appeared behind her grandmother with Allar's knapsack and a basket hurriedly piled with biscuits and fruit. Armina grunted but said nothing when she saw the food. She handed it to him with his sack, still barring Rindelle from the porch.

"Thank you, my lady," he said. "I have learned much from your example here, and I have also learned much from the light keeper who was good enough to rescue me from my night of folly. May I ask for your forgiveness before I leave?"

Armina broke her silence. "Any man who takes six days to sober up best be gone," she said scowling with even more ferocity. "The lightkeep would be one to know about that."

"As you wish lady Armina, but may I please say goodbye to Rindelle? She also has been good to me."

Rindelle broke through Armina's barricade. "Allar, Allar y' can't leave us!" she cried ready to fling herself into his arms but he held her back.

"Walk me to the gate." He looked back at Armina. "If she may, my lady?"

"To the gate and no further," she gave in, her anger beginning to dampen with memories and regrets.

Allar and Rindelle walked slowly hand in hand through the garden to the gate. There was so much to say but no words came. Armina watched from the porch, grateful that they had eyes only for each other and could not see her tears.

"We would give y' a parting gift," said Rindelle stooping to pluck a sprig from the rosemary shrub beside the gate. She pulled the ribbon from her hair, tied the sprig and handed it to Allar. "Rosemary is for remembrance."

"I will remember you always," he said accepting the gift. He opened his knapsack and took out the seashell with the star sign

Fallsveil had given him. "This was given once before as a parting gift from friend to friend."

"We will always remember y' as more than friend," she said as he pressed it into her hand.

They stood a long moment holding each other's gifts, holding on to the moment, wishing it would stay.

"I want to kiss you," Allar whispered. "But your grandmother is watching."

"We want to accept your kiss, but Granny is watching."

"Then I must speak the kiss though words can never be as sweet."

"And we must speak its return though the pain of parting would want us to keep it always," she whispered up to him.

"That's enough!" Armina barked from the porch.

"One more minute, Granny, please."

Allar took her hands. "Remember the home spell," he said. "Love is home, home to Love." He squeezed her hands once more and let her go.

Rindelle fled back to the house weeping.

"Goodbye to you too, my lady," Allar called to Armina. He waited a moment but she did not respond. The woman he saw in the doorway looked old and weak, not formidable at all. "Thank you again for everything," he added with a wave as he walked away. He did not look back. The journey pull was strong but his feet felt heavy and slow. The lines of one of Dell's songs ran through his head.

"Each new love expands the heart,
Though paths diverge
And friends must part."

Rindelle threw herself sobbing onto the bed. "We love him. We do!"

Armina sank down onto the porch step. She was tired and the pain in her chest would not stop. She listened to the sobs inside the house and remembered being young. The sobs changed to angry cries.

"How can y' just sit out there and not care, Granny?" Rindelle shouted. "He wants us and we want him."

Armina stood up slowly and went inside. She pushed back the bedroom curtain. "Men be all alike, child. They take a woman's heart then break it in one way or another. Come to your granny who loves y' best."

Rindelle pushed her away.

"What did he give y'?" I saw him give y' somethin'." She reached for Rindelle's closed fist.

"It's ours and you'll not take it from us."

"I'll not take your trinket, child. It were a sand dollar, somethin' his Sealie girl gave him if old Armina's eyes saw true. Wonder what woman he'll pass on the rosemary to from friend to friend."

"We won't take no more of this!" Rindelle screamed. "We're leaving. We'll leave and follow Allar."

"You ain't gonna do no such thing."

"We will and there's nothin' y' can do t' stop us."

Armina raised her hand to strike but put it down. "Y' be a grown woman but I still have say over y'. Settle yourself down till y' can talk sense."

"We're going"."

"You're not an' that's my final word."

"But we love him. We do," Rindelle wailed.

"The man's gone and y' are left an' that's that. No use cryin'. The man takes your heart an' your senses an' leaves but a seashell's worth to mark his stay."

Rindelle held out the shell. "It's marked with the same sign as the one on his heart. He'll remember and he'll come back. We know he will and we will wait for him."

"There be other fish in the sea, child and if none bite the hook well then y' can watch the weather for what that's worth when I 'm dead and gone."

"You'd rather us to marry Tom Netter or, the gods forbid, Dylan Breaks?"

"No child, y' ain't no fisher slut and y' shan't wed and bear to the likes of them. You're born better."

"Are we born better than Allar? Tell us, Granny, who are we?"

"I can't say what I don't know but come here an' I'll show you what I do."

Rindelle reluctantly followed. Armina drew the curtains and lit the lamp though it was still afternoon. She led the way to the small table beside her bed that served as a wash stand and turned it around. There on the side that had always faced the wall was a drawer Rindelle had never noticed before.

"Open it."

Rindelle hesitated.

"Open it if y' want to know all that Armina knows."

Cautiously Rindelle pulled out the drawer. Armina held the lamp closer. Inside was a child's embroidered dress and undergarments, and a pair of tiny velvet slippers.

"Reach further back," said Armina.

Rindelle slid her fingers into the shallow drawer until she felt something metal.

"Y' wore all them things when old Armina found y' out on the heather moor."

Rindelle turned the heart-shaped locket over in her hand. On its face was engraved a letter 'A' in graceful, flowing script. "The 'A' be for Allar," she declared. "We are for him after all."

"Or 'A' for Armina and y' be mine," said Armina with a hint of wistfulness creeping into her tone.

"Or maybe 'A' is for whoever we really are. It's not 'R' for Rindelle that's for sure."

"Who knows, child, what it means now or later. But one thing know for sure that old Armina loves y' and wants that y' be happy. And know too that there's somethin' about Allar that's wrong, I can feel it in my bones it's wrong. I feel it like the day I found y', like a great brewin' storm, contrary to the nature of things. Believe me, child, he ain't the man for y'."

Rindelle walked out of the room, out of the house, out onto the moor to the cliff by the sea. The sky was dark. A storm was coming but she didn't care.

An hour or so later Armina Weatherwatcher took the lantern. "Headstrong! Hot-blooded!" she grumbled as she bolted the door behind her. "The girl's no better than a fisher slut after all," she told the stony path. "Halloo! Halloo! Child where y' be?" she called loud across the moor. Then she resumed her monologue. "Runnin' off over a man when Armina gave her all she is."

Rindelle heard her coming. She knew she would be found sooner or later. Granny's senses could scry out most lost things and some purposely hidden. She sat on the rocky ledge and hugged her knees against the chill wind. Below her the sea slapped the strand with a decisive rhythm. She loved Granny but she was seventeen now, two years into womanhood. Allar wanted her. She could feel the bond between them. It was more than man to woman. It was soul to soul. What did Granny know but weather and fish lore? She had never loved and wed. "We will follow him," she vowed clutching the star shell so tightly it cracked and began to crumble. "It's like our heart," she wept as the fragments sifted through her fingers. "It's broken, slipping away till nothing is left."

"Y' be out there. Armina knows y' hear."

"What's this?" Rindelle said to herself, feeling the center of the shell lying in her hand. It was smooth and hard. Was it a pearl or something else? It was too dark to see. "We're here, Granny," she called aloud.

Armina came puffing up the path. Lightening cracked and thunder rolled. The wind whipped cold and wet. "Get back t' the house or you'll catch your death," she ordered.

It was morning. The sun was bright. Rindelle stretched then snuggled deeper beneath the quilt. The house was quiet. No sound of steps in the kitchen, no clank of pots, no smell of biscuits baking. She sat up with alarm. The sun stood high, slanting in the seaside window. It was late. Where was Granny? She pushed back the bedroom curtain. The kitchen was empty. The fire was cold.

A quick glance from the front door told her where to look. The buckets were gone from the porch and the garden gate was open. The well! She ran out with her nightgown flying behind her, around to the back of the house. There on the path a few paces from the well slumped a shawl-wrapped figure pinned to the ground by the bucket yoke. "Granny! Granny!" she cried.

She lifted the heavy yoke off the motionless black shawl. Her hand shook with fear as she reached to touch the pale cheek beneath the shawl. The skin of that cheek was cold and clammy. The eyes above the cheek rolled back. "Granny! No, no! You can't be dead!" She shook the still figure. She clutched it to her rocking it with a keening wail, bathing it with tears.

The body convulsed. Breath sucked in with a rattle, then stopped. "Granny please be alive! Please, please!" She shook the body, demanding an answer. The breath sucked in again, then again in an irregular but distinct pattern. The lips moved as if to speak. Rindelle bent close to hear.

"Pains...my chest," the lips formed soundless words.

"What tonic? What salve? What tea?" Rindelle demanded with rising panic.

The lips sucked in another ragged breath. "Foxglove," they said.

"Where? How much?"

"Top shelf. Just a pinch."

"In tea?"

"No, not hot. Just a pinch...a pinch on the honey spoon."

Rindelle kissed her grandmother's cheek with vigor and ran to the house. She returned in a moment with the remedy and the quilt from the bed.

She half carried, half dragged Armina into the house. Except for chores that had to be done, she spent the long tense day that followed sitting in the chair by the bed. She administered the medicine and tucked the quilt around the restless sleeper.

When Armina awoke it was almost evening. She refused to eat supper but begged Rindelle to eat for strength for both of them. Rindelle cut bread and cheese for herself and returned carrying her supper to the bedside chair.

"There's a thing I must tell y' now," Armina's voice rasped. "A thing the Captain my Pa didn't tell me till his deathbed."

"Don't say deathbed, Granny. We'll have y' well by morning," said Rindelle. "We promise."

"Better it were said too soon than too late," Armina insisted.

"Then tell us," said Rindelle almost choking on the dry bread.

"The Captain my Pa says he was fishin' off by the far side of Sealhaven one night when a squall the like of which he had never seen before come up and carried him boat and all the entire way up onto the shore. There he seen a light. He went toward it cautious thinkin' it was Sealies, but when he got a look it was the strangest man and woman arguing over a child. They was fair-skinned and ebon-haired and all round them, no he said all inside them, was a glowin' light. Then they seen him. The woman called to him without words and held the child for him to take. When the Captain my Pa took the child, who was but a newborn, the light from the woman faded. The glowin' man pulled her back. She looked sad-like and said but one word before they disappeared. That word was 'Armina,' so that's what he called me."

"Then we be alike, Granny," said Rindelle. "It's the same story, bein' from somewhere else, not belongin' here."

"Both of us," Armina whispered then gasped, clutching her chest again. Her eyes closed.

"Should we get the remedy again?" Rindelle panicked.

"No not this time," Armina answered in a flat, even tone. She began to hum softly, "Five one, one five, home, love, home..."

Rindelle kept vigil by the bed. Armina lay motionless against the pillows. In the depths of her consciousness Rindelle heard another voice humming the same melody. "Hie thee home, home to love." She felt a presence. She knew someone stood behind her, yet the door had not opened. Slowly she turned her head.

The tenuous outline of an armored man hovered by the door. As it drifted toward her the features became more distinct but the door was still visible behind him. A regal but aged face looked out from beneath his helmet. He removed his gauntlet and extended his hand to Armina. "Come sister. Come home to Love," he said.

She heard her grandmother sit up in the bed beside her but she could not take her eyes from the ghostly knight. Armina stood up and took his white, transparent hand. Her hair was unbraided. Her nightgown was white, very white, very thin and transparent.

"Arinth...my brother...my twin," said Armina's voice with a youthful lightness Rindelle had never heard before.

"Granny! Granny don't leave us!" Rindelle broke through the spell with alarm as the pale silver knight embraced the fading woman with long, long gray hair. Armina's voice floated back to her from somewhere faraway. "You too have a brother, child. Find him...find him...find him..."

The room was empty. Rindelle looked back at the bed. Armina Weatherwatcher was dead.

Chapter 12

Keilen and his man Tam Mabryson rode out across the fields. The dust rose lazily behind them.

"Sure is getting dry," said Tam.

"I have never seen such a summer," said Keilen. "There wasn't much rain before midsummer and nothing since."

They rode past a field of rye. The short yellowed grain rippled like a mirage in the heat. They passed a lumbering water wagon loaded with barrels sloshing with each bump.

"G'afternoon, sire," called the farmer. "It's sure thirsty weather."

"That it is, my good man," Keilen agreed as his eyes scanned the field. The man's wagon load of water barrels was not nearly enough to save the crop. It was hopeless. The wilting plants would die. Farther on a group of women and children carried heavy buckets along the rows. They looked dusty and tired. Keilen waved to them. They bowed but did not call out a greeting.

Ahead rose the stone wall which divided the fields of Frevaria from those of Arindon. Along the wall the plants were green. Soon they were close enough to see over the barrier. Arindon's bounty thrived among the latticed ribbons of the irrigation ditches. Keilen's face grew tight. The situation was critical. His land was parched. His people were thirsty and discontent while his cousin's land bloomed with its magic web of waterways. Had the rain come like other years the comparison would not be so obvious, but the truth was that Arindon's harvests had been fuller than Frevaria's ever since King Will and Mabry made the waterways seventeen years ago. Mabry helped with improvements in Frevaria too, but Keilen's tradition-bound kingdom moved slowly, facing change with fear and suspicion. Anything that Frevaria did not understand they labeled magic and were not eager to learn otherwise. But Keilen knew the difference. Simple engineering skills were not magic. The superb manor house Mabry built for his wife, Lady Cellina, was filled with clever devices run with levers and pulleys and clockwork gears. The great wheel of Mabry's mill that ground the flour and ran the saws and looms of Arindon was powered by the river, not magic. No one distrusted magic more than Mabry. Keilen pulled his horse to a stop when they came to the fork in the road. He watched an Arindian farmer goad his mule to walk in an endless circle. The animal was harnessed to a wheel which was connected to other smaller wheels and gears to pump the water from the ditch into the fields.

"Go on ahead, Tam," Keilen said to his manservant. "Tell Lady Cellina I will be there for dinner. I want to ride over the bridge first."

"Yes, Sire," said Tam. He knew his king had many things on his mind lately and High Bridge was where he did his best thinking alone.

Keilen reined his horse west to the now narrow track. Soldiers in his father's day had marched six abreast and war wagons could pass each other without stopping, but no longer. Now no one but Keilen came to stare at the roaring river from the old stone bridge. Here his father had fought and died, so it was here that Keilen came to fight his personal battles. He thought about his dying land and restless people. He also thought about Mabry's youngest daughter. Dulcie was often in his thoughts lately. She was a small frightened waif of a girl waiting on her demanding stepmother Cellina. What would Dulcie be like away from Mill Manor? The river rushed under the bridge giving the illusion that the bridge was moving upstream. Keilen gripped the rail and willed the vertigo to stop. When he had regained his balance he spat defiantly over the rail. "Water your damn fields with that Jasenth," he called after his falling spittle. "I will have revenge for my poor harvest. I will steal your fairest flower from underneath your upturned nose. I will have Dulcie and breed a castle full of sons. Then we will see whose fields are fertile."

It was a daring plan. He would have to think on it further. Lady Cellina would more than approve. Of that he was certain. Mabry would be cautious, but he would definitely be in favor of the idea. That left only Dulcie and she would, she had to say yes."

He swung up on his horse again. He slapped his mount to a gallop, crossed over the bridge to take a shortcut through Arindon woods to Mill Manor.

The next day King Keilen poked his head in the kitchen door. "Cook, ho Cook," he called. "Have you got something I can pack for noontime, maybe some pie?"

The Frevarian master cook set down the heavy cheese he had just brought up from the spring cellar. "Sit down, Kylie my boy, while my turnovers cool and I'll wrap one up for you."

Keilen sat on the kitchen stool that had been his regular perch ever since his arrival in Frevaria as a lonely fosterling of seven. Cook was his special friend, his mentor, his confidant. Cook was the only Frevarian who still called His Majesty King Keilen the First by his baby name. He pampered the young king with special treats and packed sack lunches for his daily outings. The boyish sweet cakes and milk had changed to a mug of ale and a slice of meat or cheese but the real nourishment Keilen sought in Cook's kitchen did not change. Keilen poured out all his troubles and Cook served up simple wisdom and love with the food he prepared.

"...and Cook don't save dinner tonight," Keilen was saying. "I'll be riding on to Mill Manor again."

"Is the food that good at Mabry's house?"

"Cook, as a man, well..." Keilen began then stopped.

"Yes Kylie?" said Cook not looking up from his cheese slicing.

"Man to man, I need your advice."

"About Mabry's daughter?"

"How did you know?"

"Recently you have mentioned her once or twice, a day that is," said Cook as he arranged the cheese slices on a plate and set it on the table in front of Keilen.

"The problem is," Keilen haltingly tried to explain. "The problem, well it's that she is Arindian and not royalty."

"She is young and pretty and well brought up, thank or blame Lady Cellina," Cook countered.

"She's so pretty, Cook, and so sweet and innocent," said Keilen. His eyes got a faraway look and his voice took a softer quality than his usual tone. "She has no idea how she can affect a man."

"So you love her, or is it only breeding season for you, boy?"

"You know I never had much time for women, Cook, and I still don't have time but..."

"But you eat dinner at Mill Manor more often than with your own house and all Frevaria is wondering why." Cook looked directly at the young man in front of him. Keilen was hunched over his plate toying with the slices of cheese. He tried to roll one up but it broke and crumbled.

"What should I do, Cook?" said Keilen as he pinched a crumb between his fingers.

"Be careful, be sure, even if she is willing," said Cook.

"Here I am, a king, a master horseman, a proven swordsman and I am more afraid of a girl than facing all of Arindon in the tournament. I could win any contest..."

"Except the longbow," Cook reminded him.

"Yeah, yeah, except the longbow, but I am terrified of facing one sweet wisp of a girl."

Cook sniffed the air, then walked across the kitchen and opened the oven door. The aroma of apple turnovers filled the room. He wadded up the corner of his apron and pulled out the pan. He smiled as Keilen's eyes lit up when he piled several golden triangles on his plate. Cook pulled up a stool and lowered his bulk down beside Keilen. "Does Mabry know what danger his daughter is in?"

"I think he knows I..."

"Does Lady Cellina?"

"She sets up all sorts of opportunities so I guess..."

"What about the girl?"

"I think she...I hope she...I don't know...not for certain anyway," said Keilen taking a bite out of the turnover. "Ouch!" he exclaimed waving a desperate hand in the direction of the water pitcher.

"My baking's not all that's hot, I think," said Cook chuckling as he poured Keilen a cup of water. "And things won't cool off until they are tasted I predict."

"Don't make fun of me. This is serious."

"Just make sure you don't get burned, Kylie my boy."

The fire crackled. Jasenth did not turn around. "Hello, Lizzie."

"You are getting so clever, Jay."

"I told you not to come here," he said ignoring her remark.

"Grandma doesn't know."

"Well I know and I was the one who told you not to come."

"Ben is asleep," Lizzie cooed.

"Your doing I suppose?"

"Well…"

"What do you want that is so urgent and so secret?"

Lizelle gave him her most winsome smile. "Just you, I was lonely."

Jasenth finally turned to look at her. Her face was pale and thin. Her large eyes were wistful and sad. "Since you're already here, you might as well stay. Have a seat," he added, his voice softening a little.

Lizelle sat down daintily on the hearth bench.

"Lizzie, I have told you again and again not to come here," he said trying his best not to let her innocent demeanor seduce him. "I'm sure Aunt Jane has told you too."

"Daily."

"Yet here you are." Jasenth paced the hearth rug.

"Sit by me, Jay. Talk to me. I just want you to talk to me like we used to when we were little."

"Alright, Lizzie, I'll talk to you," He curled up on the rug by her feet. "I'll tell you all the things that are important to me and why I want no secrets."

Lizelle folded her hands in her lap and assumed a listening pose. Jasenth pretended not to notice.

"Grandfather betrothed us," he began. "That is a fact and someday we must wed but…"

"Must wed! You make it sound so awful!"

"Lizzie please. I want a wife. I want a queen. But I do not want a selfish little girl whose only ambition in life is to play games and deceive people. I want a marriage like Uncle Jareth and Aunt Mari have. They work together…"

"You won't let me work with you," Lizelle pouted.

"I don't trust you."

"Then you don't love me."

Jasenth stood up again. He opened his mouth to reply but he stopped himself. He tried to think of something better to say. Finally he looked at her and said, "How can I love a will-o-the-wisp? I want something real, something solid. Magic and love don't mix."

Lizelle glared at him with indignant ire. "You know what I am. You have always known. You are selfish to withhold your love."

"You are selfish to waste your gifts," Jasenth snapped back. He started to pace back and forth in front of her.

"You wouldn't let me use magic to help rebuild the castle. I would have made it ever so nice and it would be done by now and we would be married and…"

"There is no need to use magic for what strong men can do."

"Now you sound just like Grandma," Lizelle continued to pout.

"She is right. You are a lazy and selfish girl, Lizzie. When have you done an honest piece of work?"

"All the time! I wash dishes and garden and do laundry and clean and…"

"And you cheat with magic every time you think Aunt Jane isn't watching."

Lizelle jumped up and planted her feet right in front of his pacing, forcing him to stop. "And why shouldn't I use magic?" she said glaring up at him.

"You aren't just a farm girl who needs a touch of binding for a piece of broken china or a calming spell for a colicky child. Your magic is for a greater purpose. Do you think I can love and respect you when you fritter it away dancing with fireflies?"

"I like dancing…" she said in a small hurt voice. A tear rolled down her cheek.

"I like dancing too, Lizzie," he said cupping her chin and turning her face up to his. His voice became soft and gentle. "Power like yours would taint a much older, stronger woman. You are but a sweet child who has not yet learned to use her awful gift. I know you can be generous and selfless. You help with births and healings. Even your weather tampering helps people when you don't frighten them to death. Remember when Aunt Avrille's mirror bird Trebil died and she was so heartbroken, you transported a whole nest of mirror birds through time and space to her garden. That was a beautiful act."

"I was exhausted for a week after that!"

"I'm sure Aunt Jane lectured you the whole time too."

Lizelle rolled her eyes.

"You've got to take care of yourself. Each time I see you, you are paler and thinner. Magic has…"

"A price, I know," she snapped but when she saw his look of genuine concern she smiled sweetly and said, "Then you do love me?"

"I think you are capable of learning what love really is," he said turning the question around.

"By doing what, washing dishes the hard way and walking all the way from Woodsmeet to Arindon?" she said with an arrogant toss of her curls.

"That's what Aunt Mari does. It's by finding joy in ordinary human things that she and Uncle Jareth share their love," said Jasenth laying a gentle hand on her shoulder.

"Will you love me if I walk all the way home tonight all by myself?" she said shrugging off his hand.

"That could be a start."

"Then I'll leave now," she said and darted for the door.

"No, Lizzie, wait," said Jasenth rushing after her. "Please stay for a while. I'll put another log on the fire and if you would like some tea, I already have a pot brewing."

Lizelle sat back on the bench. "Jay," she said, not quite sure of herself. "Does this mean we are courting?"

"This can be a beginning, Lizzie," he said cutting two thick slices of bread. "Lady Lizelle would you like butter or jam on your bread?"

"Butter, if you please."

"Sugar in your tea?"

She nodded.

"Cream?"

"None thank you."

Jasenth smiled to himself as he poured. He did love her. She was his childhood companion, his friend. Why did she have to bear such a heavy burden of power in the cause of the Light? He handed her the big, blue china cup. Lizelle looked like a delicate white snowflake against the dark wood of the bench. Such a frail little thing, how could she be a weapon against the Dark? What epic event lay ahead to put them to the test?

When they had finished Jasenth's simple hospitality he rose and said, "It will be a long chilly walk for a lady unused to night outings." He pulled a blanket from the foot of his bed. "Here, wrap up in this and I'll take you home. That is if you don't mind riding double."

"I don't really like horses," she said smiling up at him. "But if you hold me tight..."

Jasenth laughed. "You don't like horses? Be glad you aren't betrothed to Frevaria."

Janille was restless. Lizelle was gone again. The scry bowl remained dark. The cards were silent. Where was she? Had all her years of guardianship been thrown away on a child's whim? This was the third time she knew her granddaughter had disappeared recently. The first two times it had only been for an hour. Those times she questioned the girl but her inquiries had met with sullen silence. This time was different. Lizelle had been gone since mid-afternoon. Tea had been put away untouched and the supper pot was already boiling.

Her hands snapped the ends of the string beans in her apron with mechanical precision. Her mind raced. Was Lizelle spying on Allar? No, she would not have to leave to do that. Was she harassing Kylie? Now that was a possibility. Lizelle's knack of fire-flitting was especially troubling to her brother. She had often warned her granddaughter about over using magic. That power has a price was one lesson Lizelle did not take seriously. The strain on her health was obvious. As a child she had been able to draw energy from any source, but thanks to the drug Firerill the danger of her power was limited. Only fire could fuel her magic now, and that caused problems enough. Usually Lizelle worked obediently to discipline and develop her gifts. She had been willful at times, playing petty tricks and her sassiness was downright disrespectful. But until now she had been open and honest. Where was she?

Hoof beats broke into Janille's reverie. She folded the corners of her apron around the pile of beans and stood up to look out the window. A horse with two riders, one dressed in white was coming down the road. The pair cantered into the yard. Jasenth slid off and helped a beaming Lizelle to the ground.

"So that's where you've been!" Janille called from the doorway.

"I hope you didn't worry. Jay asked me to stay to tea."

"He did, did he?"

"Lizzie has been showing up in my firelight recently," Jasenth hastened to explain. "Not by my request I assure you, Aunt Jane."

"But you did ask me to stay today."

"Come in both of you," said Janille. "It seems we have some talking to do."

Janille dumped her apronful of beans onto the kitchen counter then pulled out a chair. "Lizzie, you have disobeyed me and

Jasenth you have done right to bring her back but I am afraid that is not all of…"

"Grandma…"

"Let me do the talking, Lizzie," said Jasenth as he pulled out a chair for her. "Lizzie wants to learn about love, Aunt Jane. But for one with so much power the simple truths about love are difficult to learn." He stopped and smiled at Lizelle. "We all know the gods have plans for her power but I also need to make plans. I need a wife and a queen, one who will love me and all Arindon, not a spoiled witch brat.

"Jay!"

"Let me finish, Lizzie," he said laying his hand on hers. He turned back to Janille. "The two of us have talked at length today. I have asked her to forgo the use of magic. If the gods call her to use her power, so be it, but she is not to use it for selfish tricks."

"You agreed to this, Lizzie?" said Janille quite startled by the proposal.

"I want Jay to love me," said Lizelle with a low, intense voice.

Jasenth continued, "I have told her if she cooperates in this I will call on her like a courting gentleman until the time is right for us to marry."

"This is music to my ears," Janille exclaimed. "You have done more with her in one afternoon than I have in all these years."

"I still love you Grandma," said Lizelle flinging her arms around Janille. "But now I am going to love Jay too."

"That is as it should be, Lizzie. You are a grown woman now. You need more than I alone can give you. It has been difficult for you with all the isolation and rejection and no friends your age…"

"Except Jay."

"Except Jasenth, yes. I am grateful for your loyalty to your grandfather's wishes," she said nodding to him.

"It's much more than that I assure you, Aunt Jane," Jasenth said quickly. "Lizzie and I have always been the best of friends. Our betrothal has nothing to do with it. So now with Uncle Jareth and Aunt Mari's love as an example I want to teach Lizzie what real love is."

"Then I must trust you, Jasenth, to not teach her all of love too soon. Power changes at best, and is often lost altogether when a sorceress weds. The Light needs Lizzie's full power if the world as we know it is to survive. Do not jeopardize it."

"You have my solemn word," said Jasenth.

"Mine too," said Lizelle.

Jasenth pushed back his chair and stood up. "With that settled I'd best be going..."

"Won't you stay for dinner," Lizelle begged.

"Not tonight, Lizzie, but with your grandmother's permission and a good report on your part of our agreement I would like to call on you for tea on let's say the day after tomorrow. If the weather is pleasant we could also go for a stroll."

"I would be delighted, Your Majesty." Lizelle bobbed a playful curtsy. "He can of course, right Grandma?"

Janille smiled her answer.

Jasenth took her hand and briefly raised it to his lips. With a nod of farewell to Janille and an undisguised smile of satisfaction he left Woodsmeet Cot and galloped away to Arindon.

It had become their custom after dinner was done for Keilen to take Dulcie for a stroll across the garden to the gazebo. Each time it became easier to take her hand, to kiss her fingers, to lean close as they spoke. He told her about life in Frevaria, of his love of horses and combat games. He boasted of his skill with the sword and the lance and complained about his failures with the Arindian longbow. He told her of settling small disputes throughout the kingdom and confided his fears about the drought in his fields. Tonight he was giving her a room by room description of the castle. Dulcie sat meekly on the bench beside him. Her hands were folded in her lap. Her face turned up to his. Keilen stopped talking in mid sentence. Night birds rustled in the arbor above. Their coos fluted in the stillness. Keilen's eyes wandered down Dulcie's moonlit throat and shoulders. The pink ruffles of her bodice quivered with each breath. He lifted her chin.

"Kiss me Dulcie."

Her breaths quickened.

"Sweet Dulcie, How I wish I were king here too. Then I would just command and have everything I want. But in Arindon I have no power. Here I am only a common man wanting what every man wants." He slowly traced the curve of her neck with his finger. When she did not resist, he grasped her shoulders and pulled her toward him. Her shawl slipped off. She made no attempt to retrieve it. Keilen kissed her cheek, her neck, and her pure white shoulders. He kissed the small swell of her breasts. He dropped to his knees before her. "Dulcie, come to me. I would be king in this small part of Arindon."

She sat demurely smiling, making no move or answer to his plea.

"Please, Dulcie. I cannot command you as a king so I must beg you as a man in desperate need."

"You have not asked father for me," she said with unexpected resistance.

"I will speak to him, I promise. Just say you're willing, please Dulcie."

She looked down at him. Her hands were still folded primly in her lap.

"Dulcie, come to me now. I'll ask the gods themselves if I must to have you."

"If I am willing tonight then what will be tomorrow," she said still holding back.

"Tomorrow I will carry you to Frevaria to share my bed and crown," Keilen declared. His hands cupped the curve of her hips pulling her gently toward him.

Dulcie dug her heels into the ground to resist his pull. She clasped and unclasped her long white fingers in her lap.

"Dulcie, sweet, soft, lovely Dulcie," Keilen pleaded. He laid his head in her lap and kissed her fingers one by one. "Come to me. I need you here, now!"

"Here?"

"Yes, yes!"

"You will make me queen, not just mistress?"

"Yes queen and more…"

Amethyst, Jasenth's little mirror bird, huddled with the tolerant family of gazebo doves until almost morning. She had heard the tender vows of the lovers as in a disarray of ruffled skirts and discarded leather the strength of Frevaria tasted the sweetness of Mill Manor. Bursting with news the little bird hurried out into the faint gray light toward home. "Ame hungry," she said. "King Jay give good treat for story, good, good treat."

Keilen did not take his usual midnight ride back to Frevaria that night. The staff at Mill Manor buzzed with speculations as they set out breakfast. Lady Cellina was taking hers in the upstairs sun room with Dulcie to wait on her. Tam had left early to visit Don and Darilla at the mill. Mabry and King Keilen were to be served, then left alone in the study. Something definitely was afoot.

"I'll take it from here," said Mabry taking the steaming tray from the kitchen boy. He set the bowls of bacon-sprinkled porridge on the table and poured two mugs of spiced tea and cream. "Eat up, Kylie. Whatever is on your mind will come easier with breakfast in your stomach." He picked up his bowl and blew on a spoonful. "But be quick about it. I have a busy day ahead of me at the mill."

"Then I won't keep you long," said Keilen. He took a sip of tea and cleared his throat. "Your daughter Dulcie pleases me," he began. "I told her last night that I would ask you for her."

"She is willing then?" asked Mabry unable to hide his joy.

"She was willing enough last night," Keilen blurted it all out at once.

Mabry roared with laughter. "We were all wondering what was taking you so long out there," he said giving Keilen a slap on the back. He laughed again. "Then all you need is my blessing and you have it." He clinked his tea mug to Keilen's. "To the future!" he declared and drained his mug. "Now we should tell Cellina. Women need lots of time to plan things."

"I don't know...maybe you can just tell her. I need to get back..." said Keilen becoming more and more afraid and confused as the impact of his decision began to take affect.

Mabry laughed and slapped Keilen on the back again. "You'd best give in to the women once they have given in to you. Life will be much different for you from now on, much different, but good I hope."

Chapter 13

Keilen rode through the kitchen gate about mid morning. Cook noted the difference in his young king's stride but he continued rolling out pie dough and fitting it into the pie tins. "Are you hungry Kylie?" he said without looking up. "Breakfast is put away but I can set out a few leftovers when I finish these pies."

"I ate at Mill Manor," answered Keilen. He helped himself to a dipper of water from the cistern.

"I served ham and cheese biscuits, potatoes and onions and one of my best apple pies this morning," said Cook. "What did you have at Mill Manor?"

"I don't remember," said Keilen as he paced nervously across the kitchen.

"Yes, when the dessert is sweet it spoils the appetite for anything more," said Cook trying to catch Keilen's eye.

Keilen hung the water dipper back on the hook. "I think we need to go down to the spring cellar to get some cheese, Cook," he said.

"What and leave my pie shells here to dry out? If you want cheese there is some in the cupboard."

"Leave your damn pies," Keilen exploded. "Cook I need to talk to you."

Cook spread a clean cloth over his work and sprinkled it with water. "If they're all dried out and burn for dinner, don't complain to me," he said. Then he smiled. "Alright, Kylie my boy, to the spring cellar to cool off it is."

"Don't tease me Cook," Keilen snapped. "This is important."

"I'm sure it is," the big man answered as he waddled down the steep stairs behind Keilen. When they reached the cool white-washed room below Cook wiped his floury hands on his apron and began to inspect the neatly piled wheels of cheese on a shelf. "She said yes, now what else do you have to tell, Little King?"

"Oh Cook is that obvious? She not only said yes she…she…"

Cook turned over a cheese wheel and scraped off a minute fleck of mold. "And...?"

"She let me of course, but not until I promised to make her queen," Keilen told him.

"And...?"

"She was so warm, so soft, so sweet, so innocent..."

"So it will be marriage then?"

"What do I do now?" said Keilen, panic rising in his voice. "She said yes, Mabry said yes, and I'm sure by now Lady Cellina knows everything. What do I do with a wife and maybe a son on the way?"

Cook started to laugh but when he saw the real terror in Keilen's face he stopped himself. "My dear boy, your first concern should be for the troop of nobles camped on your doorstep since this time yesterday. Until Frevaria's fields are watered, your planting seeds in Arindon will not be good news."

"What do they want?"

"The gatekeeper says they have a letter."

"So what should I do?" said Keilen.

"Go talk to them, then swallow some pride and ask Arindon for help."

"Ask help from Jay!" Keilen swung his fist wildly. Cook stepped with amazing quickness for a man of his size to rescue an endangered row of canning jars.

"How sweet is Mabry's daughter?" asked Cook laying a hand on the young king's shoulder to try to bring him back to reason.

Keilen kicked over an empty barrel and sat down. "Are you sure there's no other way?"

"Not unless the gods send rain."

"I'll do whatever I have to," said Keilen. "I'll even ask Arindon if it comes to that."

"Women always come with a high price, Kylie, and the higher the man the higher the price." He patted Keilen's shoulder. "Shall we go back up now? You have petitioners waiting and I have my pies."

Keilen re-read the letter the nobles had given him. "Damn!" he shouted. "Why now?" He pounded his desk. He crumbled the letter and threw it across the room. His feet paced the floor with angry strides. Tears of desperation welled in his eyes. A sick fear gripped his stomach. He picked up the letter again and tried to smooth out the sheet of awful truth. With shaking hands he read the message a third time.

Summer Solstice Day 53

Be it known to King Keilen the First that the people of Frevaria are thirsty. Our farms wither and our beasts collapse while our neighbors in Arindon endure no such hardship. What evil magic threatens us and nourishes them? Be it also known that the people of Frevaria are concerned by their king's frequent absences from the kingdom. Does he consort with evil in Arindon thus causing punishment to be meted out to us by the gods? Hear us and answer us.

In humble petition,
The stewards of your land

All the triumphs of last night's conquest were tumbled with that one letter. "I am king," Keilen yelled at the walls of his office. "I have power." But only as long as my people are willing to serve me, he added silently. What will they do now? Will they revolt? Why did this have to happen now? Ask Jay for help? The very thought galls me. I'm three years older. I've been king three years longer, he argued with himself. Damn him. His kingdom thrives. His people are content.

Keilen's blood curdled with anger and envy, yet the truth of the situation would not go away. He would send for Mabry. He would ask him to design and build a water system and a mill and maybe even extend Jasenth's infernal communication line. Mabry would help. After all, his daughter's future was at stake.

"Tam! Tam!" he shouted for his manservant. When Tam appeared in the doorway, Keilen thrust a hastily scrawled note in his hand. "Take this to Mill Manor, now."

"Shall I greet my sister for you while I'm there, sire?" said Tam when he saw the note was addressed to Mabry.

"No Tam, from now on I will deliver all messages to Dulcie personally. Now get going. The matter at hand is urgent."

Tam obediently nodded and hurried out. Keilen sank into his chair. He was exhausted. He closed his eyes but try as he would, even thoughts of Dulcie could not blot out his fears.

King Jasenth arrived at Woodsmeet Cot by mid afternoon. The day was sultry. Janille greeted him at the door with a glass of cool mint tea.

"Where's Lizzie?" Jasenth asked between gulps.

"She is out in the meadow."

"She remembered I was coming?"

Janille smiled at him. That was answer enough.

"Thanks, Aunt Jane," he said handing back his empty glass. He stood a long awkward moment searching for something else to say.

"Go Jay. You did not ride all the way out here in this heat to talk to me."

Jasenth climbed the rail fence beyond the garden. He could see Lizelle's blonde head just beyond a clump of mustard flowers. He hurried out into the fragrant meadow, stopping only long enough to pick a handful of daisies. He laughed at himself. The King of Arindon picking daisies! But a woman likes flowers, especially when a man picks them. He had agreed to court Lizelle and he was prepared to play the game.

Lizelle did not look up from the book she was reading when he approached. She looked like a wildflower herself as she lounged amid the white semicircle of her skirts.

"Little Lizzie with golden hair," Jasenth sang out. "Sitting in the meadow fair. Doesn't know her lover's there or is it that she doesn't care."

Lizelle laughed and closed her book.

"Didn't you hear me coming?"

"Of course I did."

"Then why did you pretend you didn't?"

"I wanted to wait until you had picked me a nice bouquet," said Lizelle as she tipped her head coyly to the side and pursed her lips.

Jasenth just shook his head and handed her the daisies. Lizelle made no motion to accept his offering.

"My attentions cannot be bought for anything less than a whole armful of daisies and at least one primrose," she said looking away across the meadow.

"A primrose?"

"There are some over there by that rock." She waved her hand toward the hedgerow.

"Do you expect me to...?"

"You want me to be pleased that you have come to court me?" she said still looking away from him.

He bent down and took her hands. "Walk with me and I will pick your primrose."

Lizelle leaped to her feet. "Catch me if you can," she called as she raced away.

Before they reached the hedgerow Jasenth had easily caught up with Lizelle. "Where are your primroses, Lizzie? I don't see any flowers here."

"You're not looking in the right place," she giggled.

"Where are they?"

"Right here," she said pursing her lips. "You can pick them as often as you like and still there will be more and more and…"

Jasenth tumbled her into the grass. "You little witch brat!"

"Kiss me Jay or I will spell you."

"You already have, Lizzie, but what about your promise?"

"What report did Grandma give?" she asked as her face went suddenly sober.

"I didn't ask her. I want our relationship to be built on honesty and trust."

"I was very good," she said turning her large innocent eyes up to him.

"I believe you," said Jasenth.

"Will you kiss me then?" she asked simply. Her coyness had vanished.

Jasenth kissed her. He was terrified but the response of her tender lips quickly dispelled his fears.

"I love you Jay," she whispered.

He kissed her again. Lizelle's small arms tightened around his neck. He held her close, until he felt her frail shoulders begin to shake with sobs. "Lizzie what have I done to you? Have I hurt you?"

"I love you. I am just so happy to love you," she sobbed and clutched him tighter.

"I love you too, Lizzie," he heard himself saying as he leaned back and brushed the tears from her cheeks. "Let me pick one more primrose and then I think it will be time to go in for tea."

Janille watched them from the open window. There was no need to put on the teapot just yet she told herself as she turned away. The war inside her between the grandmother and the sorceress raged anew. Her heart wept for her own love denied in the cause of the Light. If only Lizelle could be spared that pain! She measured out the tea from the canister and set it aside. The weather was too hot for anything but mint. Memories and regrets clouded her eyes and choked her throat. She wept for her daughters, for Elanille whom she had barely known and now was forever lost. She wept for Avrille severed from both her husband and her children but still not free to love. She wept for herself and the awful secrets she kept inside her heart where love should reign. Must her granddaughter also be denied every woman's dream of love and marriage and babies? Janille wept for Lizelle and her awful burden of power.

She dried her eyes with the corner of her apron and looked out the window again. The sun blazed bright and hot. Not a leaf stirred. There was no breeze to cool the land as evening approached. She saw Jasenth and Lizelle walking down the path toward the house hand in hand.

"Come inside and cool off," she called to them. "Jay there is a cloth by the sink if you want to wash your face and Lizzie you are wrinkles and grass stains from head to toe. Go to your room and come out looking like a lady."

When Lizelle emerged from her room, her face had been washed, her hair brushed and she had changed into a clean white dress with a dainty, embroidered apron. Janille was pleased. This courtship was not just a new game. She could feel the press of approaching events. The time they all both longed for and feared was not far away. Would Lizelle be ready for the test?

"Grandma?"

"I must have been miles off," said Janille realizing she was standing in the kitchen doorway holding the teapot.

"I'll pour since I am hostess," Lizelle announced.

"Then I'll get the scones," said Janille.

"Just wait till you taste the scones, Jay," Lizelle chattered gaily. "We baked them this morning before it got too hot for the oven. They have blueberries inside and we have cream and honey to put on them and…"

"Lizzie slow down," said Jasenth a bit overwhelmed. "I have been here to tea lots of times before today."

"But not as a courting king," said Janille coming back with a plateful of scones wrapped in a tea towel.

Jasenth said very little from then on. There were enough scones to keep him busy but his eyes never left Lizelle. She is so thin, he thought, yet she has taken only one bite of her scone. She drank her cup of tea and she did put sugar in it but that is not enough to sustain a healthy girl....

"Jay you're staring."

"Eat your scone, Lizzie, you're much to skinny," he said suddenly.

"That's not a romantic thing to say!" she exclaimed indignantly, but she did pick up her scone. "I didn't know you liked fat women."

Jasenth wiped the crumbs from his chin. "I want you to be strong and healthy."

"Like Auntie Maralinne?"

"Aunt Mari is beautiful. You would do well to learn from her example."

"Don't be too hard on her," Janille cautioned. "It's the Firerill that kills her appetite and the magic that saps her strength."

Jasenth looked serious for a long moment. "Does she still need to take it, Aunt Jane, if she doesn't do magic anymore?"

"Do I Grandma?" said Lizelle.

Janille carefully weighed her answer. So much was at stake. Lizelle was still a child in mind as well as in body. The Firerill that controlled her magic also held back her womanhood. Could Lizelle be trusted if she stopped taking the drug or would she slip in a moment of folly? Now that Jasenth's ardor had been kindled, would they destroy the purity she needed to wield her full power when the Light called? "I don't know," she said. "Lizzie's magic is so powerful and there is so much to consider..."

"You know best, Aunt Jane," said Jasenth. "But love and trust are also powerful. Uncle Jareth and Aunt Mari..."

Lizelle stamped her foot. "I am not Auntie Maralinne and you are not Uncle Jareth. Stop always saying that we have to be like them."

"Lizzie! Jay!" Janille ordered stepping between them. "You are adults, royalty, a respected king and a powerful sorceress. Must I remind you of your importance to the world and to the Light? For now we will keep things as is. Lizzie will continue the

Firerill. But she will also promise to eat better, won't you Lizzie?"

Lizelle stamped her foot again. "Grandma you are so unfair!"

"I do think honest housework has made her a bit stronger, don't you think so Jasenth," said Janille ignoring Lizelle's outburst.

"Certainly Aunt Jane," said Jasenth handing Lizelle a scone.

She crammed the scone in her mouth and reached for another.

After tea was cleared, Jasenth and Lizelle strolled out to the garden. The sun slanted at a lower angle through the trees and the day had begun to cool slightly. He missed living at Woodsmeet Farm though his lodgings in Arindon's gatehouse were comfortable. He thought of the castle. The reconstruction was almost complete. Soon he would have to give up peace and privacy. He would have to marry Lizelle and hold balls and parades and formal courts. Is that what he really wanted?

"Will you stay for dinner?" said Lizelle breaking into his thoughts.

"No Lizzie, I said I would just come for tea this time."

"But we have plenty and Grandma won't mind," she begged.

"No Lizzie..."

"But Jay..."

"I need to stop in with Uncle Jareth on business before I go home. I can't stay."

She grabbed his hands and looked pleadingly up into his face. "Can't you just tap out a message on your line when you get home?"

"No," he said gently releasing her grip on his hands. "This is a personal matter."

Lizelle's eyes welled with disappointment. "Will you call on me tomorrow?"

"No, but the day after tomorrow is our birthdays, Aunt Mari has a special dinner planned. I was supposed to invite you and Aunt Jane but I almost forgot."

"I wanted to celebrate with you, alone," Lizelle pouted.

"Lizzie we had a lovely afternoon, don't spoil it now or I won't come courting again," Jasenth threatened then immediately regretted saying it.

Lizelle burst into tears. "It's so hard to be good. You can't know how hard it is," she wailed.

"Yes I do, Lizzie sweet, and if I may call on you again..." He stopped and grinned at her. "If I may, Lady Lizelle, perhaps we can go for a carriage ride, to the falls perhaps and then if it is not inconvenient for your grandmother I will stay for dinner. In the meantime we both have obligations to our families."

Lizelle threw her arms around his neck. "I love you. I love you. Of course you can call again."

Jasenth kissed her. She was warm and delicately sweet. He wanted to stay, but he was afraid to stay. He wanted to stay, but he had to talk to Uncle Jareth before things went any farther. "Goodbye Lizzie," he said and with one more quick kiss broke away from her embrace. Jubilantly he ran all the way to Woodsmeet manor.

When Jasenth arrived home at the castle gatehouse Ben was entertaining a visitor. "Hello Tam," he said. "Am I interrupting a brotherly tete a tete?"

Tam jumped to his feet. "No Your Majesty, I am on official business for King Keilen. I am to..."

"What does Kylie want now?" said Jasenth somewhat annoyed.

"I am to deliver this message and wait for a reply." Tam handed him a sealed letter.

"Official business, everything Frevarian is official business," Jasenth remarked breaking the wax the seal. "Don't you sober people ever relax and have fun?"

But it was Jasenth who sobered when he read the letter.

Summer Solstice Day 54
Dear Jay,

Forgive the informality but I would speak to you as a kinsman and a friend. Frevaria is dying. You have seen my fields. My nobles speak against me and I have no reply for them. I need your help. I have spoken to Mabry about constructing a water system. He will not proceed without your consent. I am asking you as one young king with tremendous responsibility to another. I am asking you as a cousin. Please help me. Help my people.

In gratitude,
Keilen

Jasenth refolded the letter. "Tam do you know what is in this letter?"

"No, Your Majesty."

"Then simply tell Kylie my answer is yes. I will take time to think through the details and I will respond at length soon."

The next day Jasenth sat all afternoon at his desk. Writing did not come easy for him. He paced the floor and read the draft of his letter aloud to Ben who had kept a patient vigil beside him.

S.S.55
To King Keilen the First of Frevaria,

Arindon will assist Frevaria in this time of drought under the following terms and conditions:

1. Frevaria will construct and maintain their half of the inter-kingdom communication line between the Star Spring gatehouse and Frevaria castle to facilitate future discourse.
2. Frevaria will construct and maintain an irrigation system to service all farm manor fields.
3. Labor for the above projects will be provided by the Frevarian military and any unemployed peasantry. Design and supervision will be provided by Mabry of Mill Manor and subject to approval of Arindon.
4. Until said projects are completed and Frevaria is again independent, Arindon will sell food to Frevaria in exchange for coin, goods or credit. In addition, Arindon will wavier the customary exchange for all Frevarian children sent to Arindon for fostering or apprenticeship.

Arindon extends the hand of kinship and friendship to Frevaria in this time of need. May the obligations imposed be short and the benefits so gained be long and enduring,

King Jasenth of Arindon

"What do you think, Ben? Does it spell out the facts without being rude?"

"You drive a hard but fair bargain, sire, and the wording is formally appropriate."

"I hope Kylie appreciates this," declared Jasenth.

"He has no choice in the matter and he knows it," said Ben.

"Why do I find so much pleasure in doing this, Ben?" said Jasenth with a smug grin spreading across his face.

"The competition between the kingdoms has always been keen," Ben replied trying to sound neutral.

Jasenth dripped sealing wax on the folded letter. "No, this isn't about kingdoms. This is personal," he said stamping the wax with his signet. "I have never liked Kylie, until now that is."

"Shall I carry the message for you?" Ben offered.

"Yes, that will be formal and official enough for King Keilen the First."

"Shall I take the little bird along so you can have an accurate report of his response, sire?"

"Ben you are clever, a man after my own heart." Jasenth embraced his co-conspirator then called to his mirror bird. "Ame my dearest little spy, how would you like to visit Frevaria's cook?"

Chapter 14

Lady Cellina had not had such a glorious opportunity since she left Frevaria for Mill Manor. Life was good since her marriage to Mabry, very good in fact, but she missed the excitement and the even exhausting preparations for royal events. Her mind was racing. First there would be a harvest festival at which Frevaria could express their gratitude for Arindon's generosity when the gods had shown none through the summer's drought. At the Autumnal Equinox they would gather together to celebrate. A new age of cooperation between the kingdoms would be heralded and the crowning moment would be when Keilen and Dulcie announced their betrothal.

"And after that..." Cellina said her face growing brilliant with enthusiasm.

"One event at a time, dear," cautioned Mabry fanning her heated cheeks.

"But Mabry, this is only the beginning. The wedding will be at Winter Solstice. Dulcie will be the returning Sun, dressed in gold, bringing prosperity back to Frevaria."

"I'm sure it will be a grand wedding if you are planning it, Cellina dear." He kissed her forehead. "But now I think I should get you a cool drink. Even mornings are hot now."

"A cool drink would be good," she panted. "Wheel me to the porch. The sight of the river always cools me."

"I'll get you a cool face cloth too," said Mabry as he wheeled her to a shady corner of the wide verandah.

Cellina's mind snapped back to her plans. For the betrothal Dulcie should wear her new yellow dress and Keilen should be in full armor.

Dell and Rogarth shared a table at Beck's Tavern. The clockwork fan Mabry had installed whirred overhead. Armon Beck refilled their pitchers of ale and asked, "How fares the lady queen if her bard and her champion have abandoned her to sit under my new fan?"

"She fares as well as can be expected on such a hot night," Rogarth answered.

"Ale and male company are cooler than mint tea and women," said Dell. "We are grateful Her Majesty gave us leave to come."

"Cooler it is," agreed the tavern keeper. "Whose tab is this round on?"

"Put it on mine," said Rogarth.

"You paid for the last one," said Dell.

"Let's keep it simple. I'll pay for tonight and you pay next time."

"On Rogarth's tab then, two pitchers," said the tavern keeper. "Will you be wanting any food?"

"It's too hot to eat," said Dell. "Just keep us wet and cool. I'm as dry as a Frevarian field."

Armon Beck went back to his dish washing and the two companions relaxed together as had become their custom in recent months.

"Lately I have been worried about our lady's health," said Dell.

"I take it you are not referring to the weather," said Rogarth.

"The weather of the heart, you could say."

"Yes, with Allar gone she says she has nothing left."

Dell took a swallow of ale and wiped his brow with his sleeve. "I also feel his loss. It was a joy to have such a congenial lad for a student."

"I miss the boy too. We all do," said Rogarth. "But all Lady Avrille's card casting for the boy and mirror watching for King Will does her more harm than good." He leaned back his chair against the wall and lifted his face to the breeze of Armon's new fan.

"It's especially the pining for King Will that concerns me," said Dell draining his mug and pouring himself another.

"Not that things were all that good when they were together," said Rogarth. "But fifteen years can soften a memory I suppose." He picked up his mug, saw that it was empty and handed it to Dell. "Pour me another while you're at it." After a long, refreshing swallow he continued, "What does she see in that mirror of hers except a reflection of her own desires?"

"Don't mock what you don't know, my friend. I have seen the image shift but not as clear as she evidently does. We all have our gifts and yours is to not see so that you may be an anchor for the rest of us."

Rogarth shook his head. "It is better to suffer the loss of separation once and be done with it, than to relive it every day."

"You should know, my friend," said Dell. "First a princess and then a queen you have loved but never wed."

Rogarth sighed but did not answer.

"Our Lady Avrille should look to her own needs now that the boy is gone," said Dell. "What she needs most is a man to love again."

Rogarth answered in a low, sad voice, "But those who love her most are either too old or two low born to do more than weep in their ale and lie alone."

"You were good enough for King Arinth, gods rest his soul, to offer you his daughter once," said Dell.

"But she loved another."

"True enough, but our Lady Avrille loves you."

"And I love her."

"Then take her, my friend, and be happy together. You have both done your duty to the boy and the kingdom."

"Dell the ale fuzz in your head makes you forget that she is my queen and another man's wife."

"King Will is gone…"

"And her heart with him. I am her trusted friend, no more, and I would not betray that trust. She dreams of Will and I dream of Maralinne. The love Avrille and I share is pain, not passion."

"I had ladies too in my day. And I had losses, cruel bitter losses," said Dell putting down his mug and picking up his harp.

"Green were her eyes
As green as the sea,
But the lady I loved
Is lost to me.

Smooth was her skin,
As smooth as a wave,
Deep as the sea
Was the love that she gave.
Gone is the tide that kisses the strand.
Gone is my love from this sad land.

Woe to the bard
Who heals with his harp,
The woes of the kingdom,
But ne're his own heart."

"I've heard you sing that one before but I never realized it was your own tale you were singing," said Rogarth.

"It was over forty years ago. I have never loved a lady since except my harp," said Dell giving his instrument an affectionate caress. "It was my lady love who taught me to play."

"Where is she now?"

"She's gone, just disappeared."

"There was no sign, no trace?"

"None."

"The heart never heals from such a loss," said Rogarth throwing his arm around Dell's shoulders.

"Nor does it heal from never having what it desires like yours, my good friend," said Dell returning his embrace.

"Never were two men as different as you and I," said Rogarth. "But our duties to rear Prince Allar, and our love for our lady queen has bound us together."

"Yes the harp and the sword, two mighty weapons wielded in the same cause, that's us," said Dell shakily refilling his mug. "Have another?"

Rogarth pushed his mug toward Dell. "I think we are both a little drunk tonight."

"It must be the heat."

"Or our third pitcher…"

"Let's order another," said Dell. His face was flushed and his eyes were wet with tears.

"Why not?" said Rogarth. He turned and waved the empty pitcher. "Armon, we're dry again."

The tavern keeper brought them another pitcher of ale. "Sing us a song, Dell, that is if you still can. My patrons are getting restless."

Dell fisted his chest and belched. "What shall it be, lads, a ballad or a bawdy?"

"Sing whatever you like, just get their minds off the heat," said the tavern keeper.

The bard moved unsteadily to the center of the room. "Lend an ear, my lads…I'll sing you my tale…" He stopped to tune a string. The room hushed and he began to sing.

"There was a woman…" his harp wailed.
Who gave to me,
The song of love,
The song of the sea…"

The harp rolled like the waves. The listeners in the room had never heard the sea but still they knew the timeless rhythms deep in their hearts.

"The song of love
In the wail of the gull,
And the wind in the sail…"

The harp's voice rose and fell. The roomful of men rocked and wept for their own lost loves and Armon Beck kept the pitchers full.

Tonight Queen Avrille brushed her hair before the mantle mirror as she did every night. Gold fingers of the setting sun stretched across the floor behind her and retreated into the shadows. Avrille had dismissed her little girls' reading class early. No child could concentrate on learning their letters in such weather. Dell and Rogarth were out. The house was empty and quiet. The time alone was precious. She laid down her hairbrush and tied the thick length of her hair back with a scarf. It was so hot! She unbuttoned her dress and let it fall in a rumpled heap on the floor. There was no one to censor her as she stood in the middle of the room in just her shift. "I am High Queen. I can do anything I please," she said aloud. She kicked her dress out of the way and did a little dance, but it was so hot she could not get her breath and had to stop. The room was almost dark. She lit the mantle candles and sat down by the cold hearth with her thoughts.
"April! April!"
The candles flickered.
"April!"
The mirror swirled with patterns of light and shadow.

"April! April! April!"

Her head jerked up. Her eyes flew open. Had she been dreaming? She stood up and stretched. Then she headed to the kitchen for a drink of water. An awareness prickled her back as she left the room.

In the kitchen the mirror birds were quiet. She filled their water dish and covered their cage. "Nighty night, little friends," she whispered. Jest gave a feeble peep.

She took her glass of water back to the living room. All the windows were open but there was no breeze. The candles beside the mirror flickered again.

"April," came the faintest whisper.

"April." She heard it again. The mirror was dark though she strained to see. Was it Will calling? Why would he call to her now? Was he really in the Dark Realm as she feared? Could he see into her world at the balances of dusk and dawn as her mother had seen from that sunless prison? Fifteen years of loneliness and sacrifice weighed heavily especially now that Allar was also gone. Her healing and teaching in the village and the devotion of Rogarth and Dell eased her pain, but she desperately missed Will. Did he need her too?

She searched the mirror in vain. The calling was silent and the candles burned with straight, tall flames. Outside she heard men's voices singing. Rogarth and Dell were returning. She picked up her discarded dress and retreated up the stairs.

Janille awakened suddenly. The moon shining through the high loft window was half full. She sat up and wrapped the quilt around her. The night was warm but she felt herself shivering. She groped for the bedside candle. The small flame she kindled did nothing to dispel the chill or the hovering shadows. Something was in the room. She could feel it. She lit another candle, then another and another. When she had lit the fifth candle the air began to tingle. Quickly she arranged them in a circle on the floor and stepped back. The candlelight caught the mirror. Images danced on the silvery surface. She could hear the rush of the sea and men's voices, one young and vibrant and one old and weary. Was one Allar? It sounded familiar but before she was sure the images shifted. A small light bobbed this way and that...a lantern? An old woman's voice called, "Child! Child, where y' be?" Again there was the sound of waves crashing on rocks. The mirror swirled white. Tendrils of mist danced in the candlelight. The air filled with humming. Soon it was joined with a counter harmony. The song was of joy and sweet relief, somehow familiar, like a lullaby out of the past. She joined the humming until at last the words rang clear and true. It was the home spell. "Home to Love," she sang with all her heart.

The white mist rose from the mirror in two pale columns, balancing and turning in a stately dance. One took the form of a woman in a long white gown. The other became a knight in gleaming armor. The woman paused before Janille and spoke.

"The girl loves the lad. She doesn't know. She follows him, but he's long gone."

"They will find each other, sister," said the ghostly knight. "They will find each other as I have found you."

Janille suddenly recognized the knight's features. "Arinth!" she exclaimed.

"That I was but now I am much more. Now that I and my sister, my twin, lost at birth and found in death, are one again. The lad and the girl will also meet again in the Dark."

"In death!" Janille cried.

"Dark yes, death no," said Arinth's shade. "You guardians must let them go. The Light will have its way but first there must be Dark."

The candles flickered wildly. The two figures embraced each other and faded into the shadows. Janille was left in the dark room alone.

Dell's harp sang merrily in the firelight. Woodsmeet Manor was alive with celebration. Today Jasenth and Lizelle were twenty year's old. Maralinne prepared a grand dinner. There was roast chicken and corn on the cob, carrot and cabbage slaw, summer squash and stuffed green peppers, and when they had eaten all they could hold they squeezed in a piece of peach cobbler. After that they pushed back the furniture and danced. Lizelle demanded reel after reel. Jasenth begged for a slower pace but to no avail. Jareth and Maralinne, and Avrille and Rogarth reeled with them but soon dropped out to catch their breath.

Lizelle and Jasenth danced on. Janille watched from the kitchen doorway, toes tapping. It was good to see the people she loved best in the world so happy. Lizelle flitted like a firefly. Jasenth nimbly countered her steps as they balanced and twirled across the floor. Dell's fingers flew over the harp strings. His voice was gay and clear. The fire sparked higher and higher. The dancing feet beat faster. The room began to shimmer with magic. Janille started with alarm. Quickly her fingers wove a calming sign. Avrille glanced at her mother, but the rest of the group seemed unaware. The song slowed as Janille moved into the dance. The steps shifted to a stately promenade. Rogarth took Avrille's hand and joined her. Jareth and Maralinne followed across the floor.

Jasenth escaped to the kitchen to get a glass of water. When he returned Lizelle was dancing alone. Janille pulled him aside.

"How does she keep going, Aunt Jane," he said between gulps.

"See how high the fire burns when she nears it?" said Janille.

Jasenth looked. The fire leaped and swirled in time to Lizelle's dance. When she neared the fire her dance intensified. When she skipped away her steps lengthened and slowed.

"She promised me," said Jasenth with profound disappointment. "She promised no magic. How could she betray our love...?"

"Jasenth, she does not know what she is doing," whispered Janille. "Don't blame her. Tonight she is so happy that she is just doing what is her nature to do..."

"Then her promise means nothing," said Jasenth.

"She did not break her promise," Janille assured him. "Instead of worrying about promises, it is her health that you should be concerned about. She must be as exhausted as the rest of us. Get her a glass of water and take her out to the porch. I'll speak to Dell."

Jasenth hesitated. The hurt of betrayal was slow to subside.

"Go on if you truly love her," Janille said kindly. "And say nothing of this. Do not betray your trust in her love."

This time Jasenth obeyed though he did not fully understand what had happened or why. He poured two glasses of water from the pitcher in the kitchen. Outside on the porch Lizelle collapsed onto the swing. He handed her a glass and sat down beside her. "You should drink more, Lizzie," he told her. "It's not good for you to dance so much without drinking. Aren't you thirsty?"

Lizelle sipped her water and leaned her head on his shoulder. "You didn't give me a birthday present," she pouted.

"Do you think that I forgot?"

"I hope not," she said with a coy tip of her head.

"Well finish your drink and I'll show you."

Lizelle jumped up and set her half empty glass on the porch rail. "Show me now."

Jasenth pointed to her glass. He waited and ignored her pained expressions until she drank the remaining water.

"Where are you taking me?" shouted Lizelle as she raced after him.

"To the barn."

"Why did you hide my present in the barn?"

"You'll see," said Jasenth as he lit the lantern by the barn door and led the way up the ladder to the loft. A soft mewing greeted them. "Tabby, show Lizzie her birthday present," he said as he knelt and gently lifted the old orange cat aside. There on the straw wriggled four scrawny balls of fur. "The white one is yours."

"Oh how precious!" Lizelle squealed with delight as she scooped up the kitten and held it close.

"Uncle Jareth says it will be another week before they are weaned. Then you can take her home."

"I just love her! She will be our baby until we marry and have babies of our own," she said reaching for him.

Jasenth held back and did not answer.

"When can we name the day? Please say when," Lizelle begged.

"Now is not the time to talk about that."

"Why not? We are betrothed and now we are courting. I like courting," she said wrapping her arms around his neck.

Jasenth sat still and said nothing.

"Please Jay, why not?"

"Because I'm scared," he said pulling away from her.

"Am I that awful?"

Jasenth shook his head but would not look at her.

"I'm trying so hard to be good. For you," she said leaning over so that she could look up at him.

Jasenth cupped his hands around hers. The kitten snuggled down with a squeaky purr. "The future is in our hands," he said. "And I am so scared. So much depends on us, all these people, our whole world, and we are barely more than children. How can we know what to do? I know Aunt Mari and Uncle Jareth will help and Aunt Jane too but is that enough? I'm just scared that's all. Dare we name the day? What happens if the Light calls on your power? I can't have you until…"

"Grandma says it will probably be when Allar comes home."

"When will that be, next year? How long can this go on?"

"Don't be scared Jayjay. I'll help you," she said with innocent belief that saying so was enough to insure their future.

Jasenth took a deep breath and looked into her eyes. She was as pure and naïve as the kitten in their hands, so unaware of the responsibilities ahead. He leaned closer. He wanted her and needed her as much as he feared her. He took her and kissed her. The kitten squealed and tumbled from their laps. Frantically it searched the straw for its mother. Old Tabby picked it up and carried it back to its brothers. Jasenth kissed Lizelle again.

"I promise you, Lizzie, if our duty to the Light is done by Midsummer, on that day we can call our love our own."

"Almost a whole year!" she wailed as she clutched him tighter.

"I promise to marry you on Midsummer's Day."

Lizelle covered him with fierce kisses mixed with tears of joy. "Jayjay, I love you! I love you! Oh Jay let's go in and tell Grandma right away."

"No! Let this be our secret for now," he choked as fear again gripped his throat.

"A secret, how exciting!" Lizelle exclaimed.

"What can we do to seal our secret?" said Jasenth now really starting to panic.

"I know, take my hand," she said bouncing up and down. "First I'll say my promise and then you say yours."

As Jasenth took her hand Lizelle dramatically cleared her throat. "I Lizzie, promise to love Jay and keep our secret until the Light no longer needs us. Now you say it."

Jasenth sat silently for a moment then started with a rush of emotion, "I Jasenth, King of Arind…"

"Don't be so formal, silly."

"Alright," he said with a nervous laugh. "I Jay promise to love Lizzie and keep our secret until the Light has called upon us and sets us free."

"My kitten will be our witness, won't you Primrose?" she said searching the straw for the little animal.

"Primrose?" said Jasenth shaking his head.

"Primroses, you know, kisses..." she said lifting the sweet bud of her lips to his. "Seal our promise with a kiss..."

Jasenth tumbled her into the straw. "Lizzie you are impossible! One kiss, but only one and then we must get back to the house."

Avrille yawned and sat up in bed. The day was already hot. It was hard to get moving. Downstairs she could hear Verity and Jest singing. Dell must have already fed them. He always got up at dawn. She padded over to the wash stand, poured water into the basin, splashed her face and rubbed her eyes. Why was she still so sleepy? It must be this heat, she thought. She slipped into her coolest dress minus the petticoat and braided up her hair.

"Lady Avrille?" Dell called up when he heard her stirring.

"I'll be down in a minute Dell."

"Verity and Jest have something to show you."

"The egg!" Avrille's bare feet flew down the stairs.

"Pretty chick chick," Verity cooed to a naked little blob squatting amid bits of golden eggshell in the corner of their cage.

"Oh Verity I'm so proud of you!" Avrille exclaimed.

"Jest too," chirped Verity's mate.

"Both of you, all three of you, I'm so proud. Here I'll give you a special treat," she said opening their fruit and nuts canister. "I'll set out my morning bread and tea right here with you and we can celebrate."

"I have a pot brewing already, My Lady," said Dell.

"You're a darling, Dell," Avrille gushed. "This is so wonderful! I must run next door to tell Rogarth."

"Jest go," said the little green bird and streaked out the window.

Rogarth came running. "My Lady, what is it? The bird just said, 'Come quick' and I..."

"Shame on you, Jest, frightening poor Rogarth. It's Verity's egg, it hatched. Rogarth we're grandparents!"

Still breathing hard Rogarth followed Avrille to the mirror birds' cage.

"After breakfast let's ride out to tell mother the news," said Avrille.

An hour later Rogarth lifted Avrille down from the carriage. She started to take his arm but unable to contain her enthusiasm, she dashed on ahead. Janille met them on the porch and hugged them both.

"Who do I thank for this unexpected but most welcome visit?"

"We have some wonderful news to tell you...Verity's egg hatched...she is so proud and Jest is so funny, panicking just like a first time father."

"What color is the chick?"

"I think she is going to be white. She doesn't have many feathers yet, just around her head."

"White," mused Janille, "That is unusual. I didn't think mirror birds could be white. Perhaps it's a sign of something..."

"I'm going to call her Pearl," Avrille babbled on. "Verity and Jest approve."

"So you think it may be a sign, Lady Janille?" said Rogarth.

"It's about time something good happens," said Avrille. "I have felt so restless lately. I've been horrid to live with haven't I, Rogarth?"

"Yes My Lady."

"You didn't have to agree, you meanie!"

Janille laughed at them. "You wouldn't want your most trusted friend to lie to you, would you?" She took their hands and drew them inside. "I'll put on a pot of tea."

"Where's Lizzie?" said Avrille. "She will want to hear our news."

"I sent her over to the manor early this morning to help Maralinne with the wool dyeing. She should be back by noon."

"Then, Mother, before she gets here I have something else I want to talk over with you."

"I thought so," said Janille as she measured out the tea into the pot.

Rogarth pulled out a chair for Avrille. Then he turned toward the still open door.

"Stay Rogarth," said Avrille. "This concerns you too."

Rogarth pulled up another chair for himself while Janille hung the tea kettle over the fire.

"Have you done the cards lately, Mother," Avrille began.

"No, you're the one who relies on the cards," answered Janille. "But I have scried a few things the past few days that I would rather not know."

"Like what?" asked Avrille, her tone rising with anxiety.

"What do your cards say?" said Janille avoiding her question.

"Let's ask them here to see if they say the same." Avrille reached up to get her mother's deck of cards from the mantle. She shuffled them rapidly then handed them to her mother.

"Five for the future I suppose?" said Janille shuffling them again. She laid out five cards. "You pick the first and ask."

"Where is Allar?" said Avrille turning over the first card. She slammed it down on the table. "There it is again, the Earth card!"

Rogarth chuckled but Avrille ignored him.

"This is not the first time it has come up for Allar, Mother," Avrille complained. "Ever since his manhood night it comes up regularly. Why? Earth is a woman's card."

"A farmer might draw the Earth card," said Janille. She grinned at Rogarth. "Or it could be drawn by a man in love."

"But Allar is only..." Avrille started to argue.

"Let's draw the other cards. Perhaps when they are all laid out their message will be clearer."

Avrille turned the second card and asked, "Where are my twins? The White Knight, now this is a new twist. Has Allar found them?"

"He does not know what he has found, Avrille. He still has much to learn."

"But has he...?"

"Draw again," said Janille.

"Mother, you're avoiding my questions. What do you know? Tell me."

"I know nothing for sure," said Janille choosing her words carefully. "Let's lay out the rest of the cards.

"Alright but when we are done here..." Avrille sighed. "Rogarth you ask this time and if it is the Black Dragon again I'll just give up."

Rogarth drew the next card and handed it to her without looking at it.

"The White Queen? This is new?" said Avrille puzzling over the card.

"Perhaps Rogarth's loyalty and patience is to be rewarded at last, daughter," said Janille.

The queen's champion did not smile, although he did look longingly at Avrille. She did not notice.

"Mother is it your turn to draw or mine?"

"Either way," said Janille leaning back to make room for Avrille to reach the cards.

"I know what it will be anyway," said Avrille picking up the fourth card. "I always draw the one I want and fear the most." She turned over the Black Queen. The image quivered glowing brightly. The face of the card mirrored Avrille's own.

Janille sat in painful silence. The memories of her lonely sojourn in the Dark Realm clouded her eyes.

"He calls me," Avrille said scarcely above a whisper. "He calls me from every mirror, every drop of water, and every darkened pane. At every balance of sun and moon he screams into my head. I have done my duty to the gods. Allar is grown and gone. Why does Will haunt me when finally I am free?"

Rogarth started to reach out a hand to comfort her, but thought better of it.

"Does the image speak?" asked Janille.

"He just says my name 'April,' over and over with such urgency. Have you seen him too, Mother?"

"I have not seen Willy but I have scried for your children. The images keep doubling and shifting. It is all so confusing. All I know is that they are not together, not yet, not anymore."

"What must we do?" Avrille wailed.

"We must wait," said Janille embracing her daughter. "We have done our part. The rest is up to Allar."

"I know that but it doesn't explain about Will. What does he want? Where is he really? Is he alright?"

"There is one more card, ladies," said Rogarth trying to ease the tension.

"Yes, the seeker's card," said Janille with a sigh. "What future does an old woman need?"

"Draw it, Mother, and stop talking like that."

Janille held the last card a long time before she turned it over. She took one look, smiled, and slipped it back into the deck.

"Well, what was it? Mother, tell me!" Avrille demanded with sudden alarm.

"Compassion."

Rogarth looked from mother to daughter trying to understand.

"Don't be afraid, Avrille," said Janille hugging her. "I already know my future. I know that love is stronger than our fear. I bear such dangerous secrets, that the thought to be relieved finally…"

"Mother! …It can't mean…Your not going to…to…"

"No, my darling I am not going to die, not for a long time anyway." She gave a little laugh. "No, on the contrary, I will live. I will more than live, oh such a glorious life gift that only the god of Compassion can bestow. It was his card I drew as always." Her voice was filled with emotion. "You cannot understand it all now. Just know that for me the future will be beautiful."

"What about Allar and the girls?"

"That we must work on." Janille thought a moment then resumed. "Perhaps there is something I can do. Let me think on it. Let's put the cards away for now."

For the rest of the morning they talked of simple, everyday things until they heard Lizelle come running down the path to the house.

"Grandma, Grandma. Look what a gorgeous color we made!" Lizelle sang as she burst into the kitchen. Her arms were full of red-dyed hanks of yarn.

"Just look at you!" Janille scolded. "You're beet red from head to toe!"

Lizelle giggled. "Only my hands and face are messy, Grandma."

"Get the soap and bleach and scrub until you're decent for polite company."

"If Jay could see you now," teased Avrille.

"Oh hi, Auntie and you too Rogarth," said Lizelle skipping around the room.

Rogarth nodded to recognize her greeting and headed for the porch.

"Isn't he friendly?" Lizelle complained. "How can you put up with such a sour old man, Auntie?"

"Enough smart talk, young lady" said her grandmother. "I told you to scrub. Do it now, before the whole house is colored

red. And when you are done your aunt has some news you'd like to hear."

A few days later Janille carried the heavy watering can to the herb garden. She was worried. Today all the mirrors were dark and the water in the scrying bowl lay still. Even the cards were lifeless pictures. Lizelle had kept her promise to Jasenth not to use magic so that window to knowledge was also closed. Allar was gone from Westshoren and he was alone. That was all she knew.

She sprinkled water on the thyme and the savory. She skipped the sage and emptied the rest on the mint. She soaked the dark green leaves, freeing their refreshing fragrance. It was almost noon. She would try the mirror again this evening just as the sun balanced on the rim of the hills. Events had taken a different turn in Westshoren than she had anticipated. She had to know if her grandson was safe and on the right road. Without Lizelle to watch and guide Allar, what would become of him?"

She carried the watering can to the porch. Her thoughts turned as they often did to Avrille and Will, her children who were separated from each other by much more than time and space. Lizelle was inside working on her embroidery. Maralinne had taught her to work with metallic threads and today she had given her some new linen to begin some pillow shams for her bridal bed.

"Grandma, my French knots look gobby. Come help me please," called Lizelle.

"Just a minute," said Janille. "I want to lay out these herbs while they're still fresh." She untied the bundle she had made with her apron and laid out her bunches of cut lavender.

"Oh forget it then," said Lizelle laying down her work. "I'm sick of embroidery." She walked out to the porch yawning and stretched her arms overhead. It was still warm but a hint of autumn was in the air. Overnight the tips of the sugar maples had turned orange and the fields were dotted with golden sheaves of grain. Lizelle picked up her shoes by the door and sat down on the steps to put them on.

"Where are you off to?" demanded Janille.

"I didn't say I was going anywhere," Lizelle said with a sassy toss of her head.

"You never put on shoes unless you are walking somewhere far. What are you up to?"

Lizelle meticulously tied her shoe laces in a bow before she answered. "I thought I'd go calling at Mill Manor today," she said. "Perhaps I'll stay for tea."

"What mischief are you plotting, Lizzie?"

"Mischief? Me?" Lizelle assumed her most innocent expression.

"Don't play games with me, missy misrule," Janille said sternly.

"I just thought I'd see what my brother thinks is so special in Mabry's daughter," said Lizelle with nonchalance.

"Kylie can dally where he pleases. It's no business of yours."

"Jay's Ame has seen more than dallying, Grandma, so I need to find out if the security of Arindon is at risk. I need to look out for my future husband."

Janille thought long and hard. "What goes on at Mill Manor is not your concern but that Mabry would put one of his daughters in the way of a king is not without precedent I agree."

"I'll just make it an innocent social call," said Lizelle slyly.

"You will not tamper."

"Jay trusts me. Why don't you?"

Janille let her thoughts probe again into the web of things for an answer. Possibilities and probabilities swirled through the web canceling each other out. Finally she said, "Brush your hair and put on a clean apron."

"Love you Grandma!" Lizelle called as she raced away.

The walk was three miles from Woodsmeet to Mill Manor. By the time she arrived Lizelle was tired and her left shoe had begun to rub a blister on her heel. She stopped at the gate to run her fingers through her short blonde curls. She could see Dulcie reading in the garden gazebo. This was more than she had hoped for. There would be no need to fend off Lady Cellina. If she was lucky she could fulfill the purpose of her visit and be gone before the formidable mistress of the manor knew she had an uninvited caller. She boldly opened the gate. "Good day Dulcie," she called as she came up the carefully graded, marigold-lined path Mabry had designed to accommodate lady Cellina's wheel chair. "What a lovely place to take a book on a sunny afternoon."

Dulcie looked up from her book to see who had invaded her vine-covered retreat. "Lizzie, good day, come in, though I'm afraid I may not be such good company. I'm not feeling very well today, but do have a seat."

Lizelle sat down on the wide bench and arranged her skirt. Dulcie did look ill. Her eyes were hollow and her cheeks were flushed. "Oh I am so sorry to hear that," she said. "Perhaps I can recommend an herb or tea. I help Grandmother with medicinals you know."

Dulcie was obviously uneasy with her caller. Lizelle politely pretended not to notice that Dulcie slipped a folded paper inside her book but the Frevarian golden seal on it was unmistakable. Was it a love letter from Kylie? How amusing, thought Lizelle.

"Will you stay for tea?" said Dulcie trying to overcome the awkwardness.

"Perhaps I shouldn't stay if you aren't feeling well…"

"No, no, you have walked all this way. That is the least I can offer. I'm sure Mother Cellina won't mind."

"She doesn't like me much," said Lizelle.

"Mother Cellina does have her opinions," Dulcie agreed as she started to stand up but before she gained her feet she turned suddenly pale. Dizzily she grabbed for the gazebo post.

"Dulcie, dear, you are quite ill," exclaimed Lizelle as she sprang up to help her. "Let me call someone…"

"No, no, I will be alright," Dulcie was quick to say. "Mother Cellina does not know. She worries so over every little thing. I don't want to alarm her."

As Lizelle stood with her arm around Dulcie another presence fluttered into her thoughts. She smiled to herself, so that is how it is. "We girls can have our little secret, for a while at least." she said.

Dulcie shot her a quick, questioning glance then she tried again to stand up, slowly this time.

Tea at Mill Manor was strained that afternoon to say the least. It was not until Dulcie gently reminded Lady Cellina that Lizelle was the betrothed of their king and would one day be their queen that the mistress of Mill Manor had backed her wheel chair from the doorway and permitted their caller to enter.

Lizelle and Dulcie chattered about girl things, embroidery, what flowers were in bloom and the weather of course. When the table was set Dulcie poured the steaming mint and chamomile from the painted rose teapot into delicate white porcelain cups. Her hand trembled as she spooned two lumps of sugar into her stepmother's cup.

"Don't you spill it, not on my new cutwork tablecloth," Cellina warned her.

"What a lovely tea service," said Lizelle trying to rescue Dulcie. "Grandmother's set is squat and heavy compared to this."

Dulcie's hands shook even more as she set the cup at just the right place on Cellina's left with the handle at just the right angle. Then it happened. One tiny telltale drop of tea sloshed over the fragile cup rim onto the tablecloth. Dulcie froze. She glanced first at Lady Cellina then at Lizelle. Her stepmother had not seen. Dulcie moved her fingers in a discreet pattern. The tea stain sparkled a moment and disappeared.

Lizelle smiled at her. "When I am queen," she said. "I will invite you to tea in Arindon Castle. But since we seem to have so much in common, you need not wait until then. You are welcome to visit Grandma and me at Woodsmeet Cot anytime."

"I would like to take tea and chat with someone my own age," said Dulcie. "But I do have obligations here." She glanced at Lady Cellina as she set out the rest of the teatime fare. Then she sat down with a tired sigh.

"We all must respect and care for our elders," Lizelle agreed as she took three of the jam-filled biscuits Dulcie offered.

Lady Cellina's eyes widened.

"Jay says I'm too skinny so I have to eat lots," said Lizelle by way of apology for taking more than might be considered appropriate.

"I don't have much appetite of late," said Dulcie breaking her biscuit in half. "It must be the weather."

Lizelle nodded knowingly. Dulcie gave her a startled, frightened look in return but when Lizelle did not say anything more, she relaxed and smiled with relief.

Lady Cellina soon began to doze over her second cup of tea. The girls cleared the table and brushed the crumbs from the cloth.

"Does my brother often call at Mill Manor?" asked Lizelle when they were alone in the pantry. "We regularly see him riding by Woodsmeet in this direction."

"Your brother?"

"My brother Kylie...His Majesty King Keilen the First of Frevaria I mean," said Lizelle with a mocking curtsy.

"His Majesty does call often at Mill Manor," said Dulcie with a wistful smile. "He still confers with Mother Cellina and father on matters of state and....Is he truly your brother?"

"Of course he is, not that he claims me," Lizelle told her. "He hates me, like a true Frevarian, because of my magic. But I don't do magic anymore now that I'm going to marry Jay someday soon."

"His Majesty told us that his sister died in the Arindon fire," said Dulcie. Interest and confusion warred in her tone.

"Grandma rescued me from the fire," Lizelle explained. "Then I lived in another place with her for a while. We came back to the kingdoms when Auntie Avrille needed help with Allar."

Dulcie sat for a long moment and puzzled over what she had heard. "Is magic wrong for queens?" she asked, carefully choosing her words.

"Only if it is used selfishly, that's what Jay says anyway."

"But if His Majesty King Keilen..."

Lizelle rolled her eyes. "Kylie is such a simpleton. He hates what he doesn't understand." She winked and smiled at her companion. "We girls have several secrets so it seems. Don't worry. We can trust each other."

When Lizelle had finally said goodbye and scampered out through the garden toward home, Dulcie returned to the gazebo to retrieve the book she left on the bench. She unfolded the letter hidden inside the pages and began to read the message again.

"To the sweetest flower at Mill Manor..."

"Dulcie! Dulcie!" Cellina's call interrupted her.

"I'm coming," said Dulcie. She reluctantly tucked the letter inside her bodice and hurried back to the house.

Chapter 15

The heavy Frevarian wagons rumbled down the road to Arindon's harvest festival. This year they had reaped in their neighbor's fields. There had been nothing worth harvesting from their own lands. The newly dug ditches scaring Frevaria's farmland would not carry water until next year's spring rains. The farmers in the wagons waved and shouted to the ditch diggers. The holiday mood was welcome even if it was a little strained. The diggers laid down their shovels and climbed aboard the wagons. Everyone was headed toward Arindon, grateful that two kingdoms could be fed this winter from only one harvest.

Keilen rode his massive, brown war horse at the head of the wagon column. He had rejected Lady Cellina's idea of formal military dress for the occasion. No armor could protect him from the humiliation he felt from having to beg his cousin for assistance. He did not want Jasenth to have any more reason to gloat or at worst, laugh at him. What made things even worse was having to announce his betrothal to Dulcie today. He wanted Dulcie, of that he was sure, but in order to get her he had been forced to give in to formalities. Dulcie made it clear that she would be queen not just a mistress. Mabry and Cellina supported her resolve. Even Cook had sided against him this time. Keilen rode along in sullen silence. The fact that he would have sons and heirs before Jasenth was only a small compensation. The weight on his shoulders this morning was almost unbearable.

The carriage rolled sedately along the road. Inside Lady Cellina, swathed in blankets and padded with cushions, clutched Mabry's arm with a vice-like hold. Getting ready for the unaccustomed trip to Arindon had taken hours. Both the staff at Mill Manor as well as the occupants of the carriage breathed a great sigh of relief when they finally drove away with Cellina's chair tied securely to the back.

"Watch out for that rut, Mabry!" Cellina cried. "You know how bumps make my poor joints pain."

Mabry gently freed his hand from her grasp and reined the horses to a slow walk. The carriage eased over the rut and they continued toward Arindon. Cellina adjusted her parasol as they rounded a curve. "Pull your bonnet down, Dulcie," she ordered the frightened girl in the back seat. "You will be red as a beet from the sun for your betrothal. You surely would not want that."

Dulcie tugged at her new bonnet which her stepmother had trimmed with gold straw flowers for the occasion.

"Don't crush your curls!" Cellina barked. "All those we spent hours putting them in, don't ruin them before we get there."

"Cellina dearest," Mabry intervened in his daughter's behalf. "Kylie already thinks she is beautiful. No sun or wind today could change his mind."

"But a girl must look perfect for her betrothal," she insisted.

"Our Dulcie will," he said winking back at his daughter. "She looks like a big yellow chrysanthemum in her new dress."

"But her hair..."

"You can fix her curls if need be when we get there." He patted a small case beneath the seat. "I brought the bag of combs and pins just like you asked."

"Oh my!" Cellina exclaimed as they hit a bump in the road.

Mabry squeezed her hand. "We are almost there, dear."

"I never remembered Arindon was so far," Cellina complained.

Mabry patted her blanket draped knee. "Now that the weather is cooler, we should drive out more often. The air would do you good, dear."

Cellina blushed and pushed his hand aside. "I don't know how much this jostling and bumping I can take today. I surely wouldn't do it for pleasure."

Mabry gave her a sly wink and put his hand back on her knee. "With Dulcie moving to Frevaria soon you and I must begin to think of how we will spend our time alone."

"I dread to think of it. What will I ever do without my Dulcie?"

Mabry leaned over and brushed her cheek with a kiss. "I will take good care of you dear." He straightened up and gave the reins a little flick. "Look Dulcie, there's Kylie riding ahead of his wagons, right there, just entering the gate."

"What on earth is he wearing?" Cellina exclaimed with horror.

"It looks like a brown shirt and trousers to me," said Mabry.

"But it's his betrothal day!"

Mabry retrieved the blanket that had slipped off Cellina's knees. "Kings have a right to wear whatever they please, even on their betrothal day. You worry too much, dearest. Everything will be fine."

"His brown will look good with my yellow," said Dulcie with a small but confident voice.

Mabry laughed and flicked the reins again, harder this time. The carriage sprang forward toward the village gate.

"Slow down, Mabry! Slow down! Slow down or you'll run over somebody."

Arindon was bustling when they finally arrived. The tents for the harvest fair were already billowing brightly along the river. Farmers and merchants from every corner of the kingdoms and beyond lined the streets. Arindian reds and Frevarian blues intermingled in joyous cacophony.

Jasenth and Keilen sat on opposite sides of the royal reviewing platform waiting for the harvest parade to start. Two benches had been set up and decorated as thrones for them. Jasenth sat and watched the wagons line up. Keilen stood up, paced back and forth, then sat down again, all the while anxiously watching until his eyes caught Mabry and Dulcie wheeling Cellina's chair through the crowd. He jumped down off the platform and when Mabry had finished positioning Cellina's chair he strode to greet them. Cellina gave Dulcie a little push. The girl dropped a deep curtsy. Keilen lifted her up and slipped his arm through hers. With a brief nod to Mabry and a formal kiss to Lady Cellina's outstretched hand he led Dulcie to the platform.

"Tam, bring a chair for your sister," he ordered his manservant.

Tam grabbed a stool from a nearby booth and set it next to Keilen's makeshift throne.

"So Kylie is making his dalliance at Mill Manor public," remarked Jasenth to himself. "Where is this all heading and why today?" He searched the crowd for his Aunt Jane and Lizelle until he found them standing on the butcher's porch. He caught Janille's eye, then he nodded toward Keilen and Dulcie. She smiled her agreement and after a brief word to Lizelle, she stepped back into the shadows. Jasenth stood up and raised his hands. The people hushed each other until it was quiet enough for their king to be heard.

"Will the Lady Lizelle accept the honor of attending me today?" he said loud enough for all to hear.

Lizelle walked demurely through the wide path the people opened for her and stopped at the edge of the platform. "As you wish My Lord," she said extending her hand to Jasenth.

He lifted her up although she could have easily climbed up unassisted. When they sat down on the bench throne side by side the people whispered nervously for a moment but soon they resumed their merry making. At last everything was ready and the harvest caravan began its joyous trek through the village. Dozens of wagons laden with ripe fruit and grains, musicians, banner carriers and the combined palace guards of both kingdoms made their way through the crowd. Queen Avrille rode in an open carriage attended by Sir Rogarth, her champion. Behind them the village children ran singing and waving colored ribbons. The queen's carriage stopped. Rogarth lifted her down and escorted her to the platform. The people clapped and cheered.

"My good people," Queen Avrille began as she held out her hands to them. "Today we have a double harvest. There is food enough for two kingdoms. I command you to put aside your reds and blues and make merry today as one people."

Keilen sat in stony silence, tightly holding Dulcie's hand.

"Now, Kylie," Lady Cellina mouthed.

Jasenth also read her words. "What is your annoying brother up to?" he whispered to Lizelle.

"Dulcie is pregnant," Lizelle whispered back.

"What!"

"Dulcie is pregnant," she repeated aloud.

Jasenth began to laugh. He cupped his hands around his mouth and called, "Hey Kylie, I hear you have found more than grain in my fields."

Keilen shot him a terrified glance but did not answer."

"Does he know she is?" Jasenth whispered to Lizelle.

"Not yet,' she whispered back.

A broad grin spread across Jasenth's face. "Kylie," he called again. "There's a price to pay for planting in another man's fields."

"Gloating is not honorable, cousin," said Keilen. His voice was shaky. His whitened face was blotched with red. He did not meet Jasenth's eye.

"Neither is thievery," said Jasenth. He was beginning to enjoy this.

"We had an agreement," said Keilen. Now his face was more puzzled than fearful.

"Our agreement was about harvesting, not planting," Jasenth continued.

"What the hell are you talking about?" Keilen yelled. His face was brilliant red.

"You have not asked for the flower at your side."

By this time the people were crowding close to the platform. The rivalry between their two kings was well known but it had never been so public until now.

"I asked her father for her."

"But you have not asked her king."

Dulcie gasped then she started to cry. Keilen's attempts to comfort her were awkward and useless. By now the people stood gaping as they listened to the exchange between their kings.

Jasenth surveyed the onlookers with a smug smile. "I Jasenth, King of Arindon," he said then he stopped and waited a mercilessly long time. "I grant permission for my subject, the maid Dulcie, Mabry's daughter, and ward of the Lady Cellina to be courted by and if the maid so wishes, to marry Frevaria. I will recognize any and all children out of that union as legitimate heirs of Frevaria under one condition..." he paused to look at Keilen who had jumped to his full height. Dulcie wept pitifully, holding on to his hand and feebly trying to pull him back. Jasenth looked at Janille who was still watching from her shadowy vantage.

"What conditions give Arindon the right to decree anything to Frevaria?" Keilen yelled.

"That Frevaria recognize the Lady Lizelle, betrothed of Arindon, and call her sister before this assembly."

Jasenth gloated as he waited for an answer. Keilen paced and cursed and fumed but he did not answer. Jasenth waited. The people waited. Then Jasenth calmly took Lizelle's hand and said, "Would My Lady Queen-to-be like a glass of fruit punch while we wait? The weather has suddenly become rather warm."

"Yes, I would My Lord," said Lizelle.

They walked hand and hand through the awestruck crowd almost as far as the fruit vendor's stand before they burst out laughing.

The decorated wagons rolled two abreast through Arindon, alternating red and blue. All the fruits of the harvest were divided equally. Workers from both kingdoms tied sheaves of grain with colored ribbons and carried them in a serpentine dance through the maze of market stalls. Young women adorned their hair with fall flowers. Everyone was singing.

King Keilen sourly stalked through the festivities alone. He poked at the baker's tarts and inspected a farmer's apples and onions without really seeing them. He stopped to watch a blacksmith shoe a horse and ended up in the Wandren trader's saddlery. There a dark wisp of a man sang with a lilting tone as he hawked his wares. The fine tooled and studded leather goods in his stall were as sturdy as cowhide and as supple as deerskin. To own Wandren leather was the privilege of only the wealthiest gentry and kings. Keilen's fingers followed the intricate floral design pressed into the smooth brown leather of a saddle.

"She's fit for a young king to carry home a bride," said the saddler.

"Then sell the damn thing to Arindon," Keilen growled.

"It's Frevarian horsemanship that is worthy of this piece and none other," the saddler continued still hoping to make a sale. "There is a matching bridle and ..."

Keilen cut him short. "Then hand it over to Arindon with everything else I want and value. I couldn't buy it if I had to. Arindon owns Frevaria, at least until next year's rain." Keilen kicked the sawbuck that held the saddle almost knocking it over.

The saddler laid down his tools and squinted at Keilen. "My woman scried a young king sitting in this saddle..."

Keilen spit on the shop floor, narrowly missing the saddle he was admiring. "Damn your woman. Damn your saddle and damn you." He turned on his heel and left. The saddler shook his head, muttered something about "young hot heads" and resumed his song.

Keilen had to find Cook. There was no one else he could talk to. He fought his way rudely through the market until he found his mentor laden with brimming market baskets, bargaining in a good-hearted debate with Armon Beck about pie pumpkins and squash.

"Kylie, Your Majesty," said Cook when he saw him. "Tell this swill slosher he has no need for fine pumpkins when all his patrons are either too ignorant or too drunk to taste the difference."

"Leave them," ordered Keilen.

"What do you say, Kylie, pumpkin pie by royal Frevarian decree or squash?"

"I said leave the damn pumpkins. I've got to talk to you."

Cook gathered up his many baskets. "Later Armon, I'll best you later," he said to Arindon's tavern keeper and followed Keilen toward the stables.

"Cook, you heard the bastard. You saw it all," Keilen began when they were barely out of earshot.

"Arindon made a right fool of you," Cook agreed. "And what is worse he brought the maid to tears."

"This means war. I mean war, Cook."

"War over a woman?" said Cook. "Now Kylie, no woman is worth the expense of war." He opened the door to Arindon's stables. The sweet scent of straw and the hearty scent of horse greeted them.

"It's not about her," Keilen fumed.

"Then it's all about Frevarian pride?"

"Damn Jay. Damn his witch."

"Some say that Lady Lizelle is indeed princess and sister to Frevaria," said Cook arranging his bulk on a bale of straw. He scooted to the side to make room for Keilen.

"My sister died in the fire. You know she did. Tell me you believe she did."

"Lizelle the babe had fearsome magic and Lizelle the child that returned almost a year after and now is grown to womanhood, also wields power. Who am I to say they are one in the same or no?"

"Cook I'm scared."

"Of Arindon?"

"No damn Jay and all of Arindon!"

"Then are you scared of Frevaria or of yourself?"

Keilen choked back tears. "I can't call Lizzie sister. I won't. Frevaria would dethrone me. They're discontent enough already." Keilen pulled bits of straw from the bale and threw them angrily on the floor.

"Kylie my boy, take my advice. Forget Arindon's slap at your pride. Forget Lady Lizelle, be she sister, or witch or whatever and go ahead and wed Mabry's daughter. Get her pregnant if she isn't already and dangle your firstborn in Arindon's face. Then who will laugh at whom?"

"But Jay said..."

"Arindon has a clever wit and a strong family to back him up, but he is no more than a boy, younger and newer to kingship than yourself. Do as you please, my little king. Wed the girl. No one can stop you. Wed her today and be done with it."

"I can't." Keilen wailed. "Dulcie wants a big wedding. Aunt Cellina has it all planned for Winter Solstice."

"So Frevaria bends his will to please a woman?" Cook grinned at Keilen.

"Dulcie pleases me."

Cook slapped Keilen's knee and smiled at him kindly. "Such a pretty golden flower she looked today. Put your anger away, Kylie. Don't give Arindon what he wants. Show him true Frevarian pride. Parade Frevaria's queen-to-be at the solemnities tonight and remember she is no more than a child herself. Women like tenderness in a man. Hold her hand. Buy her sweets. Talk soft to her and kiss her. That's the things that make a woman happy."

Keilen stood up and brushed the straw from his breeches. "Thanks Cook," he said. "And by the way shall I tell Armon Beck you really make your pumpkin pies from butternut squash?"

"You won't unless you want to take all your meals in Beck's Tavern from now on."

It was a long exhausting day. Janille and Lizelle retired with Jasenth to his bachelor quarters in Arindon Castle gatehouse for a quiet tea before the Equinox festivities climaxed at moonrise. The castle stood completed but still vacant behind them. The rooms were for the most part already furnished. Only the hiring of the staff and the decorating of the royal apartments had yet to be done. Jasenth said he was just waiting for the right time to move in. He wanted what was right for the kingdom and for himself. The glory he sought was simple justice and modest respect, not the decadent opulence of his grandfather's court.

Janille took over the tea making as soon as she arrived. Ben had been given the holiday off. Lizelle spread the tablecloth and set out the cups. Jasenth sprawled across his bed and had almost fallen asleep when a knock at the door interrupted them. It was Mabry.

"Ladies," he nodded briefly to Janille and Lizelle before he knelt in front of Jasenth who yawned and sat up on the edge of the bed. "I come in humbleness, sire. I come as the father of a weeping child, seeking only to restore her happiness."

"Poor Dulcie," said Lizelle. "What has Kylie done now?"

Her remark passed unheeded as Mabry waited for Jasenth to reply, but it was Janille who spoke first.

"Mabry come sit and have some tea. Talk is always easier over tea."

"Did Kylie send you?" said Jasenth now fully awake.

"No sire, he did not."

"Did Aunt Cellina?"

"She knows I have come but she did not send me. I come as a loving father, nothing more. My Dulcie loves Frevaria's king and he loves her. What a joy it has been for my dear Cellina and I to watch their love blossom and grow these past months. Today they were to announce their betrothal and now all that is spoiled. Dulcie is in tears and Kylie has gone off who knows where. I beg you, Your Majesty, to please reconsider the conditions you have placed on their union."

Jasenth looked first at Janille and then at Lizelle. Janille busied herself at serving tea. Lizelle cocked her head and bit her lip. Neither one gave him a clue to the answer he should give.

"Mabry get up and drink your tea before it gets cold," said Jasenth. "I assure you my sport at Kylie was not intended to hurt your daughter."

Mabry took a chair but he did not pick up his cup. "Dulcie is my last, my baby girl," he said. "It tears my heart to see her cry."

"Dulcie is a sweet girl, Jay," said Lizelle. "I called on her recently for tea and we had a lovely conversation. I hope we can still be friends after today."

Jasenth gave her a look of annoyance but with a hint of panic. "Then advise me as a woman, as my queen-to-be, should I retract my conditions to spare Lady Dulcie's feelings and honor, or should I remain adamant and assert my strength to my fellow king?"

Lizelle thought a moment. "You cannot retract the resolve outright but you could modify the conditions," she said as she sweetly offered Mabry a plate of bread and butter. When Jasenth did not say anything to respond she continued. "I have a grand idea. Mabry has Dulcie chosen her bridesmaids yet?"

"They will be her sisters I suppose," Mabry answered somewhat puzzled. "I let all that sort of arrangement up to Cellina."

"Well," said Lizelle clapping her hands with delight. "Since I am Kylie's sister, after the wedding I will be Dulcie's sister too. Tell her that I will be delighted to be her bridesmaid. That will be recognition enough won't it Jay and it will depend on, not prevent, their wedding."

Jay raised his eyebrows and looked from her to Mabry to Janille.

"You know it's a grand idea, Jay. Say you agree. I just love wearing pretty dresses and I love weddings…"

"Lizzie you are a clever little witch," said Jasenth. "Come here so I can give you a hug."

Lizelle held her ground. "You called me a witch and I didn't do any magic."

"Yes you did, but it was the right kind of magic this time."

Lizelle threw herself into Jasenth arms and hugged him wildly. When Jasenth could extract himself from her embrace he picked up the teapot and topped off Mabry's cold cup with hot tea. "Drink up, man. We accept your petition. It seems I too am at the mercy of the ladies in my life."

When Mabry left, Lizelle and Janille cleared the table and washed the cups. Outside the shadows lengthened along the castle walls.

"Tomorrow Lizzie and I will be moving to Arindon," Janille announced. "We will stay with Avrille until the castle is ready."

"Is it time Aunt Jane?" Jasenth asked with both fear and anticipation.

"It is time for many things," she answered.

The people left the booths and stalls of the fair. The merchants dropped their tent flaps and covered their wares. Women called to gather their tired and dirty children. The taverns emptied and the lamps were snuffed out. As the drums began, the chatter and laughter stopped. The populace of both kingdoms assembled in front of Arindon's gate, shuffling and groping to join hands. In a somewhat skewed circle they began to move together. First one voice then another joined Dell's song.

"One harvest, one kingdom,
No hunger, no hatred,
No fear, no want, and no fast.

One harvest united two kingdoms divided,
One land, one kindred at last."

The heralds trumpeted. The castle gates opened. High Queen Avrille rode out in her open carriage with her champion. The people pressed close to greet her once again. Rogarth steadied the horse. The queen stood up and motioned for silence.

"Where are my two nephew kings? They're out dallying again I'll wager."

The crowd roared with good-hearted laughter.

King Keilen's war horse carved a path through the crowd. The young king dressed in blue silk and gold trappings, was greeted by cheers of approval, some sincere, some ribald, all well meant. When he drew abreast of Mabry and his family clustered around Lady Cellina's chair he stopped. Mabry gave Dulcie a kiss and handed her up to Keilen.

"So that's what you've been up to," called Queen Avrille. "Come and attend me and introduce me to my niece-to-be."

Keilen rode like a conqueror returning home with his prize. His new Wandren leather saddle and harness gleamed in the setting sun. Dulcie clasped her small arms about his neck and pressed her cheek tight to his gold-armored chest.

"That's one wayward nephew accounted for," Avrille declared. "Now where is the other? Jasenth, your High Queen commands your presence."

King Jasenth stepped out onto the castle wall. Shouts of "Hurray for King Jay!" thundered to the sky.

"Attend me," said the queen. "And bring my sister's child with you, if you have her up there."

Jasenth and Lizelle descended the stairs and walked through the gate to the waiting crowd. The cheers started slowly but soon they rang out with unrestrained joy.

"Arindon and Frevaria had better get used to celebrating together," said Queen Avrille. "This year will see two weddings and next year two namings and the year after that…"

"Look!" someone shouted pointing to the sky. The moon rose like a golden lantern above the tree-lined horizon. Its silver twin sparkled in the river below. As one voice the people sang.

> "One harvest united,
> The kingdom divided,
> One land,
> One kingdom,
> At last."

Faraway in the hills above Westshoren, Allar huddled by the sheepherder's fire. Stars pierced the sky overhead. He had never seen them so clear or so bright. The thin mountain air chilled his bones and sharpened his senses. In the shadows the baaing and bleating of the flock rose and fell with the wind.

"They come swoopin' out a nowhere on wings five paces wide," the sheepherder was telling. "Clutchin' up man or beast or whatever takes their hunger."

"These eagles, where do they nest?" asked Allar.

"Way up in the crags," the herder said jerking his head toward the north. "They keep their wimmin up there in the crags."

"Women?" said Allar.

"Broad an' strong as a man them wimmin. They all kin eat a sheep at one stint." He poked Allar in the ribs with a crooked finger. "Not thinkin' a havin' one are y'? You're no more than a yearling yourself. A full-horned ram of a man would have a hard time rut wrastling an Eyeren ewe."

"Eyeren ewe?" puzzled Allar.

"That's what the eagle folk call theirselves, Eyeren."

The sheepherder stirred up the fire. Allar inched a bit closer to the meager flame.

"Cold are y'?"

"A bit," Allar admitted.

The man picked up a forked stick and poked a pot out of the coals. He spit on his fingers and lifted the lid. "Belar's breath she's hot!" he exclaimed as he ladled out near-boiling milky tea into a leather mug and handled it to Allar. "Drink up, lad. Nights be long up here."

The drink was strong-flavored but its warmth was welcome. Allar sipped it slowly, grateful for the small fire and his rough host's generosity. The wind sent a shiver straight through the sweater his Aunt Cellina had knit for him as a parting gift. His coming of age and leaving his family all seemed so long ago, and the Twin Kingdoms so small and very faraway. Only the expanse of cold black sky seamed real tonight. He took another sip, cradling the mug to warm his hands and thought of all that had passed in the last half year. Fallsveil still haunted his dreams and Rindelle his waking thoughts. The sea rhythms had become a part of him, but the mountains called him north. He shivered again.

At the edge of the firelight the sheep stirred uneasily. Their scent intensified as panic spread. With a rush of wind a scream of death curdled the silence. Enormous wings rose above the camp. With a thunderous rhythm the wings beat northward, blotting out the patterns of the sky.

Appendix I

Characters

Twin Kingdoms

Allarinth (AL ar inth) Allar. High Prince of the Twin Kingdoms. Son of Avrille and Will.

Jasenth (JAY senth), Jay
King of Arindon. Betrothed to Lizelle. Nephew of Maralinne. Cousin of Allar.

Keilen (KI len) Kylie
King of Frevaria. Cousin of Allar. Brother of Lizelle. Grandson of Janille.

Avrille (AV reel), April
High Queen of the Twin Kingdoms. Daughter of Janille. Mother of Allar and twins Arinda and Arielle.

Janille (jan EEL), Janie, Aunt Jane
Former wife and queen of Frebar. Mother of Avrille and Elanille. Foster mother of Will.

Lizelle (liz EL), Lizzie
Betrothed of King Jasenth. Granddaughter of Janille. Sister of King Keilen and cousin of Allar.

Maralinne (MAR a lin), Aunt Mari
Princess of Arindon. Consort of Jareth. Guardian of nephew Jasenth. Twin sister of Analinne.

Jareth (JAR eth)
Consort of Maralinne. Former gamekeeper of Arindon wood. Advisor to King Arinth and later to King Will. Guardian and advisor to King Jasenth.

Lady Cellina (SEL in ah),
>   Former regent for King Keilen of Frevaria. Wife of Mabry.

Mabry (MAB ree)
>   Miller of Arindon. Husband of Lady Cellina. Father of Darilla, Tad, Tam, Ben, Belle and Dulcie.

Dulcie (DOOL see)
>   Mabry's daughter. Beloved of King Keilen.

Rogarth (ROE garth)
>   Former Captain of the guard in Arindon, later Master of War. Queen Avrille's knight champion and friend. Mentor to Allar.

Dell (Del)
>   Bard of the Twin Kingdoms. Companion to Queen Avrille. Mentor to Allar.

Cook
>   Master Cook of Frevaria castle. Mentor to King Keilen.

Armon Beck (AR mon)
>   Innkeeper of Arindon.

Tam
>   Manservant to King Keilen. Mabry's son. Twin to Tad.

Ben
>   Manservant to King Jasenth. Mabry's son.

Varen. (VAR en), Starbelly.
>   Bastard son of Darilla, Mabry's daughter and King Will.

Darilla (Dar IL ah)
>   Daughter of Mabry. Former mistress to Will. Mother of Varen. Wife of Don the miller.

Don.
>   Miller journeyman of Arindon, husband of Darilla.

Tad
> Mabry's son. Twin to Tam.

Timmy,
> Grandson of Mabry.

Saddler
> Wandren leather trader in Arindon market.

Amethyst, Ame (AH me)
> King Jasenth's mirror bird.

Verity, Jest and Pearl.
> Queen Avrille's mirror birds.

Thatchmeet

Fallsveil
> Friend of Allar. Granddaughter and apprentice to Cranecall.

Cranecall
> Headwoman of Thatchmeet.

Willow, Tidesong, Lily and Springbud.
> Women of the Crane's nest council.

Piper, Puffin Sandy and Skeeter
> Children of Thatchmeet.

Carinna (Car IN ah)
> Goddess of the sea.

Westshoren

Armina Weatherwatcher (Ar MEE na)
> Weather forecaster, herbalist and healer. Grandmother of Rindelle.

Rindelle Twovoice (rin DEL)
: Friend of Allar. Granddaughter of Armina.

Dylan Breaks, Tom Netter, Davy Grimm, Sharky, Burly and Pier
: Fishermen of Westshoren.

Lightkeep
: Keeper of Farwest lighthouse.

Barkeep
: Keeper of the Gull's Breath tavern.

Tessy, Felicity Spinner and Rose Burnie
: Women of Westshoren.

Historical:

Willarinth (WIL ar inth), Will, Willy
: High King of the Twin Kingdoms. Husband of Avrille. Father of Allar. Disappeared at the Star Castle Equinox ceremony 15 years ago.

Kyrdthin (KURD thin), Hawke
: Magician. Beloved of Janille. Died battling Belar the Dark Lord 18 years ago.

Analinne (AN a lin),
: Princess of Arindon. Twin sister of Maralinne. Mother of Jasenth. Killed by husband Prince Tobar of Frevaria at Avrille and Will's coronation 18 years ago

Elanille (El an eel)
: Princess of Frevaria. Daughter of Janille and Frebar. Sister of Avrille. Mother of Keilen and Lizelle. Drowned in Star Spring Pool, 16 years ago.

Marielle (MAR ee el)
: Queen of Arindon and Allarion. Mother of Will. Died at Frevaria 16 years ago.

Arinth (AR inth)
: King of Arindon. Father of Analinne, Maralinne and Will. Died at Arindon 19 years ago.

Gil
: Consort of Marielle in Allarion. Advisor to Arinth and later to Will. Accompanied Marielle on her death journey 16 years ago.

Belar (BAY lar)
: Dark Lord of Bellarion. Defeated by Kyrdthin at Avrille and Will's coronation 18 years ago.

Frebar (FRAY bar)
: King of Frevaria. Grandfather of Keilen. Former husband of Janille. Twin to Tobar. Killed by lightening on the battlefield 16 years ago.

Tobar (TOE bar)
: Prince of Frevaria. Father of Jasenth. Husband of Analinne. Twin brother of Frebar. Killed at Avrille and Will's coronation 18 years ago.

Keilen (KI len)
: Bowman of Arindon. Father of King Keilen of Frevaria. Killed at the battle of High Bridge 19 years ago.

Arinda (Ar IN dah) Rindy
: Princess of twin Kingdoms. Sister of Allar. Daughter of Avrille and Will. Twin to Arielle. Disappeared at the Star Castle Equinox celebration 15 years ago.

Arielle (AR ee el) Rella
: Princess of twin Kingdoms. Sister of Allar. Daughter of Avrille and Will. Twin to Arinda. Disappeared at the Star Castle Equinox celebration 15 years ago.

Varan (VAR an)
: Bastard son of Will and Darilla. Twin to Veren. Disappeared at the Star Castle Equinox celebration 15 years ago. Only one twin returned named Varen.

Veren (VER en)
Bastard son of Will and Darilla. Twin to Varan Disappeared at the Star Castle Equinox celebration 15 years ago. Only one twin returned named Varen.

Appendix II

The Cards

The House of Light
    White King, White Queen, White Dragon, White Knight, White Fortress

The House of Darkness
    Black King, Black Queen, Black Dragon, Black Knight, Black Fortress

The Gifts of the Gods
    Beauty, Wisdom, Strength, Honor, Compassion

The Abodes of the Gods
    Sun, Moon, Star, Rainbow, Fountain

The Elements of Creation
    Fire, Water, Air, Earth, Time

Appendix III

The Prophecy

When the sun and Moon
Shine double in the sky,
Then shall the cask be opened.
Then shall the three be Five.

Twice two shall weep
When the eclipse is done.
Magic will die
When the darkness is chained.
And the star arches alive.

The Chant of Life

Light and Death are one.
Love and Dark are one.
Truth and Time but move
Eclipsing each other in tune.

We live and are of Earth.
We die and are of Fire.
In the Air we fly free
In the Circle of Time
To our birth in the Sea.

None can change what we are.
None can change what we must be.